Devil House

Phillip Strang

BOOKS BY PHILLIP STRANG

DCI Isaac Cook Series
MURDER IS A TRICKY BUSINESS
MURDER HOUSE
MURDER IS ONLY A NUMBER
MURDER IN LITTLE VENICE
MURDER IS THE ONLY OPTION
MURDER IN NOTTING HILL
MURDER IN ROOM 346
MURDER OF A SILENT MAN
MURDER HAS NO GUILT
MURDER IN HYDE PARK
SIX YEARS TOO LATE
GRAVE PASSION
THE SLAYING OF JOE FOSTER
THE HERO'S FALL
THE VICAR'S CONFESSION
GUILTY UNTIL PROVEN INNOCENT
MURDER WITHOUT REASON

DI Keith Tremayne Series
DEATH UNHOLY
DEATH AND THE ASSASSIN'S BLADE
DEATH AND THE LUCKY MAN
DEATH AT COOMBE FARM
DEATH BY A DEAD MAN'S HAND
DEATH IN THE VILLAGE
BURIAL MOUND
THE BODY IN THE DITCH
THE HORSE'S MOUTH
MONTFIELD'S MADNESS

Sergeant Natalie Campbell Series
DARK STREETS
PINCHGUT
ISLAND SHADOWS

Steve Case Series
HOSTAGE OF ISLAM
THE HABERMAN VIRUS
PRELUDE TO WAR

Standalone Books
MALIKA'S REVENGE
VERRALL'S NIGHTMARE

Copyright © 2024 Phillip Strang
Cover Design by Phillip Strang

All rights reserved. No part of this book may be reproduced, stored in a retrieval system, or transmitted in any form or by any means (electronic, mechanical, photocopying, recording or otherwise) without the prior written permission of the publisher, except by a reviewer who may quote brief passages in a review to be printed by a newspaper, magazine, or journal.

All characters appearing in this work are fictitious. Any resemblance to actual events, locales, or persons, living or dead, is coincidental.
All Rights Reserved.

This work is registered with the UK Copyright Service.
ISBN - 13: 9798333003348

Dedication

For Elli and Tais, who both had the perseverance to make me sit down and write

Chapter 1

'I thought they used virgins,' Sergeant Wendy Gladstone said. She was in her late fifties and not in good health after too many years pounding the pavement in the inclement English weather. She had a lifetime of valuable experience, first as the only child of a subsistence farmer and his wife in northern England and then as a police officer for over thirty years.

She thought she had seen it all, but a naked man spreadeagled on a bare floor in a suburban house in London was a first for her.

Dead bodies, even if mutilated, no longer fazed her, but the man, in his thirties or early forties, had. He was surrounded by candles that had since burnt out, and on the cellar floor, crudely painted in red, was an inverted pentagram, the Sigil of Baphomet, the official insignia of the Church of Satan.

Wendy surmised middle-class affluence, pagan worship, and human sacrifice. She had read fiction and watched the occasional late-night horror movie, but to be confronted by reality made her feel uneasy.

'He might have been,' Inspector Larry Hill said, responding to Wendy's initial comment on seeing the body. Hill, in his forties, was an alcoholic, one month since his last drink. He had twenty-two years as a police officer and was highly regarded in Homicide for his investigative skills and commitment to policing. However, one more drunken bender and his days in Homicide would be numbered.

He had seen more of man's depravity than his sergeant, but she thought his remark was flippant. Although Wendy knew, as any police officer did, especially in Homicide, that flippancy often defused the situation. It was for them to be dispassionately professional, not to be melancholy or disheartened by humanity's ability to inflict terrible actions against another.

Detective Chief Inspector Isaac Cook, the senior officer in Homicide at Challis Street Police Station, close to Paddington in London, arrived within the hour. He took one look at the body and walked outside the house. The crime scene investigators, Forensics, and Pathology would provide the details.

One look at the man gave Homicide enough to commence a murder investigation. Proof from the knife in the man's chest that it was murder. Whatever the reason behind the death, ritual or not, it was a sadistic slaying. The perpetrators might claim they were practising their beliefs and offer an explanation for a sacrifice. However, murder was murder, whether it was ritualistic, a crime of passion, or a crime committed in agony.

Wendy and a couple of constables began interviewing the crowd gathered outside, asking what they had seen, what they knew, and who had lived in the house.

There were the signs of a couple who had rapidly left the place. Upstairs, an unmade bed, an emptied wardrobe, clothes strewn on the floor. In the bathroom, no toothbrushes or soap. And downstairs, in the kitchen, an open suitcase, still full of clothes that had not been taken.

'Loss of blood,' Gordon Windsor, the senior CSI, said when he took a dispassionate look at the body.

'But why?' Isaac asked.

'You're the detectives, not me.'

Isaac realised it was a dumb question. Whoever had committed the crime was not a typical suburbanite. Devil worship, satanism, and violent rituals did not belong in England.

Isaac knew he would not tell his wife, Jenny, about the latest murder. When they had moved in together, he had explained to her his reluctance to bring his work home with him and that she would be disturbed if he told her too much about his day.

To him, the home was a sanctuary, and on his return to the marital home, all he wanted to do was to kiss her, eat his meal, and then watch an inane programme on the television, whereas she wanted to talk about their life, the day she had had, the house they were buying, and especially his current murder investigation. He satisfied her once with details of another murder investigation over a pizza one Sunday. They were in the park with their young son. It was sunny, people were relaxing, and dogs were fetching balls.

She had been determined, and he relented, told her about the body they had found slowly dissolving in acid, the manner of the victim's death before entering the barrel, the reason he had died, and that a young constable had vomited at the sight of it.

After that, she asked, but there was no pressure for the gruesome details. If told of what they had seen at that house in suburbia – a spreadeagled naked man, his body covered in blood – she would have been upset and would not have slept that night. And then, for several days after, conversations about London and how she wanted to go and live somewhere quiet, where the neighbours were friendly, coming round to borrow a cup of sugar or to have a natter over the garden fence. Isaac knew they would not come round, and neighbours might be friendly one day but antagonistic the next. The illusion was better than the reality, which begged the question of how a satanic ritual of such malevolence could occur in a suburban detached house.

***

Phillip Strang

Although Homicide at Challis Street Police Station in London had dealt with terrorism, gang warfare, organised crime, and bombings where innocent people had died, this was the first time with satanism, apart from Wendy interviewing a woman conducting a séance in the backroom of her house. But a Ouija board and a group of lonely women were frivolous compared to the violent death of a hapless individual.

Bridget, Homicide's resident computer guru, spent two days studying ritualistic killings. She researched voodoo from the Caribbean, human sacrifice, and cannibalism amongst primitive peoples, immersing herself so much in the subject that she needed solace with a bottle of wine at home. Wendy worried for her and called for a halt to her research. Bridget struggled to comply.

The CSIs had concluded that four persons had been in the house when the victim had died.

Larry and Wendy were spending time out on the street, knocking on doors, waylaying people in the immediate vicinity. Larry had contacts, informers who would pass information for money, criminals who would talk in return for leniency or for the police not to cast a critical eye on their criminal ventures. But they were coming up with blanks. Satanism and ritual death were not the actions of the criminal but of the insane.

The pathologist conducted the autopsy, revealing that the man was between thirty-one and forty-five and English. Apart from his appearance, his ethnicity had been confirmed by DNA. The contents of his stomach, the pallor of his skin, and his poor physical condition lent weight to the theory that the man had spent time on the street and that he had been homeless for extended periods, surviving on scraps of food scrounged from those passing by or out of rubbish bins.

Wendy Gladstone thought, based on the man's appearance – unsavoury, with a broken nose, four missing teeth, bad dental hygiene, and a sallow appearance – that he had been a petty criminal and had spent time in prison, as well as being homeless. This proved true after the man's fingerprints were checked on a police database.

The murder house was now identified as the residence of Harold and Elizabeth Colson, and they had a clear title to it.

In one of the adjoining houses, a couple in their seventies, the man, hard of hearing, the wife, fit and agile. Wendy and Larry sat with them.

'Never spoke to them, but that's us. We do not look for company and prefer to stay indoors. We knew that someone lived there, saw shadows on the curtains at night, and there was a car, but they had one of those automatic garage doors: press a button, and it opens. Occasionally, we would see someone take out the rubbish or walk around the garden, but we did not talk to them, although we sometimes waved.'

On the other side of the murder house, a group of young people shared the rent, the lease in the name of one. The house was poorly maintained. Larry thought it looked more like a squatter's dive than someone's treasure.

'The owners don't care, as long as we pay the rent,' a barefooted young woman said. She had a towel wrapped around her, which should have indicated hygiene, but she was far from clean. Wendy and Larry realised the situation: in bed with a man or possibly a woman, rampant sex fuelled by illegal drugs. The odour of marijuana hung in the air.

'Next door?' Larry asked.

The young woman's lifestyle was taking its toll. Her complexion was pasty white, with no colour in her cheeks, tattoos on both arms and an eagle tattooed underneath her neck, its wings extending out over the top of her breasts. In another couple of years, she would either be dead or recovering from her addiction. Wendy hoped for the best; Larry did not concern himself with those who chose self-destruction. He had seen too much of life, and so had Wendy. Once a person was on the slippery slope down, there was not much hope of coming back, and when the social services failed to support her increasingly expensive drug habit, she'd be on the street selling herself.

'No idea. Never looked, don't care.'

'You're aware of what happened?' Wendy asked.

'Sort of. Barry lives here, he told me that someone had died there. He didn't say much, but that's Barry.'

'Anyone else in the house?'

'Barry, but he's indisposed.'

Larry could hear that, even if garbled, her speech was cultured, the result of an affluent upbringing and a good school. Drugs were her downfall, as with many others. However, it didn't alter the fact that the number of people residing in the house was still uncertain. Someone must have seen something.

A voice from upstairs beckoned the woman to come back. Larry was up the stairs, stepping over detritus as he climbed, not concerned either. It wasn't his house, and he wanted answers. Devil worshippers were unlikely to be good neighbours who kept to themselves, tending the garden on weekends and working during the week.

'Who are you?' a heavily tattooed man said as Larry entered the bedroom. There was a mattress on the floor, a bottle of whisky nearby, drug paraphernalia on the other side of the mattress, a candle on a windowsill, and the tattered curtains were drawn closed. Larry's wife had been keen on buying an investment property, but he had resisted. In part because he didn't have the capital, but mainly because he had seen inside other houses destroyed by the renters, if they ever paid, and then the trouble of evicting them.

'Detective Inspector Hill, Challis Street Police Station, Homicide. Who are you?'

'I don't have to give my name; I've done nothing wrong.'

Downstairs, the towelled woman, Cheryl Hastings, who had finally given her name, sat with Wendy. Larry thought that the young woman, her mental faculties impaired by drugs, had gone downmarket in her choice of men. This was a nobody, a reprobate, possibly with a criminal record, who could be hiding out from the police. He was certainly not a reliable witness, but he might know something.

'You probably have, but that's not why I'm here,' Larry said. 'Next door, do you know who they are?'

'No.'

'I've not said which side, have I?' Larry had met this type before. Politeness wasn't the way to get cooperation.

'I saw the police vehicles outside. I heard what the officers were saying.'

'And you don't feel you need to assist and help with our enquiries?'

'What for? Why should I help the pigs?'

Larry had heard worse. The man was drunk and high on one illicit substance or another, and his amorous intent had been disturbed. Larry could not blame him for being upset, not that he cared whether he was or not. It was answers he wanted.

'We have a problem here, don't we?' Larry said. 'It's criminal to have some of these drugs, and you don't want to give me a name.'

'You've got nothing on me.'

'I do, but that's not important. I'll give you a break. I'll look the other way, and you tell me who you are and what you know about next door. It's murder, violent and depraved, and the dead person could be one of your friends.'

'Could it?'

'Either it is, or it isn't. Who owns the house next door? Have you met them?'

Larry knew who owned both houses. Bridget, in Homicide at Challis Street, had found that out within twenty minutes of the murder being discovered.

'English, in their fifties, maybe older. They own this house as well. We pay the rent to them.'

'Or supply them with recruits? How much rent do you pay?'

'Not my interest. I only squat.'

'And fornicate with the woman downstairs. Got it made, have you?'

'I reckon so. Free drugs, a willing woman, what more does a man want?'

Larry could have said respect for the woman, who had now changed from the towel into a pair of jeans and a loose top. She was coming off the high, and Wendy, a sucker for someone down on their luck, was calmly talking to her and offering to help.

Their chief inspector, Isaac Cook, had spoken to Wendy about her susceptibility to becoming emotionally involved with persons she met. Still, it was a habit of a lifetime, going back to when she was a constable in Sheffield in the north of the country, tasked with finding missing children. Disturbing stories of abuse at the hands of a parent or a friend of the family. Unless the circumstances were conclusive, the children returned home, and one of them, a young girl, had died within weeks at the hands of her father.

Wendy could see a troubled soul in Cheryl Hastings. Although this was early in the investigation, she would heed Isaac's warning, as he should know, having been conned by two women in his early days in the force, believing them to be innocent. Both proved to be murderers. One was psychopathic, the other was in the employ of Her Majesty's Government, and she had killed one of the people in the murder investigation. Homicide had been investigated, although that crime, courtesy of the Official Secrets Act and senior political influence, had been swept under the carpet, and the woman had disappeared out of the country.

'You know the people?'

'Cheryl deals with them.'

'But you've seen them.'

'Seen, not spoken. This person they killed, a homeless drifter, dossed down here for a couple of weeks. I don't know his name, but he told us it was David. I'm not sure if it was.'

'And you didn't care either. Did he pay money to stay? How do you know it's him?'

'I didn't, but he never returned last night. He gave some money for the rent and paid the remainder in-kind.'

Devil House

The man's attitude changed once he realised the inspector wasn't about to arrest him. He got out of bed, grabbed hold of an old tee shirt and a pair of shorts, and put them on. He was barefooted and smelled of body odour. He was an unpleasant sight compared to the young woman downstairs, who had combed her hair and washed her face.

'Drugs?'

'Not drugs, alcohol. He might have stolen them, not that we cared.'

'Who is "we"?'

'Those in the house.'

'How many?'

'Four or five, three at the moment, or maybe two if it's David next door.'

'Doesn't that upset the neighbours?' Larry said. His initial approach to the man had moderated.

'Nobody makes much noise here. Cheryl rules the roost and ensures those staying understand the rules and pay in advance. She doesn't like it here or like me much, so I can't blame her. She's a good person, better than this life, but drugs destroy us all. Not that I ever had much, a council housing estate, left school at sixteen, was expelled, and never returned. And then, my father, strait-laced, worked for the council, disapproved of me, kicked me out of the house the second time I was arrested for drugs.'

'How long here, in this house?'

'Five months, maybe six.'

'With Cheryl?'

'I met her here. She's long-term. The house was in better condition back then, but she was in rehab, back on the drugs now.'

'Because of you?'

'Not me. Once a drug addict, always a drug addict; there is no point denying it. It doesn't take much for a person to fall off the wagon and to start shooting up.'

'Heroin?'

'For me, not for Cheryl. Cocaine and amphetamines with her. She could break the habit and get a decent job, but she's got issues. I don't know the details, never asked, never cared.'

'As long as she sleeps with you?'

'Not that. You're a police inspector; you know what it's like. Skeletons in the cupboard, hidden trauma. I don't know what hers is, although it's probably abuse.'

'You're not as dumb as you look,' Larry said. 'Drugs, where do you get the money?'

'We manage. Cheryl works, and so do I, casual in a fast-food joint, flip hamburgers. And then those who stay pay extra, and the rent for this dump isn't much.'

'As long as you supply the occasional sacrifice.'

'Don't try to pin that on us. Okay, he went around there, fifty pounds to mow the lawn, tidy up around the place. No idea he would get himself killed, or they were into murder.'

'Blood everywhere. Not your cup of tea?'

'Not me. They offered me work there once, but I didn't go.'

'Tell me about them.'

'Not much to say. A married couple in their fifties. They drive a nondescript car.'

'Can you be more specific.'

'I didn't look, nor am I interested. We live here cheaply, and they don't bother us. There's no need to rock the boat; they told Cheryl they were intensely private and didn't want to be disturbed.'

'Who else apart from the dead man went around there?'

'No one since we've been here. Might be the first death.'

Larry felt he had exhausted the conversation, but there would be more questions. 'We need to be able to contact you, just in case.'

'No problem, take my phone number.'

'I'll need an ID. A driving licence and a home address.'

'Neither. I don't drive, and I'm never bothered to learn. And you won't find me at a home address. I haven't been there since I was kicked out.'

'Always someone to cadge off?'

'Something like that.'

'Your home address. Give it to me anyway.'

Larry entered the address into his phone and dialled the number given. A man answered the phone. 'Ted Sorell,' he said.

'Detective Inspector Larry Hill. Do you have a son, name of Barry?'

'Did, once. Kicked him out of the house. Is he in trouble?'

'Not trouble. We need to confirm his identity. Do you want to talk to him?'

'Not me. His mother might.'

Larry handed over the phone; mother and son spoke for five minutes before Barry Sorell returned the phone. 'Thanks for that,' he said.

Chapter 2

The nondescript car that Sorell described was a 2012 VW Golf. The registration was known, and the vehicle was registered and insured. According to the insurance company, there had been no accidents.

Harold and Elizabeth Colson appeared to be an average middle-class suburban couple. He was an accountant, and she was a housewife. He worked from home, although none of his clients had ever entered the house. There was only one issue: they had disappeared.

It was mysterious that two mild-mannered and inoffensive persons could be devil worshippers, although Bridget, in her research, had found that they fitted the profile. The ability to be regular and boringly average while keeping their dark side secret.

The dead man's name was David Grayling, the son of a vicar and his wife in the north of England. Wendy, on phoning the parents, found out that he had left home fourteen years previously, called home once a month, did not ask for money, and told his parents not to worry, and no, he wouldn't be coming home soon, not until he had sorted himself out.

To his parents, when he had left at twenty-one years of age, that had meant sowing his wild oats, drinking too much, experimenting with drugs, and chasing women, although they failed to mention his time in prison. And they had prayed every night for his safe return to the bosom of the family, to embrace the Lord, but now realised that their prayers had been in vain.

Isaac thought being the son of a holy man might have been important to those who had killed him.

It was de rigueur when there was a murder to solve – an early-morning meeting in Homicide. It was Isaac who stated the obvious. 'Find the Colsons. Did they kill David Grayling? And was he a willing victim? It seems illogical that he was, but it's happened in the past, or was he in the wrong place at the wrong time?'

Isaac could see that Larry had had too many drinks the previous night. He hoped the man wasn't slipping back into bad habits. One more reprimand and he was out of the force, and he needed him, as good a detective as any he had worked with.

'These people don't display their beliefs openly, as malevolent as they are, as violent as it was. Did he suffer?' Bridget asked.

'There appears to be no sign of resistance, although the man had consumed alcohol and injected heroin before his death.'

'Mr and Mrs Average, they don't sound,' Wendy said. 'I've asked in the street; nobody had much to say, and no one had been in the house. I found a plumber who fixed a leak in the upstairs bathroom. He said the house smelled damp and that it was dark and drab. He offered to check for them, but they declined. The CSIs have been through the place, clean and tidy, but neglected, with rising damp and mould in a couple of rooms.'

Isaac, as the senior officer in Homicide, was frustrated by the lack of progress. Two persons, crucial to the investigation, were the possible murderers, although there was proof that other people had been in the house, either on the night of the murder or a few days earlier. But out on the street, nobody was talking. One person had slammed the door in Wendy's face, and another, red-faced and drunk, had muttered incoherently that you don't get involved if you know what is good for you.

Nobody in Homicide was willing to believe that Satan had a hold over the street and that it was just the typical reaction of law-abiding persons not to become involved. But if the Colsons and whoever else had committed such a heinous crime, they were people to be frightened of. All except Barry and Cheryl, next door's amorous, drugged-out lovers, who were enjoying the benefits of not paying rent to their landlord.

It was late morning, close to midday, when Wendy entered the unlocked front door of their house. She could hear people moving upstairs, so she climbed the stairs. In one room, Sorell and Cheryl Hastings. In another room, a young woman was asleep.

'That's Mila,' Sorell said. He was dressed casually and was clean-shaven, a transformation from the man Larry had met.

'Barry works a casual job,' Cheryl said as she kissed him.

'According to my inspector, you are a layabout. Was he wrong?'

'Not wrong. Cheryl and I are trying to sort ourselves out, get rid of the drugs, and find somewhere better than this.'

'Which you're not paying rent on now,' Wendy reminded him.

'Except for the police presence outside, and your people intend to rip this place apart.'

'It shouldn't bother you, or should it?'

'Not us, but it's inconvenient.'

'What about her next door?'

'Eastern European, not that she has said much.'

'Illegal? Selling herself?'

'She paid for the night. If she doesn't bother us, we don't bother her. Does a hotel ask if someone has the money, and why do you think she is selling herself?'

'A lot do. Do you get many in like her?'

'Not a lot, most nights on our own. Single women or a couple, male and female, can stay, but not single men. We can't trust them, although we did with David.'

'With Cheryl?'

'With drugs. The men are more likely to OD, and then we have the police asking questions. She's slept since she arrived. She might be selling herself, but that's not our concern. What about those who want to rip up the floorboards?'

'It won't be as drastic as that. Will they find anything?'

'They might. We've never seen anything, although we've not been here long. It could explain the cheap rent.'

***

The search for the Colsons continued. Reports from Scotland and Cornwall of possible sightings. The airports and the cross-channel ports had been updated to be on the lookout for two people matching their descriptions. What was of concern and made no sense was why two persons who had lived in the house for sixteen years had suddenly decided to sacrifice a hapless victim and then disappear. Since then, no credit cards had been used.

This was, to Homicide, suspicious and a clear indicator, if not of murder, then of a calculated deception.

The car, registered and insured, was found ten miles from the house by an eagle-eyed hiker down a track in the forest he was walking through. It was in perfect condition, clean inside and out, with no trace of what had happened to the occupants, whose fingerprints were easily found. A police team had searched the forest, and divers were checking a pond there.

David Grayling, his body formally identified by his father, was in the morgue, awaiting release for burial. His parents were found to be solid citizens, salt-of-the-earth types, who had raised their son well and ensured he had a good education. He was a gifted rugby player who had played for the school and his county as an under-16. But then, life intervened, and whereas he had taken a job and committed himself to further education, a Bachelor of Engineering under his belt, he had also discovered recreational drugs.

In the end, he had drifted away, phoned home occasionally, but never visited, preferring the anonymity of the street, euphoria, and melancholy, surviving on unemployment benefits, a hostel when he could afford it, and casual work to supplement his income.

'Always a dreamer,' his father said.

'We warned him that he would end up dead if he did not change his ways. Believes us now,' his mother said. She was a small woman, barely up to her husband's shoulder.

Larry could read the signals. The father ruled the house with an iron fist and brokered no dissent. The wife was timid and frightened of his wrath. Two people, not loving but unable to separate, and the young Grayling, in the middle of a fractious relationship.

Larry had seen it before: the toxic household, not a place of nurture, and in their teens, most go through a difficult time with raging hormones and the need to experiment, to take risks, to get laid, to drink too much alcohol, and to try drugs. David Grayling had probably been a decent person who, when he had needed his parents, found out they were not there for him, and he had drifted away, and now he was dead. But was his death voluntary?

Bridget's research showed that sometimes it was the victim's choice, but if David had willingly given his life, why? It was still murder, premeditated, and punishable by a lengthy prison term, and the Colsons were in their fifties, with no chance they would experience freedom again once convicted.

***

Barry Sorell and Cheryl Hastings's departure occurred earlier than expected. They had intended to stay on at the house to allow the crime scene investigators free access. After all, they had nothing of worth, and, as Wendy observed, the drug paraphernalia was gone, and they had cleaned their bedroom with clean sheets on the mattress, a picture of loving bliss.

The woman in the other room, pretty and Slavic, when she was brought to Challis Street Police Station, was found to be illegal and would be passed over to immigration. An unfortunate choice of accommodation with Sorell and Cheryl. It was her bad luck that she had been caught. Her English was passable, enough to be understood. She wasn't turning tricks, just taking casual jobs when she could get them and sending money home to her mother in Bulgaria. Her deportation wasn't immediate, and if she could prove good intent and difficulties if she was repatriated to her home country – she said there would be, as the economy was in tatters, and she would be forced into prostitution – she would be given temporary residency in the United Kingdom.

She could then apply for full-time employment, as she had a degree in economics from a university in Sofia, which would be much better than stacking shelves in a supermarket or cash in hand in a coffee shop.

Initially, after the murder, it had been decided that only a cursory inspection of the leased house was warranted and that it wasn't urgent. The situation changed rapidly when a sniffer dog entered the house. It wasn't customary to use a dog, but the damp, not-so-noticeable upstairs was more apparent in one corner of a room downstairs. There was a rudimentary bed in there, but those who slept on it for one night would not for a second. The two incumbent residents had just locked the room and left it alone, enduring the dampness and the smell with disinterest and copious quantities of air freshener. Until the sniffer dog latched onto the smell and wouldn't move away.

The floorboards were ripped up, and a set of stairs was discovered leading down, a room at the bottom. The house was Victorian, 1857, but the room was much earlier. Why and how made no sense. The street, thankfully a cul-de-sac, was closed at the junction to the main road, entry only on presentation of a badge or a signed document from Challis Street. Residents in the street were allowed access. The situation was grim, the possibilities mind-boggling.

An expert in basements and architecture of the period confirmed the date of the house, with proof that before the house, the area had been agricultural, and the house was positioned where a farmhouse had once stood. A geologist, an architectural expert, and an expert on satanic rituals confirmed that the hidden room was from the seventeenth century. The expert on satanic rituals confirmed that it could have been used for worship of the devil, but it could also have been for Catholic worship in the early eighteenth century when it had become illegal to conduct Catholic services.

Chapter 3

It wasn't unusual for the past to be uncovered in London. A new office block, another skyscraper, a residential home, and below them, as the foundations were established, there would be ancient Roman ruins from when London was known as Londinium. Also, Black Death burial sites, mass skeletons lumped together, a mosaic, proof of the many ethnicities that had helped to make the city what it is in the twenty-first century.

However, a room below ground level, hewn from the soil and used for religious or irreligious purposes, was unusual. Isaac had a healthy respect for religion but could not countenance devil worship. Yet, the Colsons were an average couple, secretive and solitary but otherwise nondescript. And now, they had vanished, and no amount of searching could find them.

Wendy believed that after their dastardly deed, they had taken themselves somewhere remote and committed suicide. Larry wasn't so sure. He was not a fatalist and knew that people don't usually commit suicide after killing. He thought they were lying low and might have changed their appearance, going from middle-aged, unsociable, and conservative to youthful, sociable, and liberal, the life and soul of the party. Isaac did not choose either option, and theorising without a factual reference offered no advantage.

'Find the Colsons,' Isaac said, to make them focus in the office. Wendy noticed the irritability and realised their chief inspector was under pressure. Commander Goddard, DCI Isaac Cook's mentor for many years and senior officer, was not coming into Homicide as often as he had in the past, not at all for the last three weeks, as he was friendly with Commissioner Davies, the head of the London Metropolitan Police, and sucking up to the slug of a man.

She had not approved of the previous draconian measures championed by Davies, and after seven months, they had been discarded because impinging the freedoms of law-abiding citizens and arbitrary arrests did not sit well with the majority.

Davies remained in his position, even if he had opened himself to criticism for his heavy-handed approach. Nobody could take him down, and the man still revelled in the improved crime statistics. He had been on television, and Isaac had to admit that the man had the gift of the gab, charismatic when needed, firm when under pressure, condescending when required. It was a masterful performance, although he had skirted around questions about excess violence by the police.

'How?' Larry said. Isaac had had another chat with him, the usual, to curtail his alcohol intake, or he would be out of the police force. He thought of reinforcing it with a disciplinary report but decided against it. The man was in enough trouble as it was, with his wife berating him for his lack of ambition.

She was a social climber, determined to rise in status and wealth, but according to her, she was held back by a mediocre husband. However, she still loved him, adored their children, and would not leave. She was comfortable with her family but not with her lifestyle. Even after the husband of one of her upwardly mobile friends had been arrested for trafficking drugs, she had stood by her friend. 'Bad eggs in any society,' she said.

Larry knew some of the others his wife clung to, and if she looked past the Range Rovers and the expensive holidays, most were up to the hilt in debt. A dip in the economy was coming, and they would be sent to the wall, forced from their SUVs into small runabouts, holidays in England, or a discount package in Spain, which previously they would have regarded as suitable for the plebs but not for them.

'What about this area underneath the floorboards?' Isaac asked, getting away from further discussion about his inspector's drinking. 'How long since anyone had been down there? Any sign of sacrifice? Any further evidence that David Grayling's death wasn't a one-off?'

'The Colsons had lived in Sorell and Hastings' house for eleven years before they bought the house next door. No signs of recent use.'

'No more bodies?'

'Not yet. The CSIs are checking both gardens with ground-penetrating radar. They believe they have found one burial site and are slowly opening it up, sifting the soil just in case.'

'How soon?'

'Later today, maybe tomorrow,' Wendy said. 'They are working through the night, in shifts. The neighbours on the other side have complained about the floodlights and reckon they can't sleep. I've told them it's murder, and they'll have to deal with it. The lights are on until we are finished.'

'Agreed,' Isaac said. 'Bridget,' turning to the office guru, 'anything to add?'

'Two missing persons, known to have been near the Colson house. One is known to Sorell and Hastings, while the other is a local junkie who lived one street away. His parents assumed he was squatting somewhere.'

'Police report?'

'They never registered his disappearance, on probation for drug use, a history of shoplifting. Caring parents, dealing with an impossible situation.'

'Body in the backyard, male or female? Or can't they tell? The soil impaction test should give an approximate date of how long it has been there. What do we have? Phone one of the CSIs to get an update. We need it now.'

There was a nervousness about her DCI, which Wendy had been the first to see, but it was now apparent to the others. A man, very much in control of himself, now suffering from anxiety about his and his family's future.

The son of Jamaican immigrants who had come to England in the sixties and who had suffered prejudice, dead-end jobs, and forced to live in slum dwellings infested with rats and lice. They had come to love England but had since retired to Jamaica. Their son, Isaac, was a proud Englishman who did not want to leave. But it was proving difficult with Commissioner Davies in charge and Commander Goddard grovelling to him, and the obsequious Superintendent Seth Caddick, who was always hovering in the background, ready to pounce as a cat would with a mouse, and Isaac knew he was the mouse.

Two men who feigned friendship. Caddick, because it came naturally to him and Isaac because he had to. It was an impossible situation with no resolution.

'Two hours,' Wendy repeated on the phone to the CSI.

'Level with us. I reckon we deserve that,' Larry said to Isaac.

'Does it relate to us?' Bridget asked.

'Firstly, Wendy, what happens in two hours?' Isaac asked.

'The body in the garden. The CSIs are certain it's human. They'll phone when they have any more information.'

'Good, keep us posted. Okay, this is the situation, at least with me. Davies has had to back down with his new anti-crime campaign. The man's a master at shifting the blame, and those who had given him tentative support have pulled back and are sitting on the fence. There will be scapegoating, and blame will be apportioned where it will be easier to stick. Davies will fight to preserve his position. He's been there before and always managed to weasel his way out. This time, his defence will be more difficult, and the pressure on him will be more virulent.'

'And Commander Goddard's thrown his hat in the ring and come out on Davies's side. More difficult for him,' Larry said.

'He's adept, plays the game better than most. I only gave tacit agreement to go along with Caddick, who is as dirty as they come. He would throw you under a bus to protect his skin. I'm not the only one under threat, or maybe I am. Whatever happens, I'm not going to play their game.'

21

'You weren't responsible, opposed it the best way you could,' Larry said. 'Whatever happens, we're behind you, all the way.'

Isaac knew they were, but they would have little influence. The best defence against censure or removal was performance and good policing. He needed a win, and the biggest win at the present time would be solving the murder of David Grayling. Permission had been given to his parents to claim the body, and his burial would be in two weeks. Under normal circumstances, there might have been a request by the police to keep the body in cold storage, but due to the nature of the death, Isaac had agreed to hand the body over.

'We've been down this road before. Our best defence is to do our job and to get a result. What do we have? Bridget, you first.'

Bridget gave a folder to each of the other three. 'In there, you will find my research on devil worshippers, the type of persons involved, the rituals, some sexual, some murderous, others frivolous, Hammer horror movies fare. The Colsons might have a family history of obscure beliefs, not that I've found it; unsure if Colson is the family name.'

'If it isn't, what can we do? There were fingerprints in the house.'

'And in the car, but we've no reference.'

'No criminal record, and not on file. Are you looking further?'

'We are; it takes time.'

'I've spoken to people in the street,' Wendy said. 'They continue to say nothing, vehemently stating that they know nothing. The house backs onto a park. There is a street on the far side.'

'Get a couple of juniors, door knock, and see if someone is not scared out of their wits. Mention the devil and people are superstitious, brings out primordial fears in them, things that go bump in the night, or did the Colsons put out the frighteners,

Halloween, that sort of thing?' Isaac said. He had forgotten his early melancholy. There were actions to take and things to do.

Regardless of office machinations and whether the Met was going to hell or would be resurrected as the august institution it had been once, they were not the primary focus of Homicide. There was a murder to solve.

***

On her way out of the office, Wendy grabbed a couple of junior officers. One, from the Middle East, was a new recruit to the department, twenty-three years old and female. Life had been brutal in her homeland. She had confided to Wendy and Bridget that she had had limited opportunities, a job in a shop, and not even the minimum wage. She was never sure if she would be paid or if the shop owner would try to proposition her.

Nadia Hussain was adamant she hadn't succumbed to the latter, but neither Wendy nor Bridget was sure. Life was tough, even in London, and working in Homicide, they knew that depravity and abuse, mental and sexual, was never far away. Either menial labour, standing on your feet during the day for a pittance and the probability of lechers aiming to take advantage, or out on the street or in a cheap hotel prostituting.

Everyone in the office could see that Nadia was attractive, aiming to protect her dignity, and now dating a constable from a floor up from Homicide, planning to move in together, and talking about marriage.

The second junior was from Liverpool, a tall, well-built lad who boxed at the weekend as an amateur and won more than he lost. A police officer with a black eye on most Mondays was not a good look and hardly inspired the public, but he had a disarming smile and a courteous manner.

'You've been updated,' Wendy said, 'Read the case files. Devil worshippers don't usually meet in twos. On the street, everyone is keeping quiet. They don't know anything, although I believe they are scared.'

'In my country, they would be,' Nadia said.

'And you?' Wendy asked.

'Terrified. Maybe it's nonsense, but I will do my job, don't worry about me.'

Wendy didn't. She hadn't travelled much, a few times to Spain or Greece, a chance to get a tan, to lie in the sun, and to dream about the lotharios who passed her by. But she had read that superstition and belief in the old ways, coupled with the fear of the unknown, still existed.

'Don't worry about me,' Constable Jim Drayton said. 'Nothing a bunch of fives won't solve.'

Wendy knew which of the two would freak out first, and it was not Nadia. A boxing ring was one thing; proximity to evil was another, and even if the Colsons had not invoked the devil, their heinous act was a quantifiable sin.

Wendy outlined where to concentrate their efforts and the questions to ask, careful not to rouse the people and make them fearful. Also, to be persistent but non-threatening as the natural state of people is to not want to become involved.

Wendy parked on the other side of the park. The three paced the route from the vehicle to the back of the Colsons' house. The crime scene investigators had scoured the route previously, and there was no concern they might be treading on evidence. It wasn't a large park, and people walked their dogs there. Nadia reckoned she could feel a chill in the air, but Wendy reassured her that it was chilly, a weak sun that struggled to shine was hidden by the trees, and that closeness to death, especially violent death, made anyone feel a presence and that Grayling's death – Nadia and Jim Drayton had seen the photos – was violent in the extreme.

On the road and near her car, Wendy focused on a row of neat, tidy semi-detached houses. Nadia would focus two streets back, and Jim Drayton would check several cul-de-sacs nearby. Wendy remained optimistic, conscious that her days of pounding the streets were behind her. Once she had revelled in the opportunity to be out of the office, policing at the coal face, she would have said. But now, her legs would ache at the end of the day, only to be soothed by a long soak in a hot bath and a few too many glasses of wine.

'Nothing unusual,' the occupants of the first house told Wendy.

At the second house, a sprightly lady in her eighties. At her heels, there was a small yapping dog. 'Is what they said on the television true?' she said.

'It depends,' Wendy replied. Sprightly old ladies, experience told her, were often a wealth of knowledge and regarded it as their responsibility to check on the neighbourhood, to see whose dog was fouling the footpath, who was having an affair, and who was worshipping the devil.

'Devil worshippers, ritual sacrifice?'

'We don't know if the people believed in the devil, but yes, signs of a ritual, and there was a naked body.'

'I sometimes saw them in the park or in the street. They seemed strange, or maybe they weren't. In hindsight, I could say they looked evil. Why would they do something like that? I suppose you've seen it all before.'

'Too often, I'm afraid. It would take a lot to shake me these days.' However, Wendy couldn't be sure if what she said was true. Seeing David Grayling's naked body on the floor, she had felt physically ill. 'Did you see anything? Any reason to be frightened?'

Wendy realised that traipsing up one street and down the street, asking the same questions, receiving verbiage at times, monosyllabic responses at others, or providing the chance for someone to vent their spleen about their neighbours and the parlous state of the police force – 'in my time, a policeman was a friend, but nowadays…' – was tiresome.

On and on some people would go, wasting time, but not the old lady. Parking was at a premium in the cul-de-sac where the murder house was. And possibly those involved had parked near the woman's home.

They could have been bank managers, civil servants, or unskilled labourers. Wendy could not imagine a police officer, but then, she could not imagine anyone debased enough to participate in human sacrifice. But in her younger years, as a junior constable in Sheffield, a long way north of London, she had seen criminality in the police station. She had been hit on more than once for sexual favours by her superiors, rejecting them all, although it had resulted in a transfer out of the station and down to London. She had seen the bribes and the doctoring of the evidence.

One thing she admired about Detective Chief Inspector Isaac Cook was that he was scrupulously honest. Although she could not say the same for Inspector Larry Hill. He mixed with criminals and arrested his quota but turned a blind eye to an indiscretion if it advanced an investigation into a more serious crime. In the last murder investigation, she wasn't sure if the blind eye resulted from the investigation or whether there was a financial incentive. She planned to talk to her DCI or maybe wait and see, and if she had proof, what then? She knew that Isaac Cook had a soft spot for the man, having seen him fluctuate between drunkenness and sobriety. He had even taken a bullet in the stomach once and spent time in hospital after a severe beating.

'Are you an educated woman?' Wendy asked.

'I used to be an insurance assessor. If you want fiction, that is the place; the ludicrous claims, some fraudulent, and a few were criminal. I sent your people a few over the years.'

'Seen it all doesn't cover what happened in that house,' Wendy reminded her.

'Doesn't it?' the woman replied. 'Arson, a body inside, burnt to a cinder, and then the husband claimed it was an accident: chips in a pan, boiling oil, and his wife had early-stage dementia and plenty of life insurance.'

'Others?'

'Cup of tea?'

Even though she was parched, Wendy would have been inclined to say no, but the woman had been an insurance assessor. That meant she had analytical skills and would have seen people and remembered who they were, what they looked like, and the cars they drove.

Wendy phoned the two constables, asked how they were doing, and received the usual – that it was slow going, no one had seen anything, or if they had, they didn't want to be involved.

'A tea, that would be great. Your name?'

'Cathy Hopkinson, widow, not that I miss him, not that much.'

'I miss my husband,' Wendy said, although it had been a few years since he died.

'I've got used to being on my own.'

The two women sat in a neat and tidy kitchen. This was the home of a woman who had seen the grittier side of life, the same as a police officer in Homicide had.

'What do you remember?' Wendy asked. 'Not generalisations, but details. If the Colsons had visitors, they could have parked near your house and walked through the park, hopped over the back fence, and then into the orgy, the chanting, the ritual sacrifice of a chicken or a goat. It's hard to imagine that they killed many people over there, although we're looking for others who have gone missing.'

'Two doors up, husband and wife. They used to go to the Colsons, saw them walk through the park more than once.'

'Are they still there?' Wendy said as she gulped down her tea and ate the biscuit on a plate nearby.

'They are. A lovely couple, Janice and Bob McCarthy. They moved in eight years ago, and I've seen the Colsons go into their house on more than one occasion.'

'You believe them to be involved?'

'Not them, no reason to. The Colsons were remote if you saw them in the street, and they were not the types to stop for a chat. But you cannot judge a book by its cover, can you? They acknowledged you, commented on the weather, and that was it.

Janice and Bob were communicative and came over here a few times, although it was Janice more than Bob. He works for a company in their financial department. She's a teacher at the local school.'

'And devil worshippers?'

'Strange if Janice and Bob are involved in devil worship.'

'Why?'

'Janice goes to the occasional church service.'

'Bob?'

'Not sure, although I don't watch what they do, only that I like to walk on a Sunday. Often, I pass the church. Can you believe in both God and the devil?' Cathy Hopkinson asked.

Wendy wasn't sure of the answer, only that in the Bible, it said that Jesus had spent forty nights and forty days in the wilderness, tempted by Satan. 'I think so,' she said.

Wendy left Cathy Hopkinson and wandered up the street, phoning the other two, who were still having no success, to tell them where she was going, and if she didn't message them in fifteen minutes, to bang on the door and smash it down if there was no response.

Wendy had a premonition and knew the most benign person could often be the most aggressive if riled. She also phoned Isaac, told him what she had found out, and that she was about to confront the people.

Isaac offered Larry Hill to accompany her, but she wasn't waiting, and besides, Inspector Hill would not act with the decorum required, accusing people of devil worship, bacchanalian orgies, and ritual sacrifice. Wendy would be more circumspect in the lion's cage, attempting to calm the savage beast.

She phoned the two constables again. 'Ten minutes, not fifteen. Keep out of sight. If you don't hear from me, or you hear shouting or banging, then smash the door down and raise the alarm.'

Wendy couldn't understand why she was being alarmist. She had faced off murderers before and stood firm while a man pointed a gun at a woman with a knife. But for some reason, she felt fear. Was it the stuff of nightmares? Whatever it was, it disturbed her.

Chapter 4

'Any friend of Cathy's,' a small bespectacled man said after Wendy introduced herself. Hardly Vincent Price or Christopher Lee, she thought.

Wendy sat in the chair of honour in the sitting room. On the mantlepiece was an old-style clock in a wooden frame. On either side, framed photographs of the McCarthys and a young girl.

'That's Beth,' Janice, thin, with drawn skin and shoulder-length hair, said.

'Your daughter?' Wendy said, unsure if she should respond. Cathy Hopkinson had not mentioned a child, and in the room where she sat, there were none of the usual signs of someone young in the house.

'She died,' Bob said. 'It was six years ago, a tragic accident.

'A lovely child, but we never know when we'll be taken, do we?' Janice said.

Was that the reason for the occasional church visits? A prayer for the daughter? Or was it to ease a guilty conscience, to get absolution from worshipping evil, or for killing a person in cold blood? Wendy thought.

'You're friends with Cathy Hopkinson?' Wendy said.

'We are, and the Colsons. Is this what this is about?' Bob McCarthy said.

'It is. You knew them better than most. We are told that you were friends.'

'They had experienced tragedy. You would not understand. Besides, you are a police officer. With the Colsons, our heartbreak was not mentioned, only that we understood each other's anguish.'

'Are they devil worshippers or satanists?'

'They had a healthy interest in the occult, in alchemy, in astrology, but they were not what you think of them.'

'Are you saying that their interest was academic?'

'We are.'

Janice McCarthy sat close to Wendy and touched her arm.

'One minute,' Wendy said. She phoned Jim Drayton. 'Okay,' she said. 'Nothing to worry about?'

'What did you expect?' Janice said. 'That we would have you staked out on the sitting room floor, with a knife in hand to cut out your beating heart?'

'Is that what they do?'

The McCarthys would be investigated about the circumstances leading up to their child's death. The tragedy that befell the Colsons was not known but could be significant.

'The Colsons? Death in the family?' Wendy asked. Janice had miraculously placed another cup of tea in front of her.

'A son. We don't know the age or the circumstances, and there were no photos of him in their house. It was only once that it was mentioned. We knew, they knew, no more needed to be said.'

'Apart from that, what else can you tell me about them?'

'They kept to themselves, were polite and neighbourly. This idea that they had killed that man is insane.'

'And yet, they disappear. What is the explanation?'

'We don't have one, only that we can't believe them guilty.'

'Did you know about the cellar in the other house? Did they attempt a manifestation?'

'A visitation from the horned beast? Are you joking?' Bob McCarthy said. 'Ludicrous.'

'A perverse attempt to resurrect their son. If Christianity wasn't going to do it, might the devil? Have you considered it yourself?' Wendy knew she was baiting the husband and wife. She needed to see if they were capable of anger and violence.

Janice McCarthy quickly rose to the bait, rising out of her chair and gesticulating with her hands. 'How dare you come in here and sully the name of our daughter?' she said.

Wendy knew that sensitivity was required with a dead child's parents, but it was murder they were investigating. Subtlety and discretion were not to be considered; apologies could be made later. A message from Bridget in Homicide asked her to return to the station. Which could only mean one thing: concerns over the deaths of the two children. Wendy had messaged the updates to Bridget.

If that was the case, Wendy knew she would be sickened at the thought and that the McCarthys would feel the full force of the law: an intense enquiry into their backgrounds, their child, and association with the Colsons, who remained at large. The all-points bulletin for them had yielded nothing, not even a credit card, which meant they were probably in a remote location and lying low.

Wendy noticed that Bob McCarthy had not risen to the bait, which, considering it was their child's death, why hadn't he? Unusual, she thought, but it was not a time to pass judgement. It may be that the McCarthys were innocent of all crimes. She was sure she would talk to the McCarthys and Cathy Hopkinson again.

***

In Homicide, Bridget Halloran sat at her laptop. Initially, she had been a CCTV officer, but due to her sharp eyes and technical skills, she was now in charge of administration in Homicide. The person to go to when you need information hidden deep in a police database or on a server elsewhere in the country or overseas. Seven years younger than Wendy, the two were inseparable friends, sharing a house after the death of Wendy's husband and the rough eviction of one of Bridget's live-ins, a council worker who took what he could and did not contribute financially to the weekly costs of the house, and Bridget let him live in for services rendered.

Wendy had been married for more years than she could remember, and in the end, her husband barely knew who she was.

Bridget had never married, although she had had lovers, and even now, the occasional night away or a strange face at the breakfast table when Wendy came down from her slumber. Bridget was adamant that no one would move in, nor would she become emotionally involved, and the men were there for one purpose.

Wendy, who missed the closeness of a man, envied her friend, but she had no intent to indulge in casual sex. She'd had more than enough of that in her teens.

'Janice and Bob McCarthy, eight years in the house as you were told. Lucy, eight years old, had an accident in the park opposite,' Bridget said.

'Is there an inquest report or an autopsy? An eight-year-old child, even if a tragic accident, would have raised concerns.'

'It did. There were signs of bruising that were inconsistent with falling off a swing. Is the playground still there?'

'Not that I've seen.'

'It was probably removed after the death. According to the autopsy, she had fallen off the swing and cracked her skull, going headfirst into a concrete plinth to one side.'

'Possible?'

'There are photos, and yes, it's possible. The pathologist who conducted the autopsy found bruising inconsistent with the fall. However, accidental death was recorded.'

'Were the McCarthys questioned about the accident, especially the bruising? Any black marks against them?'

'Not against Bob McCarthy.'

'Which means?'

Wendy understood that her friend had gone for the dramatic. In a murder investigation, it could be frustrating, but it was unavoidable. If Bridget wanted the dramatic, no one in the office was about to stop her.

'His wife. It was before she married Bob McCarthy. She was nineteen years of age, mixed with the wrong crowd, arrested twice for drug possession, once for dealing, and spent two years in prison.'

'Any more?'

'In prison, an altercation with another prisoner. She spent time in the prison hospital with severe concussion.'

'The other prisoner?'

'Dead. Janice struck her, and the woman fell heavy onto a concrete floor, causing a brain haemorrhage. It was recorded as accidental death.'

'Was it?'

'I read the reports. It doesn't say who started it, only that one woman died, another lived.'

'Any bearing on the current investigation?'

'Unknown. It indicates the woman can be violent if provoked.'

'Inconsistent bruising indicates parental involvement. Or could it be more sinister? Could she have been involved in the Colsons' get-togethers, children as offerings, and sexual abuse? I assume the pathologist checked?'

'It would be best if you asked him. The reports I have indicate a cover-up. Why, I don't know.'

'The Colsons' child?'

'A boy, sixteen years of age. Drug overdose.'

'An autopsy?'

'Accidental death, another tragedy. Whether the drugs were a result of abuse and trauma is unknown. The pathologist would not have known about devil worship, and drug overdose was only too common eleven years ago.'

***

Larry Hill believed the case was going to crack open, and soon. Isaac Cook wasn't so sure. To him, there were too many variables, and proving a case against Janice McCarthy that the inquest into their child had been incorrect would be difficult.

Not that Bridget saw it that way. 'The bruising? A cover-up? Could the inquest have been a cover-up to protect someone?' she asked.

'If the McCarthy child had been abused, it's important to confirm it. And who was Janice McCarthy?' Isaac said.

'We must assume her husband knows about her time in prison,' Wendy said.

'Not necessarily.'

Two hours and twenty minutes later, a tall, severe man with horn-rimmed glasses entered Homicide. He wore a suit, a white shirt, and a bow tie.

'Randolph Featherstone. It was a whitewash,' he said as he shook Isaac's hand. 'The reason I'm here? Another death?'

'We're not implicating Janice McCarthy with that murder yet,' Wendy replied.

'You will,' Featherstone said.

It was unusual for a pathologist to express an opinion other than professional, but not for Featherstone. The man was agitated, not wanting to sit until Isaac told him to. 'We have seen your report. Also, a summary of the inquest. Why wasn't the bruising mentioned? Were you asked to present yourself at the inquest?'

'It wasn't, and I was not present. Janice McCarthy's criminal record would not have been mentioned at the inquest. It wasn't a trial but an inquest into a minor's death. The fall from the swing was the cause of death, and that was what they focused on; they saw my report on the additional bruising as irrelevant.'

'Was it?'

'She died from the fall, but it was for the judge and social services to investigate. If I had been asked to appear, I would have raised the matter.'

'But you weren't.'

'I wasn't available, laid low in hospital. It's documented. A subordinate of mine was at the inquest and presented my report. Accepted and entered into the record, with no one questioned.'

Isaac understood why. The death of a child brings out added emotions, and the court's desire would be not to place additional strain on the grieving parents and not to allow the inquest to run for longer than necessary.

'If it became relevant, assuming we arrest one or both of the McCarthys, would you be willing to testify?'

'With what? It was ruled an accidental death.' Featherstone had taken a seat, dusting the chair before he sat. Isaac saw a fastidious man, which might have been detrimental if he had given evidence. Eccentricity would be considered an advantage to the defence, as the man's foibles might lead him to exaggeration.

'I saw bruising and believed it needed to be discussed,' Featherstone continued. 'A child falls from a swing; unfortunate, but it happens. There is no disputing the cause of death, a clear indication that the child had been hurled from the swing, and even if the parents were pushing it higher and higher, with the child egging them on, it does not make them guilty of a crime. Both parents showed appropriate remorse and no reason to dispute their love for the child. All I'm saying is, and with thirty-five years of experience, that Lucy McCarthy's bruising was consistent with abuse.'

'Another child?'

'The school playground, the local bully. Yes, it happens, but not with the force applied.'

'You could tell?' Wendy questioned. She found Featherstone refreshing and not afraid to give an opinion. In recent years, experts had become careful in what they said, not wanting to open themselves to censure, not to be politically incorrect, and not to indulge in racial profiling, as their careers would be at stake if they did. Featherstone had no such reluctance.

'It wouldn't have affected accidental death being recorded. Although it might have caused the McCarthys to be investigated for child abuse. I was asked to offer an opinion today. That's what I've done.'

'Are you aware of what happened in another house nearby?'

'I am. No involvement personally or professionally, other than I like to keep abreast of the news.'

'Bruising consistent with a ritual?'

'I can't answer that question. I only saw Janice McCarthy once, and the child suffered abuse. I wasn't in their house, and it doesn't mean her parents were responsible, but they would have seen the bruising. And if they weren't responsible, if it had been a babysitter or someone else, they would have confronted or reported that person or persons.'

Isaac realised it was a quantum leap from suspected child abuse to ritualistic killing.

Chapter 5

Two persons were hunkered down in Scotland. A renovated croft with all mods and cons, they had rented the place through a local estate agent.

One was a man in his fifties. He had entered the agent's office wearing a tweed jacket and slacks. 'Back to nature,' he had said, 'although with some concessions to modern living.'

Four hours later, after a month's rent had been paid with a credit card, later discovered not to be in the name of Colson, two people moved into the croft.

The estate agent didn't care that he could have offered them better for the money. The man said it was fine. The agent thought it more than it was worth as he treated himself to a dram of whisky at a nearby pub. 'Strange,' he said to the woman behind the bar.

'Sassenachs?' she said.

'Aye, from down south. Takes all sorts.'

The barmaid made no further comment. The estate agent thought no more about the man, not for another week, not until he came across a news article that showed a couple wanted by the police in connection with a murder in London. It was then that he telephoned the local police station.

Two hours later, Isaac received a phone call.

***

'DCI Isaac Cook,' Sergeant Josephine Cameron said on the phone. 'Everyone calls me Josie.'

Isaac could only think of a Josie with her pussycats, but the sergeant was no lightweight when they met. As tall as him, with a thick Scottish brogue, she looked like she could have competed in highland games, tossing the caber.

Devil House

'Are they there?' Larry asked.

Isaac and Larry had flown to Scotland after confirming their identities. The croft could be seen in the distance, on the other side of the valley, with smoke coming out of a chimney.

'Do they know we're here,' Larry asked.

'All roads are blocked, and their car is outside the croft. Devil worshippers, are they?'

'Media exaggeration,' Isaac said, not wanting to indulge in extraneous comment, 'but, yes, signs of a ceremony and a body. Unsure whether Lucifer appeared or if the pair believed in it. Could have been orgiastic, high on alcohol and narcotics.'

'We don't get much drama around here. The occasional drunk or someone lost on the moors.'

Isaac nudged Larry, who had accompanied him. Larry understood Sergeant Cameron was a gossip, and they didn't want the pair's arrest nor a trial jeopardised by careless talk.

'Sergeant, maximum discretion to what you say to the media and the pub. You might find yourself a local celebrity after this.'

'You can rely on me, DCI,' Cameron said.

Across the valley, two persons came out of the front door of the croft and got into the car. Vehicles converged from either direction as they moved out through the gate and onto the small lane. Isaac had wanted to be in at the arrest, but now he was a reluctant observer. 'Get us down there, Sergeant,' he shouted.

'Take the vehicle. Here is ideal to see what happens. There's a farm track to their right.'

'Passable.'

'It depends on how desperate you are. I can phone those down below and keep them updated.'

Isaac and Larry, using GPS, drove to the other side of the valley. It was fifteen minutes before they arrived. By then, the drama was over.

'Glad to see you made it,' Sergeant Cameron said.

'How?' Larry asked.

'Farm, over the way, belongs to my parents. I phoned them, and one of the farmhands came over with a quad bike. We cut across the valley. They took the farm track, lost control, and drove into a ditch. The woman's fine, but the husband is banged up. He will need a visit to the hospital for a few stitches.'

Isaac and Larry walked to a nearby police car, looked inside, and saw the woman. 'Elizabeth Colson?' Isaac said.

A sorry-looking woman, her head bent low, nodded. 'My husband?'

'Minor, by the looks of it,' Isaac said. 'You've been cautioned?'

'Yes.'

'You'll be formally charged later.'

'I didn't do it,' a meek voice said.

Away from the vehicle, Larry spoke to Isaac. 'She could be right,' he said.

'Their house, their cellar, their body. We'll take them to London before discussing innocence or guilt, although hiding out in the back of beyond, using a false name, aren't the actions of the innocent.'

'Could be the actions of the desperate or frightened.'

Isaac understood that the McCarthys had history, whereas the Colsons did not.

***

Rhiconich police station in the Scottish North West Highlands served as a police station and a residence. Sergeant Cameron lived there with her husband and two children. Two storeys and painted white, it was typical of a small police station in rural Scotland.

Elizabeth Colson sat in a locked room. She accepted a cup of tea and a plate of sandwiches but said little, only to enquire after her husband.

Devil House

Her husband returned after what seemed an eternity but was closer to two hours. His head was bandaged. 'I believe you have a few questions for us,' Harold Colson said.

Hiding in the croft in Scotland had been detrimental to both husband and wife. Grey was showing in the wife's hair, and her clothes were askew and dirty. Her husband looked no better: unshaven, hair uncombed, dirt on his shirt collar and under his fingernails.

'A few,' Isaac replied.

'We didn't do it,' Colson said. His wife sat mute, holding her husband's arm.

Larry felt like saying that if you are innocent, why hide out in Scotland under a false name, but he did not. They would need to be interviewed first in depth. The small police station wasn't suitable, only for them to be charged and plead their innocence.

At four in the afternoon, a convoy of vehicles set off. In the lead car, two patrol officers. In the back seat, handcuffed together, husband and wife. Following them was Sergeant Cameron, and at the rear were Isaac and Larry in the car they had hired in Inverness. It was ninety miles, and the trip would take three hours, given that the roads weren't up to motorway standard for most of the way.

On arrival, and after they had been signed in to the police station in Inverness, the Colsons were offered food and drink, which they accepted. Even though it was eight-thirty in the evening, and the Colsons complained they were tired, they would still be interviewed.

Harold Colson said that his wife suffered in confined spaces and felt intimidated. A female sergeant trained in counselling sat with her while she waited for her husband. Sergeant Josie Cameron had offered, but she was an intimidating woman, and Isaac had put her down gently and told her that it had to be a qualified counsellor.

'A witch, cauldron and broomstick, and she requires special care?' Sergeant Cameron had answered. A rural police

41

officer dealing with drunks and hooligans, the occasional poacher, and family disputes did not understand the subtlety required in a murder investigation.

'This is a preliminary interview,' Isaac said. 'You've declined legal representation, which has been duly noted.'

'We're innocent,' Harold Colson said again.

'That is to be confirmed. You and your wife will be transferred to London on a flight at seven-thirty tomorrow morning. You will be held there at Challis Street Police Station for further questioning. Your lawyer will be present during the interviews.'

'It wasn't us.'

'Do you wish to make a statement?'

'Not here. In London.'

Another forty minutes were spent toing and froing, Harold Colson constantly stating their innocence. Isaac ended the interview.

'You'll both spend the night here,' Isaac said as he left the room.

'My wife?'

'A separate cell.'

Isaac was perplexed as to why he felt sorrow for a loving couple who might be responsible for the death of David Grayling.

***

Janice McCarthy busied herself in the kitchen; her husband, Bob, was in the garden mowing the lawn. It was a sunny afternoon, and Wendy was still knocking on doors. Not as much as when Grayling's body had been discovered, but talking casually to the locals often revealed something.

The cul-de-sac where the Colsons lived hadn't yielded much, and the house next door that Barry Sorell and Cheryl Hastings had rented was empty.

Wendy wandered over to where Bob McCarthy laboured.

Devil House

'Fine weather,' she shouted over the sound of the lawn mower.

'It is,' McCarthy replied as he switched off the engine. 'Are we still under suspicion?'

'For murder?'

'Yes. You've found the Colsons; what did they have to say for themselves?'

'I'm not at liberty to say,' Wendy said. 'Besides, I've not seen them yet. No doubt, they will claim they are innocent. What do you reckon?'

'It's hard to say. We were friendly, but you know why.' Wendy did.

'How do you deal with it, the death of a child?'

Wendy thought she should be more sensitive, but the pathologist had raised a negative against the couple. No harm needling them, she thought.

'Life goes on.' A pregnant pause. 'Somehow.'

'Your wife?'

'We thought of another child, but neither of us could deal with the guilt of Lucy.'

'Guilt?'

'It was an accident, but we were there, watching her play, and then she starts getting higher, and then she falls, or more correctly, is thrown forward. It's not there now. The council took it away.'

'Do you blame the council?'

'What for? It was there for children. Children have accidents, scrape knees, and break bones. They rarely die, but Lucy did.'

Wendy thought back to her sons, the scrapes they got into climbing trees, daring each other to jump in the river, to go faster, and with swings, who could go the highest. They had survived; Lucy McCarthy had not.

Wendy thought it macabre talking to the man in such a fashion, angling to see if he would reveal his innermost thoughts about whether he had beaten the child or his wife. The pathologist hadn't been under any illusion, nor was Wendy. She knew that children could test the patience of a saint with their demanding, constant chatter and crying, and it was on record that Janice McCarthy was far from being a saint.

'Your life before you came here?' she asked. Suitably vague, not easily misinterpreted, she thought. She was trying to draw the man out, to get him to talk, hopeful it might lead down another path, to see if he knew his wife's history.

Four years had passed after her release from prison before she married. Four years of rehabilitation, or had there been further indiscretions by the woman? Bob seemed fine, with no history of delinquency or criminality, not even a parking ticket. And if one had inflicted violence on their daughter, did the other know, condemn, or condone. Was the death an accident, although Featherstone thought it was?

'When you heard about the Colsons and what they were doing, what were your initial thoughts?'

'Disbelief. Harold can be monosyllabic, but we put that down to his nature, and he was there when their son died. Elizabeth was fine. We got on better with her. They looked after the rental next door and ensured the tenants, if not the most respectable, looked after the place.'

'You knew the tenants?'

'Not personally, a nod of the head if we saw them, but that's on the other side of the park. Are you still knocking on doors? What do you hope to achieve?'

'Someone might know or have seen something. Cathy Hopkinson keeps an eye out for what's going on.'

'A nosy woman, or hadn't you figured that out?'

Wendy replied. 'I had. If prejudiced by their jaundiced view of life, what they tell us often comes with an element of truth.'

'That jaundice was directed at us. We are not about to make a case about it, but it can be annoying. If she knew about Janice, then what? Our lives would be intolerable, and we would be marched out of the area. It would worry Janice more than me, but nobody likes their dirty linen aired in public.'

'She will not know, not from us. It was a long time ago; your wife paid the price.'

'The price was too high.'

'Did she tell you, or did you find out?'

'She told me. There are no secrets between us. Janice went through a rough period when young. No doubt most of us do, but then there was the incident in prison.'

'It never came up at the inquest, but there was additional bruising, not due to falling from the swing.'

Wendy could sense the man's hostility. He would have expected it to be a place of repose in his garden, but now, a woman sergeant was gently badgering him with questions.

'It never came up before as it would have been regarded as prejudiced information. I know what the pathologist believed, but Lucy had issues, self-harming, banging against doors, and throwing herself down the stairs once. He didn't tell you that, did he?'

Wendy realised that Featherstone had not mentioned that in his report, and he might have never been told that the child had issues. If he had suspicions, a professional man should have contacted social services or the police to investigate, regardless of the inquest. There was no record of either.

'That would explain it,' Wendy said. 'Any more we don't know?'

'I don't know what you know. All I can hear are innuendoes. Janice is damned and staying in the house, just in case.'

'I told you, we won't mention it.'

'You might not, but it's murder. Hidden secrets will be laid bare; if they aren't, lies and gossip will fill the blanks. Goodbye, Sergeant.'

With that, Bob McCarthy started the engine on his lawnmower and pushed it to the other side of the lawn.

Wendy could only agree with the man. Lies and gossip were inevitable, but sometimes the truth came with them.

Further down the road, the universal signal from Cathy Hopkinson, the kettle's on the boil, a cup of tea in the house. Wendy would have appreciated the tea but thought it not wise to be seen ducking into the home of the area's gossip, the realisation that the chat over the fence had been observed by the woman and possibly by others.

Instead, she cut across the small park on the opposite side of the road, careful to avoid the reminders that it was a place where dogs were let off the leash. Where the playground was, all that remained was a sign to only use it with adult supervision.

Another concern for Wendy was that the child's parents remained in the area. Most parents, she imagined, would have rented out or sold their house, yet the McCarthys had remained.

At the rear of the Colsons was a small gate, usually padlocked when the Colsons lived in the house; it was open. It was an oversight by the crime scene investigators. Wendy opened it and walked down to the back of the house, finding the door open. Inside were the signs of occupation, although at the front of the house, there was a sign that the place was part of an ongoing police investigation.

Wendy, who once might have ventured over the threshold alone, phoned Larry Hill, who called for uniform backup. Neither Wendy nor Larry wanted a patrol car arriving outside the house, alerting those inside and giving them time to dash out and abscond. She reminded Larry to tell the marked car to hang back and for him to come to the house.

Inside, Wendy could hear a toilet flushing.

Larry arrived eleven minutes after Wendy had phoned him, enough time for those inside to have realised that someone was outside the back door, which they slammed shut with force.

The time for holding back was gone. One of the uniforms went to the front with Larry, while Wendy stayed at the rear with the other. Wendy knocked on the back door and shouted, 'Police, open up.'

Devil House

Nothing. She tried once more before it opened slightly. 'We thought it was someone else.'

'Cheryl Hastings,' Wendy said. 'Why here? Why not next door?'

***

Larry and Wendy sat in the living room. On a couch on the other side of the room, Cheryl and her boyfriend, Barry Sorell.

'You want to know why we're here?' Sorell said.

'A crime scene, that's bad enough, but after what happened here to David Grayling,' Wendy said. The house had spooked her when she saw the dead body. It spooked her now.

'It was a dare,' Cheryl, attractive, young, silly, and with a deadbeat boyfriend, said.

'House of the devil,' Sorell said. 'Down the pub last night, five hundred pounds if we sleep in the Colsons' bed, no lights on, only candles.'

Wendy could see his dirty hair and clothes that had not been washed in a month. By comparison, Cheryl wore a white top with a cartoon rabbit on the front, eating a carrot, and a pair of jeans with the knees poking through. A fashion trend that Wendy couldn't understand.

Larry wasn't buying it. He made a phone call and gave the address. 'Twenty-five minutes,' he said after he hung up.

'What for?' Sorell asked.

'Top to bottom, the crime scene investigators. This place was off-limits, and you knew it. We need to know if you are telling the truth or there's more to it. Might help if you level with us.'

'We've been here for three days, evicted from our other place while your people went through it with a fine-tooth comb,' Cheryl said.

'Why?' Wendy asked the obvious question.

'The dare is not a lie,' Sorell said. 'No one reckoned we'd be game, but Cheryl's not easily frightened, and I don't believe in whatever the Colsons did.'

'Not much of anything,' Larry said. 'If you don't have to pay, you scrounge off family, friends, and the government.'

'Not criminal, can't hold us because I'm a burden on society.'

There was a brain in Sorell, a brain he did not intend to strain, but he was correct. Professional layabout was not a crime. Breaking and entering was, but it was minor and no more than a misdemeanour.

Not wanting to waste time, Wendy didn't need two men in conflict. She needed to know more about Sorell and his girlfriend.

Barry and Cheryl's presence was in bad taste. They had shared a house with Grayling, and the man had died. And now, Wendy had just received confirmation in the last hour that the otherbody had been recovered from the garden next door, where the two had previously lived.

It had been there for a long time: fifteen years was the best estimate due to the body's condition, clothing fragments, a receipt found in a pocket, and soil impaction.

Wendy called the two constables. 'We have got a couple of people with something to tell us. Challis Street Police Station, interview room.'

'We've done nothing wrong,' Sorell said.

'You have. You're holding back on the truth. I suggest you pack your belongings and get ready to answer questions.'

'Maybe we should,' Cheryl said.

Chapter 6

Isaac looked at the reports from Forensics and Pathology, another from the team that had unearthed the body in the garden next door to the Colsons'. 'No clear identification of the body,' he told his team.

Having taken heed of Isaac's last warning, Larry looked better for not drinking for a few days. Wendy had had a rough night due to arthritis in her legs from traipsing around the streets close to the Colsons' house.

The one piece of good news was that after a conversation with Commander Goddard, Isaac was pleased that the man who had mentored and protected him after a couple of indiscretions, was still there and fighting for Homicide, Challis Street, and the London Met; and that Goddard's support of Commissioner Davies was strategic, but not permanent.

'I play the game better than you, Isaac,' Goddard had said.

'I can't play it at all,' Isaac had admitted. 'Caddick?'

'Caddick remains where he has always been, at Davies's right hand. Davies is shifting the blame for his heavy-handed approach to policing in London.'

'It worked.'

'It did, but at what cost? It might have curtailed crime, but it didn't do much for a person's freedom.'

Isaac was always concerned about the balance between responsible policing, no policing, and too much. He had to credit Davies with reducing crime, even though he disagreed with the severe measures imposed. And now, in the aftermath, there was a reluctance for the police to act, even for a minor crime.

However, with Davies's scapegoating, was he under threat? Was his commander? Isaac should have been worried but had more important issues to consider. Homicide was in for a couple of hectic days.

In one interview room, Sorell and Cheryl Hastings sat. In the cells below, Harold and Elizabeth Colson waited.

'Male, forty to forty-five, cause of death indeterminate.'

'It has to be murder,' Wendy said.

'Check missing persons, and we assume murder. It was also the Colsons' residence before they bought the house next door. No sign of blood in the basement?'

'None. It's damp, and moisture and mould would have dealt with it.'

'Bridget, find out who this person was. And why hadn't the Colsons dealt with David Grayling, removed his body, and buried it? It would have been logical.'

'If the latest body had been in the ground for fifteen years, the idea that a sacrifice would bring back the son makes no sense,' Wendy said. 'He died eleven years ago.'

The meeting was short, as the Colsons needed to be interviewed by Isaac and Larry. Wendy would talk to Sorell and Hastings, as there was no crime against them other than bad taste, bad drugs, and, in Cheryl's case, a poor choice in men.

Harold Colson was adamant that they had not killed either man and that academic interest in a subject does not infer that they practised what they researched. The interview room was warm due to a problem with the air conditioning in the building. Larry was sweating, as was Harold Colson, although his wife, Elizabeth, was not.

'We knew the body was there,' Elizabeth said. 'We panicked.'

Before leaving Scotland, Isaac, Larry, and Sergeant Josie Cameron met Boyd Ivers, the estate agent who had rented the croft to the Colsons. 'Cool as a cucumber when he came here,' he said. 'I didn't meet his wife, but Colson was calm and polite. No reason not to believe that they wanted time out.'

'From what? Murder?' Larry said.

'From the rat race. We get a few up here in the summer who want to live a simpler life. Most want a concession for creature comforts. The croft was fine for them and me if the truth's known.'

'You recognised them and then phoned the police.'

'I did. It came as a shock. Is it true what they did?'

'The evidence points to that conclusion,' Isaac said. 'What else can you tell us about them?'

'Nothing. I saw him once, and his wife was in the car. I might have waved and wished her well through the car window.'

'You didn't go up there with them?'

'No need to. I had been to the croft several days before to check it out.'

'Which means they had contacted you.'

'I had a phone call. Not that I rushed around because of it. I get phone calls daily for one property or another, but it's the school holidays in a couple of weeks. The rent goes up then. If they hadn't taken it, another couple or a family would have. Is it back on the market?' Ivers asked.

'Not yet. We will need the crime scene investigators to go through it. Unlikely they will find anything.'

'They paid for the month, and there are no refunds. Take your time. Hopefully, your people will not rip the carpet or make an unholy mess.'

'Unlikely. We will send in a cleaning team afterwards,' Josie Cameron said. 'Good as new.'

Isaac knew it might be clean, but it would not be the same as when the team entered. The Colsons were prime suspects in a murder, and even though their time in the croft was short, the building and the grounds around it would be subjected to scrupulous investigation, and carpets would be removed, and possibly holes dug in the garden.

Elizabeth Colson stirred in her chair during the interview; her hands were shaking. Isaac could see a shy, retiring person, someone who would not say boo to a soul. But the murder scene revealed something else, and then she, along with her husband, had run before the body was found.

'We're innocent,' Harold Colson protested again.

'With no proof,' Isaac reminded him. 'You both left the house, disappearing off the face of the earth. We might not have found you if it hadn't been for the estate agent. How did you survive? Where did the cash come from? We know you also used another name, a credit card, which indicates criminal intent or fraud. The situation is grim for both of you. And now, we have a body next door, at a house you own and had lived in when the body was placed there. Who is he? How did he die?' Is it his name that you are using?'

'We came home, saw David's body, and realised that we would be blamed.'

'Why?'

'The body next door. His name is Grant Batholomew. He was Elizabeth's brother.'

'And you killed him.'

'We did not. Elizabeth and Grant were close, but Grant had issues. He was wealthy, solitary, almost invisible, and hid behind various names. He wasn't a criminal but a smart investor who played the financial markets and bought and sold property. A bona fide genius.'

'You killed him and assumed his identity.'

'We didn't kill him,' Elizabeth Colson said. 'I loved him, and Harold admired him. It was his money that allowed us to purchase our first house. His mood was changeable and sometimes depressive. He had attempted suicide before but not succeeded. But that night, dark and rainy, he did. I found him in the morning on his bed. Overdosed on sleeping pills.'

'Wealthy, everything to live for. Why?'

'Depression affects the person, not their wealth or their status. They don't give immunity. He had gone through a nasty divorce a few years before. A bitch who had tried to fleece him, but couldn't, didn't know how much he had. Grant loved me and trusted Harold.

'When Grant died, we decided that it would be best if we buried him. If his death was revealed, the bloodsucker would be knocking on the door, even though they were divorced. We just carried on with the pretence. But when we saw David on the floor and realised that someone was attempting to frame us, we panicked.'

'Even if we attempt to accept that ludicrous story, who would have killed him?'

'We have our suspicions. Not that we can prove it, only that the two houses didn't mean much to us. We're frugal people, not interested in the show, and apart from the McCarthys, we didn't socialise, and not often with them. You are aware of our son?'

'We are. Drugs.'

'We never got over it, became morbid, and would read depressing books, found an interest in the occult. Believe me, there is little happiness in our lives. Sure, we can maintain a pretence, but we found no enjoyment. The croft in Scotland suited us, and we might have bought one in time, although even more remote, living out our remaining years in solitude, in memory of our son.'

'Who would have killed Grayling?' Isaac asked. He was willing to concede the Colsons some latitude, and what they had just said would be checked.

'It was three months ago, a Friday afternoon. We were at home. I was reading, Harold was in the other room, on the internet. A knock on the door, and there, standing in front of us, Grant's former wife. We had not seen her for sixteen, seventeen years. She was older but no less aggressive, accused us of hiding Grant from her, and asked where her money was. None was due to her, but somehow she had found out about his aliases and that they were still active.'

'How?'

'She came into the house, laid out paperwork before us, and showed clearly that Grant had doubled his wealth since the divorce and that she wanted her share. Otherwise, she would go to the police, show that crimes had been committed, have us arrested and thrown on the street.'

'She knew you were involved in Grant's schemes and using his money to your benefit?'

'We used it cautiously. It seemed prudent to continue with what Grant had been doing. She didn't know Grant was dead, but she had figured it out. Whoever had found out was smart, and we had always been careful.'

'What happened?'

'We paid her off.'

'How much?'

'Two million pounds.'

'Which was a fraction of the increased assets. It must be if you were willing to leave the two houses in London and buy another in Scotland.'

'It was. We thought she would be appeased, and we'd never see her again.'

'It doesn't explain why she would murder someone.'

'She knew that we were academic and that we researched obscure subjects. She saw our book and realised we were researching the occult.'

'Books on a shelf aren't conclusive.'

'They were to her. Besides, we were civil with her and asked how she was. She asked how we were. Nobody was sincere, but shouting and calling each other names wouldn't have helped.'

'Barry Sorell and Cheryl Hastings, could she have spoken to them and gained more insight into your studies?' Larry said.

'Why not? We were being subjected to blackmail. She could have twisted our research and made it into something else.'

'Inferring that you were not only theoretical but practical. Implicating you in a murder, ensuring that you would run.'

'We couldn't come forward. How could we? It would be impossible to explain Grant, and then our fraud would be discovered. Damned if we stayed; damned if we ran.'

Isaac realised that what they were saying was valid. It wasn't what they had expected to be told, but it could not be discounted.

Devil House

However, due to the flight risk and their admittance that they had buried Grant Batholomew in the garden, they would be held in custody.

'Whatever happens, you're in a heap of trouble,' Isaac said.

'Grant never committed a prosecutable crime, nor did we.'

'You have more than enough money to survive,' Isaac said.

'What do we want? Our son is dead. We don't interest ourselves in material assets. A quiet location, with no need to interact with people, is what we want.'

***

Wendy Gladstone was anxious to meet with Barry Sorell and Cheryl Hastings. Their crime was stupidity, and she knew they would not be charged with trespass.

It was clear when Wendy entered the room at the police station that there was affection between the two people. Sorell was a slovenly man who spoke poorly and had bad diction, and his personal hygiene was woeful. What the woman saw in Sorell baffled Wendy, but then, she realised she had been attracted to disparate men in her youth. Some, if she had bothered to maintain contact, were either in jail or manual labouring with a wife and a brood of snotty-nosed kids. And even if her husband had been a plodder, nine in the morning to five in the afternoon with the council, unambitious, other than getting by, she had loved him dearly for his loyalty, apart from once when he had been tempted to stray. He was also the father of her two sons, fine and upstanding, a credit to their parents, unlike the man leaning back on his chair, his arms behind his head, the sweating armpits clearly visible, the smell of body odour wafting throughout the room.

'Did you shower?' Wendy asked.

'Not today,' Sorell replied. 'Not your concern either.'

'It's your girlfriend who should be.'

Wendy realised she was falling into the trap of caring too much. Besides a drug habit, Cheryl Hastings was an attractive young woman, clearly more suited for someone better than the man she cohabited with.

Cheryl looked over at Wendy and smiled, which perturbed Wendy. The realisation that these two people had lived next door to a house of extreme violence, that they had been spending time there, and that another body had been discovered in their garden, even if it had been there for fifteen years. It gave credence to the view that they could be involved.

After all, David Grayling had stayed in their house before disappearing and was subsequently found dead in what appeared to be a ritual sacrifice.

Jim Drayton, one of the young constables, sat alongside Wendy. She would have preferred Nadia, as she had warmed to the woman, but even though her English was fluent, she still struggled with some of the nuances. If Sorell reverted to slang and foul language, it was possible she might not fully understand.

Drayton, who boxed as an amateur in his spare time, would know foul language better than most and probably used it often.

It was expected that Drayton would not take an active part in the interview and that his attendance would be formal.

The interview was to be recorded, and whereas Wendy did not have high hopes of a revelation and that it would usually be her DCI and DI who would conduct the interviews, she did not intend to fail in the interrogation. She felt that she needed to be tough, dispassionate, and persistent, not giving the benefit of the doubt but probing, relentless, and, if necessary, unpleasant.

'Let's get this straight,' Wendy said, looking at Sorell. 'You're a reprehensible layabout. Would that be a fair summation?'

'It would,' Sorell replied, sitting up straight in disbelief.

God's gift to woman, Wendy thought.

'I don't believe you have the right to talk to Barry that way,' Cheryl Hastings said.

'I do. Not only are you taking drugs, and you could be charged for that, but you're in the Colsons' house, making out it was a dare. Nobody sleeps in a house that soon after a death, not if it's particularly violent, and Grayling was one of yours. You both knew the man. Attractive, mowing the Colsons' lawn. Not the actions of the usual reprobate. Why choose Barry here when you could have had Grayling? Where is the innate charm in this man?'

Wendy had observed her DCI and Inspector Hill do it, although her DCI was better at it. Raising the tempo makes those being interviewed nervous, and with nervousness and anger come mistakes, such as talking when they should remain quiet and not thinking before blurting out something.

Drayton kept quiet, observing the woman opposite, whose skimpy top was riding high as she gesticulated at Wendy. Wendy had seen Drayton, observed Cheryl, and realised the man could be helpful.

'Constable, let me put it to you,' she said. 'We have two people who, apart from drugs and fornicating, are not stupid. They've been in the presence of evil, have seen it close up, and are not fazed by it. What do you reckon?'

Wendy hoped the man would rise to the prompt, a baptism of fire for him, the first step in a stellar career in the police force if he got it right.

Calmly, Drayton looked at Wendy and then at the young lovers holding hands. 'I would say that they know more than they are saying, a lot more. Evil is pervasive, and its odour is unmistakable. They have seen it and experienced it in close quarters. How many were in that basement when Grayling died?'

'Four,' Wendy said.

Sorell's body shook before attempting to rise from his seat and collapsing.

'Epilepsy,' Chery Hastings said as she rushed to his side.

Wendy made a phone call, and a local doctor arrived within five minutes. By that time, Wendy had seen through the subterfuge. After all, she had seen epilepsy in her youth, a friend at school. She had also seen that the involuntary motions were not rhythmic and were created by Sorell.

'You're wasting your time,' Wendy said. 'You'll need to put on a better act than that.'

'We'll still need to get him checked,' Drayton said.

'Constable, you're correct. Leave him there, and we'll come back in ten minutes. Either he's sitting on his chair, or we'll take him to the hospital. If he's playing us for fools, what do you reckon?'

'Mr Sorell and Miss Hastings are in a heap of trouble. I've read the reports. The Colsons deny involvement and reckon they've been framed. The former wife of the dead man in the garden. Have they met her?'

'And if they have?' Wendy realised that Drayton was working with her and postulating further theories. She was impressed.

'Is there a possibility that the Colsons are innocent?'

Wendy didn't think they could be.

After an inopportune break, while the doctor checked Sorell, time enough for Wendy and Drayton to discuss the interview, it resumed.

On the way out, the doctor signed off on Sorell. No medical issues, no epilepsy. 'I'll send in a report, but off the record, the man's a malingerer. Down for murder?'

'Not yet,' Wendy said.

Chapter 7

With Drayton's assistance, Wendy uncovered complexity in the interview with Sorell and Hastings and consulted with Isaac. If Sorell and Hastings were to reveal involvement or a possible admission of murder, did he want to take over the interview?

'It's yours,' Isaac said. 'Whatever happens, this won't be the last time we speak with them.'

In the interview room, the two people were drinking coffee and eating sandwiches from a shop across the road. A constable stood in the corner of the room. On Wendy and Drayton's arrival, the constable left.

'The doctor said you were malingering,' Wendy said.

'The stress,' Sorell replied. 'I'm not used to confrontation.'

Wendy was sure he was not, the reason for his appearance and his behaviour.

'Resuming where we finished off before the unfortunate interruption. Constable Drayton raised some interesting points. We believe, due to the work of the crime scene investigators, there were more than two persons in the basement cellar when Grayling died. It would explain why you were in the Colsons' house and why you did not feel the ambience.'

'I paid the rent; David Grayling mowed their lawn. We've done nothing wrong other than be stupid when we're high,' Cheryl Hastings said.

'It's either you two or a married couple that we've interviewed. Cheryl, you are clearly the most responsible in this relationship. Are you intending to stay with Barry? Or is this talk about getting clean, off drugs, and making something of your lives, just verbiage?'

'It's what we talk about when we're not high, but I don't think Barry's got the discipline.'

'But you have, and now, whether high or not, you've become entangled in a murder investigation. Honesty is the best defence,' Wendy said, although at this stage in the investigation, with no tangible proof as to whether the woman had also been in the basement, she knew that silence was probably their best defence.

'We've done nothing,' Sorell blurted. He had looked sheepish since his ruse had been uncovered. Wendy knew the man was treading on thin ice, and he didn't have his lover's intellect to deal with intensive interrogation.

Drayton took the lead. 'What type of drugs? Did they make you psychotic? Sadism and devil worship might be seen as exciting. Was Grayling one of your lovers, Cheryl? High on one drug or another, a threesome, and then, there is this body's ex-wife.

'She was desperate for money, got plenty from the Colsons, and would have paid you two to be accomplices. And now, the Colsons are looking at a long stretch in prison.'

'Fiona Cole is unlikely to have got her hands dirty,' Wendy added.

'We met her,' Cheryl said. 'Not that we told her anything, nothing to tell. What did we know? We paid the rent, spoke to Mrs Colson occasionally, rarely to her husband, and even if high, evil is evil.'

The atmosphere in the room was stuffy. Wendy realised that it needed air and turned on the air conditioner. Sorell was becoming agitated, either due to frustration or the need to inject. Realising that fresh air would relieve him, she turned off the air conditioner. Hot and stuffy would harm him more than the other three.

'In need of a fix?' she said.

'Yes,' Sorell replied. He was picking at his nose again, running his fingers through his hair, and tapping on the table.

Cheryl Hastings remained calm. Wendy looked over at her. 'Cheryl, there is hope for you. Are you to be blighted by what you have done?'

'I've done nothing other than to be young and stupid. Barry is a hopeless case, but he's kind to me. My father was distant, and my mother was career-obsessed. I did not intend to go down that road; I prefer someone who treats me well. Barry won't amount to much, but as long as we have love, we will survive.'

Very Mills & Boon, Wendy thought.

She felt tired; Drayton did not. 'It looks to me,' he said, 'that you knew Grayling was dead before the police.'

'We did,' Cheryl said.

Wendy perked up, finally something that made sense.

'How?' Wendy asked.

'David had been missing for two days. We knew he had been around the Colsons, even inside the house. And yes, they invited him in, but not us. He thought they were okay, if a little odd. You see, David was not into drugs; alcohol was his weakness, but he kept it under control. We were never sure why they invited him in, but sometimes he would spend the night there. We used to joke; well, you know.'

'That he was into threesomes with the Colsons?' Drayton said.

Wendy thought the suggestion was amusing. It was hard to imagine the staid couple indulging in sexual adventures any more than it was to believe they were Satanists. But the latter idea was looking more robust, regardless of their denials. Behind closed doors, who knows, she thought.

'Let's come back to Fiona Cole,' Wendy said. 'You met her; you don't deny that. Tell us about your discussion with her.'

'She knocked on the door. It was eight in the evening. She introduced herself, told us who she was, and that she had not seen Mrs Colson's brother since they had divorced.'

'Was she trying to find him?'

'She said not. She told us there was animosity with the Colsons and that she knew they owned our rented house. We weren't sure what she wanted. After all, we paid the rent and didn't get involved.'

'Apart from Grayling playing footsie with Mrs Colson, or was it Mr?' Drayton chipped in.

'David would never talk about what happened in the house other than to say that it was his business and convivial.'

'The son of a vicar; devil worshippers. The Colsons were heavily into the occult. Did they tell you that?'

'Never. Our interaction with them was purely financial.'

'Do you know the McCarthys?'

'No. We did go down to where David had died. It was part of the dare.'

'And?'

'Barry threw up; I didn't.'

'You were unmoved?'

'I suppose so.'

That was the trait of a sociopath, Wendy knew, although she struggled to believe that Cheryl Hastings was unfeeling and mentally troubled. Yet, she remembered that a trait of the sociopath was the ability to seem normal. A trait that the Colsons possessed, but whether theirs and the young woman's were feigned would need to be evaluated.

'Or had you been there before?' Wendy asked.

'I had,' Cheryl replied. 'I phoned the police and gave the anonymous tip-off.'

'You found the body?'

'I did. I knocked on the Colsons' back door and found it was open, signs that they had left. I needed David's share of the rent; he hadn't paid, and she hadn't been around for the rent. I wasn't suspicious, but I needed the money from David.'

'Why didn't you tell us this before?'

'I didn't want to be involved. I checked the house and found a door at the end of the corridor, the steps leading down. That's when I found him.'

'Proof of this?'

'You found proof of other persons in the house. Was it two or more, or could it be only one? I was the one, but that was sometime after David died.'

'We didn't find fingerprints.'

'You wouldn't. I wore gloves. It was a cold day, and the house was freezing. I wore them to keep warm. I also wore heavy boots.'

'Where are the gloves and the boots?'

'After I saw what had happened and phoned the police, I put them in the rubbish bin. You can scour the local rubbish tip.'

'Yet you seem impervious to what you saw.'

'I am. Don't ask me why.'

'I must,' Wendy said.

'Not today,' Cheryl said. 'And not here. Another day, the two of us will meet. I will get drunk, and then you will know. Until then, I will say no more.'

Wendy realised there was something in the woman's past that not only allowed her to look at the body of a murdered man dispassionately but also might have allowed her to be involved in the ceremony. Could Cheryl Hastings be a murderer? It was a question to be considered. Barry Sorell had shown himself to be a weak character, who, if he had vomited in the cellar, which the CSIs would confirm, would not have the stomach for a heinous act, psychotic drug or not.

In the interim, the interview had reached an impasse. Either they were charged with a crime or free to go. The question was, which crime? Breaking and entering the Colsons' home was unclear, as Cheryl had a key, which was shown to be the same as the house she rented next door. They had entered, but breaking in, with intent to steal, was not provable, as nothing had been stolen. They had taken up illegal residence as squatters. It wasn't enough to arrest them, not enough to put them in a holding cell for twenty-four hours.

'Where will you be?' Wendy asked.

'We'll move back into the other house,' Sorell said.

Wendy couldn't be sure they wouldn't abscond, although she had no alternative but to let them go. She could have sworn that Cheryl smirked as she left, but was it from relief to be out of the station, or had she hoodwinked the sergeant and her constable?

***

DNA testing confirmed that the body in the garden was Grant Batholomew. Bridget had found out that Fiona, his former wife, had remarried after their divorce and his subsequent disappearance and was living twenty miles southeast of London. She needed to be interviewed.

Larry and Wendy made the trip down to Sevenoaks in Kent. With a population of nearly thirty thousand, it was in the commuter belt of the metropolis.

'Not for a long time,' Fiona Coles, previously Bartholomew, said. She was in her late forties, dressed expensively, and Wendy was sure she had been under the knife: cosmetic surgery around the eyes, full lips, and barely a wrinkle on her face.

'This house, Grant's money?' Larry asked.

The three sat in the living room, expensively decorated like the rest of the house.

'We divorced. I was entitled to my share. Grant paid.'

'No animosity?'

'Grant was a Shylock, never revealed his true worth. Life is good, if not perfect.'

'And now that your husband is confirmed as dead?'

'He was dead a long time ago. I assumed he had been using an alias in this country or overseas. You never met him. You have no idea of the depth of the man.'

'Tell us,' Wendy said.

'Charismatic, women found him attractive, but deep, incredibly deep. A prodigious brain dedicated to the pursuit of wealth. Not that he showed it, like his sister and her husband in that respect.'

'But not you.'

'Grant lived well with me in a comfortable house in London with a tight group of friends. But he didn't care either way; he would have lived in a council flat if he could have.

'Obsessed with money at the expense of our marriage. I never knew the extent of his wealth, and if I hadn't come to know that Elizabeth and Harold were using Grant's money and his aliases, I might never have. I was cheated, accepted forty per cent of our joint wealth at the time of our divorce.'

'And then you realise that the Colsons have the money, and you're on their doorstep, cap in hand,' Wendy said. She could tell the woman was a gold digger.

'I approached Harold and Elizabeth, laid out the facts, and what I wanted.'

'How much?' Larry asked.

'Two million pounds.'

When confronted with what Fiona had said, Harold Colson responded, 'She gave us assurances that she wouldn't claim more?'

'Why give her money? She had no legal claim.'

'We always felt that Grant had mistreated her, and even if we did not like her particularly, she had done right by him. Grant could be callous. His need to accumulate overrode his concern for her.'

'And due to your involvement in his complex schemes, you bury him in the garden. You expect us to believe that? And now you intimate that she lures a man to your house, strips him naked, and then kills him, makes out that you two had indulged in satanism.'

'It's illogical,' Colson said. 'But it's the only explanation.'

'Why the fascination?' Wendy asked.

'An academic pursuit, nothing more. The distortion of historical truth due to ignorance.'

'Obscure.'

'Esoteric, not many would understand, but much of our culture has been formed by untruths.'

Nobody in Homicide could believe that the Colsons were innocent. There was proof they had paid the former wife two million pounds, and with them convicted, she could have found more with her knowledge of the various aliases used and the bank accounts where the money was deposited. However, the question was, how did she know so much? And why commit a heinous crime? And, more importantly, what hold had she had over David Grayling? Was he the homeless drifter that he portrayed? His parents believed he was, and so did Sorell and Cheryl Hastings, but they had not known him well.

***

Confirmation of recent vomit at the murder scene confirmed what had been said during the interview with Sorell and Hastings. The man appeared to be innocent of all crimes. However, he'd had trouble with the law in his teens, shoplifting, and a one-year probation. His best defence was his apathy and disinterest in meaningful employment and bettering himself.

However, Cheryl Hastings remained a prime suspect, especially when she disappeared two days after the interview at Challis Street. The first that Homicide became aware of it was when Sorell phoned Wendy to tell her.

'Last night, two in the morning. We'd had a bender, a few too many drinks.'

'And drugs,' Wendy added.

'Okay, as you say. I thought we were staying together, but she packs her belongings and goes. I didn't see her go, only a note by my side of the bed.'

'You have the note?' Wendy asked. 'What does it say?'

'Gone, might be back. Too many issues.'

'Nothing more?'

'Nothing. I don't know why.'

Wendy did. She had opened wounds in the woman, who did not want to deal with them. If she was there when Grayling died, that made her sociopathic. If she did not want to confront the past, as grim as it might be, the woman maintained a sense of right and wrong, of what was decent and what was not. That suggested that she had a conscience and that death, whether murderous or otherwise, did prick her psyche. It was too deep for Wendy, and the only resolution was to find the woman, something she was well equipped to do after her years as a junior constable in Sheffield, looking for missing children.

Early the next day, a meeting in the chief inspector's office. Bridget had a hangover after downing a bottle of an indifferent red wine the night before. Larry Hill arrived bright and breezy. Isaac knew it would not last but was thankful drink wasn't an issue today.

Larry, feeling the heat of a tightening economy and a wife who believed that a positive attitude and hard work were the only criteria for success, continued to badger him to do better. But he knew he was at the apex. Further promotion was hampered by a lack of a degree and a lackadaisical attitude to life. At the police station and out on the street, investigating, solving crimes, and arresting were fine. At home, he wanted a break from the trauma, a chance to unwind with his wife and their children, not to endure another ear bashing as to why he was this and that. And what do we have, their neighbours, children in good schools, holidays overseas, a new car in the garage?

He was inclined to respond, but after a hard day dealing with villains and murderers, he could only nod and say 'yes' or 'no' on cue.

Wendy, who had had an early night, was alert but concerned. A sure sign that she was becoming emotionally involved.

Wendy recounted the interview with Sorell and the missing woman. Her fears that Cheryl might be involved and that her disappearance intensified that fear, although she explained that the woman had a hidden past. And until that was resolved, she would not focus on other facets of the investigation.

Isaac had his own problems. The previous night, he had been arguing with his wife, Jenny. She was interested in moving out of London to somewhere less expensive to buy a bigger house, which was logical, given that the family was expanding, with three children now. She was not like Larry's wife, fuelled by the desire to flaunt wealth, but was realistic, only wanting the best for the family.

Isaac knew she was right, and on paper, it made sense. But a provincial police station didn't feel right, even if it came with a promotion. Homicide was where the action was, where he had passion. A bureaucrat dealing with endless paperwork, confined to the office most of the time, was not him. Yet the reality was that a larger house in London was out of the question. The economy was in turmoil, house prices were escalating, and mortgage costs continued to rise.

Bridget's drinking in the last year had become worse. She was worried about it, as was Wendy. Both knew the reason. Bridget was getting older, the occasional stud did not spend the night, and she was feeling lonely – alcohol was the compensation.

Wendy realised that actively looking for Cheryl Hastings would come with its own set of problems. The most pressing was her health. The weight had come on, even though she remained active, and the aches and pains rarely left her. And traipsing the streets looking for a missing woman would play hell with her arthritis. Most times in the office, she could maintain the pretence that it didn't hurt, and she would stride out with determination. But quietly, she wanted to hobble. At home, with Bridget she could relax, sit in a comfortable armchair with a cat on her lap, drink a hot chocolate or wine, and vegetate.

'What she said was disturbing,' Wendy said. 'If we're on the fence regarding the Colsons…'

'Not on the fence,' Isaac interjected. 'Confused. We still believe that the Colsons are responsible for Grayling's death, although the reason why remains unclear. It's one thing to have an interest in the occult and satanism, and no doubt there's a university degree somewhere on the subject, but to practise it requires a quantum leap.

'We can't be sure that they have made that leap. Any truth in David Grayling and the Colsons, especially Elizabeth? I've read your report. You raised it as a possibility.'

'No proof, and probably not. But with the man's death, who knows?'

'And we need to know. Sorell, are we ruling him out for now?'

'For now,' Larry said. 'Although, if he was psychotic?'

'Timid when clean,' Wendy said. 'I saw that in the interview. However, he is a known user of mind-bending drugs, which, if used in sufficient quantity, could induce him to commit violent actions.'

'And not remember afterwards,' Bridget said.

'Research the subject,' Isaac said. 'We have records of the drugs at Sorell and Hastings' house?'

'Not the amount it would take to make a drugged-out fool commit murder.'

'Then find out. Larry, stay focused on Fiona Cole and check out her new husband. Are they financially stable? Is the marriage on the wane?'

'They are financially sound now,' Wendy said.

'That's an assumption. Two million pounds is easily consumed if there's a failing business or gambling debts.'

Wendy knew where she was going first, a two-hour drive from the city. At least she could have the heater on.

Chapter 8

Oxford, the home of the oldest university in the English-speaking world, dating back to the twelfth century, was somewhere Wendy would never have studied. She had left school at sixteen with an O level in English, and then at nineteen, she had graduated from the police academy, receiving a certificate on completion, which her parents had framed and hung on the wall in their front room.

Compared to the degrees given in Oxford, it was small fry, but, at the time, and even now, she was proud that she had passed through the police academy with no drama, apart from a twenty-years-old male in her class who she had taken a fancy to. They were an item, but the romance had withered on the vine. She sometimes read about him, a chief superintendent in Cornwall, and married with three sons.

The Hastings family home was in a leafy suburb three miles from the city centre. Wendy was impressed. A two-storey brick residence with a circular driveway in the front and a Mercedes Benz parked in front of the main entrance. She had not phoned in advance, primarily because she did not want to forewarn Cheryl if she was there.

The front door of the house swung open. An elegantly dressed woman in her fifties looked like she was about to go out. 'Yes, can I help you?' she said.

'Sergeant Wendy Gladstone, Homicide, Challis Street Police Station,' Wendy said.

'Come in. Are you looking for Cheryl?'

'You're aware of the situation?'

'We are. My husband is not here at this moment. Will we need him?'

'That depends on what you tell me and if you know where Cheryl is.'

Ushered into the front room of the house, Wendy sat down on a cushioned chair. For her, the room was too comfortable and too warm. After two hours behind the wheel, she knew the temptation to close her eyes was too great.

'I'll take the other chair,' Wendy said. With that, she took hold of a straight-backed wooden chair and sat down.

'A drink, tea or something stronger?'

'Tea would be fine,' Wendy said, although she realised that such a house and woman would not have supermarket wine but something expensive and exquisite. Even so, this was not social, and tea would suffice.

The tea arrived on a silver tray, accompanied by biscuits and savouries. A conversation ensued about the usual, the weather, the economy, and the lack of effective government.

The prelude to the main event, but Wendy knew it was necessary. Establish a rapport in a non-controversial setting and attempt to find common ground; then, the problematic questions would not be so difficult to ask, and hopefully, the answers would not be so challenging to draw out.

'Firstly, where is Cheryl?' It was round one of the questioning. Wendy started with the most immediate.

'I don't know.'

'But you knew of me?' Wendy said.

'I did. Cheryl phoned, told us what had happened next door, and that she needed space.'

'Does that concern you?'

'We would not be good parents if it did not. However, we understand.'

'You're not frightened for her safety?'

'Concerned. Cheryl is her own person. We don't always agree with her decisions, but we must respect them. We have infrequent contact, realised that she was living an unusual life in London, involved with a person of no consequence,' Adriana Hastings said.

'She told you this?'

'She did.'

'What else did she tell you?' Wendy asked.

'That she was unmoved by the death of David Grayling, and she had phoned the police.'

'She said she would need to be drunk to tell me why she was not affected by the body, something to do with her childhood.'

'And her father is stern, and I'm always socialising?'

'Words to that effect.'

'I need a glass of wine if I'm to tell you. No doubt you want to hear the story, even from me.'

'I do if it's the truth.'

'It will be.'

Wendy felt it was wise to also have a glass of wine, in a spirit of unity with the woman, but also because she wanted to savour the French chardonnay she had been shown.

'We were living in Michigan, USA. My husband is a senior executive in a large global engineering company. You've undoubtedly researched us online, but this happened in America, and Cheryl was a minor. Her name was suppressed.

'One day, coming home from school, she was grabbed off the street. She was eleven years of age. Ten days later, the police found the man and shot him at the house where he held our daughter.'

'Did she suffer?'

'If you're asking, was she raped, then the answer is yes.'

'Traumatic experience. And afterwards?'

'Nothing. She never spoke of it and remained dispassionate. We're not sure if she remembers or if she's blocked it. Best if it's the latter.'

'Emotionally scarred, no issues with seeing what had happened to a murdered man,' Wendy said.

'Nothing will faze her. I'm surprised that she mentioned what had happened to her. That means she remembers.'

'Whatever it is, it makes her impervious to violence.'

'And capable of committing it. Is that what you are inferring?'

'We don't know how or why she would do such a thing, but it must be considered a possibility. Pets, did she have any, or did she harm them? I don't want to upset or insult your daughter, but the truth is paramount, the best defence there is.'

'We tried, but she would ignore them.'

'You're remarkably open about your daughter,' Wendy said.

'Not open, but frank. She portrays normality and almost certainly believes it, but who knows? How can anyone understand the trauma that she endured.'

'And you and your husband?'

'We are there for our daughter, aware that one day she might turn, or maybe her life will never change. Experimenting with drugs and inappropriate men is a small cost for us to accept.'

Wendy left the house, aware that Cheryl's opinion of her parents might be jaundiced. As she drove, Wendy spoke to Bridget, who scoured the internet, focusing on Michigan and an eleven-year-old girl.

'What they told you is correct,' Bridget said. 'The name was suppressed, but the facts are there. They tally with what the mother told you.'

However, it didn't obviate the fact that regardless of what had happened to Cheryl as a child, it wouldn't absolve her from the crime of murder. There was still reason to believe she was capable. Wendy hoped that wasn't the case, but the law was the law; murder was murder. A crime needs someone to be punished for committing it, and if Cheryl Hastings had been responsible, she would not have served time in prison but in a high-security psychiatric facility.

***

Pathology and Forensics could find no cause of Grant Batholomew's death. After fifteen years under the ground, there were no signs of a knife tear in the remaining fabric of the suit he had been wearing and no indentations or fracturing of bones.

DNA from Elizabeth Colson confirmed his identity. No murder charges would be brought against her and her husband, although burying a body in the back garden without due process, not obtaining a death certificate, and then using the man's money as their own were crimes. They were not crimes that Homicide would be pursuing. Murder was their interest, and so far, the Colsons and Cheryl Hastings were pinned high on the evidence board in Homicide as prime suspects.

It was imperative to talk to the young woman, but with the Colsons, the crime of murder could only be proven circumstantially. The Colsons were bailed pending charges to be laid, the judge listening to the facts, deciding that based on the arguments from Homicide, he had no option but to direct that they be released.

It had been one week, and the Colsons were still in London, not at either of the two houses, but at a hotel close to the police station. Isaac and Larry had been to see them every day. Isaac found them interesting and highly knowledgeable on mythology, ancient religions, and the occult. They had also read about and travelled the world extensively. Larry, less academic than his chief inspector, found them boring. 'Up themselves,' he said to Isaac when asked.

It was derogatory, but Isaac brushed it off. To him, their release from the cell was a flawed decision. They had disappeared once; they could do it again. They had access to money, and even though they had surrendered their passports, it did not mean they did not have others.

All in all, Isaac was convinced that using a dead man's money was criminal and that the Colsons did not do it out of respect for Bartholomew but out of greed, conscious of the seriousness of the crime.

Four days later, events took an unexpected turn. In response to a notice on Facebook, a person knocked on the door of the house rented by Cheryl Hastings.

As was to be found out later, she was a recent arrival in the country from Ukraine. Oksana Akimova, twenty-six years old, blonde, and vivacious, aspired to be a beautician in one of the overpriced establishments in the city, close to Notting Hill.

Isaac, when he met her the first time, thought she had a good chance of realising her dream and not falling into the trap of others who had been lured into prostitution.

Wendy had been out of the office, following up on leads where Cheryl might be, her mother increasingly worried for her welfare, and Larry had been getting the feel of Sevenoaks, those who might know Fiona Cole and her husband, and their opinion of them.

Isaac had taken the call and driven out to the house, closely followed by two uniforms.

At the house, Oksana, whose English was fluent, sat outside on the pavement. 'Inside,' she said.

To Isaac, it could mean only one thing, although he had been updated by emergency services after she had phoned them, that inside the house was a dead body.

Oksana Akimova seemed unmoved by the body and chatted freely with Isaac, even offering to accompany him upstairs. He declined, as it was a crime scene. Police tape was strung outside, although the original tape was still in place and only needed additional tape to cover the areas where it had been torn by the locals and the elements.

Wendy had been notified. She was on the way, but Larry was staying in Sevenoaks for a couple of days, a room over a pub for the night, a chance to mingle with the locals in the bar, a chance to have a couple of drinks. He was granted permission by Isaac, who told Larry's wife that he was allowed to break ranks for one night. Larry was at his best in the convivial atmosphere of a pub, the chance to gently nudge people to open up.

Fiona Cole's husband was a builder, which explained the house they shared. Four bedrooms, worth a lot of money, prestige location, gym, and swimming pool. That was what it said in the window of an estate agent. Inside, the salesperson was more flamboyant in her description. Larry ignored the sales pitch. His wife had dragged him to enough houses over the weekend, houses he could not afford. He had heard the spiel ad infinitum. What interested him was that the house was for sale. Was that due to financial troubles, but why, if she had two million pounds from the Colsons, or were they going upmarket? Trying to get it from the horse's mouth, namely the Coles, would be counterproductive, as they would lie if going broke.

He had an appointment with their bank manager in the morning, although customer confidentiality would probably render that a futile exercise. However, body language could confer as much as an abbreviated statement imparted nothing.

Inside Sorell and Hastings' house, it was as expected. Barry Sorell was on the bed which he had shared with Cheryl. He had been stabbed in the chest.

'Another one,' one of the CSIs said.

'It looks that way,' Isaac replied, although he wasn't so sure. There appeared to be no ceremony, just a murder. Although, in bed, in a state of undress, it looked as though Sorell had been with a woman before his demise. It would require the combined efforts of the CSIs, Forensics, and Pathology to confirm.

The most likely suspect was Cheryl Hastings, who, so far, had not been seen since she left the house.

Isaac phoned Wendy. 'Focus on finding this woman. Sorell's dead, and your friend is the most likely suspect.'

Two hours later, Oksana Akimova accompanied Isaac to Homicide. She would give a statement, and Isaac would ensure she had a hotel room for the next couple of nights, courtesy of the department. There might be further questions; if there were, as her movements were transient, she could disappear at a moment's notice. He hoped his estimation of the woman was correct, aware that his prejudice favoured the attractive, which had proven his downfall in the past.

***

Larry enjoyed his time in Sevenoaks, especially drinking in the pub. The Chequers, built in the sixteenth century, enjoyed a good clientele, but as the landlord, Harry Makepeace, explained, 'Business isn't what it was. The margins are tight, and people are moving out of the area, going somewhere cheaper. Increasingly more people are working online, no need for a high-speed train link.'

'You seem familiar,' Larry said. It was early, but as he was staying at the pub, he got the bar to himself and the landlord.

'Rugby player, played for England a couple of times until I damaged my knee. Nowadays, I can walk but not run.'

Larry wasn't a rugby fan and preferred football, but he could appreciate that playing for your country was an honour.

'Aaron Cole, what do you know about him?' Larry asked.

'Is that the customer or the policeman asking?'

'That obvious?'

'Two and two. News travels, and they found his wife's first husband under six feet of soil.'

'Four, to be precise. Background information. Homicide, checking those involved. It's not that we suspect Fiona, but asking a few questions is always good.'

'Okay. Here's what I've got. Cole's a good man who plays business hard but is fair. You'll not find many with a bad word against him.'

'Fiona?'

'Likewise. Tough in business but affable, and gave to charity. She can be snooty and reckons their money affords them a degree of respect. They come in here sometimes.'

'They're selling their house.'

'As I heard it, not that I'm sticking my nose in, but I heard that she came into money.'

'A lot of money.'

Larry thought he had learnt enough and would give the bank manager a miss in the morning, meaning he could lie in and enjoy a few more drinks.

'Another drink, one for yourself,' Larry said. 'Have you got a menu?'

'Steak and chips, highly recommended.'

'Then it's steak and chips for me.'

Larry was not the only one having a night away from home. Wendy was at the Hastings' house in Oxford, this time with Cheryl Hastings's father. Upright and tall, he reminded Wendy of a stern teacher where she went to school as a child. Cheryl had said he was tyrannical, although she doubted that was true.

Cheryl, she had decided, had issues, although not of her making. When she had looked for missing children in Sheffield, she had heard and been told of terrible things committed by parents on their children, but none as dramatic as what had befallen Cheryl. She couldn't blame the woman if she was twisted and a killer, realising that the adult is shaped by the child.

Bridget had obtained a police report from Michigan. It was heavy reading and unpleasant. How the young girl had been lured by a friend of the family into his Chevrolet truck. How he had driven her twenty miles away, locked her in a room, plied her with alcohol, beaten and raped her over ten days.

If it hadn't been for the tip-off, the child's fate didn't bear thinking about.

After her release, she spent three days in the hospital and returned home. Within four weeks, while Cheryl sat silently in her room, her father's company hastily arranged a transfer to England.

Reports from the time, school reports mainly, indicated that in England, the child had opened up and got on with her life, although there had been overexuberance, promiscuity, and drugs. As her mother had said, it was a small price to pay.

As her father reiterated, 'Under the circumstances, she turned out better than we could have hoped for, but then Grayling's murder and now Barry Sorell. God knows how that will affect her. Badly, I assume, but with Cheryl, you can never be certain.'

'It's important we find her,' Wendy said. 'Not arrest. We have no proof that she's done anything, but what if somebody knew of her history and planned the murders to frame her?'

'A sick mind.'

'The world is full of sick minds. To deny their existence would be folly.'

'I can't believe it,' the mother said.

'I don't want to believe it, but I must do my duty. Your daughter must be found, either before she kills again if she's guilty or she harms herself.'

The father knew that the nightmare the family had endured in America had returned. Regardless of the outcome, their lives were irreparably thrown into utter turmoil.

Chapter 9

Wendy continued with the search for Cheryl Hastings, more so than before, as there was evidence that she had been in the house with Barry Sorell on the night that he died.

Her guilt wasn't certain, as additional persons had been in the house during that time, before or after. It was impossible to be conclusive. Pathology and Forensics confirmed that Sorell had sexual intercourse that night, as there were semen stains on the bed sheet. The logical assumption was that the woman was Cheryl.

However, additional persons were of interest, as, apart from Sorell's blood, there were traces of another person near the man but not in the bed. This caused confusion.

'Bizarre' was how Isaac Cook described it, but that seemed to sum up most of the murder investigations they had conducted in the last few years.

Wendy was hopeful that Cheryl Hastings was not the murderer – the woman had suffered enough – but there was also an underlying fear that if she had visited the house and spent time with Barry Sorell, someone else might have been in the home or seen her. Loose ends were not what a murderer wanted.

The Colsons were holding firm to their story. Isaac had told them to confine themselves to their house or the one next door, but now, one was a past murder scene and the other a current one. Ignoring the instruction, they took a train out of London and relocated back to the croft in Scotland, paying twice the rate they had paid before.

Harold Colson had phoned, reemphasised their innocence, and said that they would stay at the croft and be available at any time for a phone call or a visit, but unless evidence was presented to the contrary, they would not come to London.

Isaac knew they were still using Grant Batholomew's money and that false identities had been used to obtain credit cards and, no doubt, passports. They were involved in crime, but not murder, until clarification that they were.

With two persons out of the way, the focus was on Cheryl Hastings and Fiona Cole. With Fiona, financial issues did not seem to be the reason for her to frame the Colsons, as she had two million pounds. Proof had been requested, given that the money had been lodged in her bank account.

Larry sensed a rat, and his experience with builders, having met a few courtesy of his wife, was that they often skirted the law, whether with building permissions, a backhander to the building department at the local council, payments in cash for services rendered, and, if they could, substandard materials used in construction. His focus was on the woman, particularly as it hadn't been proven that Cheryl was Sorell's sexual partner that night.

The only fly in the ointment was why Sorell had died. If Fiona had engineered the death of Grayling in an attempt to frame the Colsons, why did she do that after she'd had the money from them? And secondly, which seemed more important, why kill Sorell when the Colsons were in Scotland. Proof had come from the estate agent who had rented the croft to the Colsons, confirming that he had seen them in the afternoon before the man's death and the following morning. That left a nine-hour window for them to return to London by plane, commit the murder and return. On the face of it, it would have been difficult to do and made no sense.

It was as if there was another person that Homicide didn't know about.

It was Isaac the following day who summated the investigation. 'We're chasing rainbows,' he said.

Wendy thought it an odd term given the context of the murders, but she understood. They were chasing shadows, hopeful that something would turn up. She knew it was the only thing they could do at the time, a process of elimination, to go through the persons they knew about and prove their innocence or guilt.

It wasn't enough.

The media, both legacy and social, were intrigued. Witches, covens, and devil worship in suburbia always made great headlines.

The idea that there were others involved gained importance. Larry was all for focusing on another person's angle at the expense of Fiona Cole, but Isaac disagreed.

'Your contacts?' Isaac said to Larry. 'The criminal underbelly that you're friendly with, the informers? What's the word on the street? Surely, it's a conversation in the pubs at night. After all, Bayswater isn't known for ritual sacrifice. They must have something to say.'

'I've been keeping away from them for a few weeks. I had a few beers in Sevenoaks and could have drunk more. I know I'm flying close to the sun. I don't want my wings to fail.'

'They will,' Wendy said.

Bridget, who had been quiet so far, spoke. 'Suffolk.'

'What's the importance?' Isaac asked.

'Higher than the national average for Satanists. I've been doing research. With the decline in organised religion in the country and the advent of social media, there's been a rise in alternate beliefs. Satanism is one of them. I'm not saying they are sacrificing a virgin every weekend, in between games of cricket on the village green and a drink down the pub. Although a few drinks, a few drugs, and no doubt frolicking and orgiastic behaviour are possible.'

'Are you suggesting we make a visit?'

'Not necessarily, but satanism, worship of evil, is on the rise. Christianity and its influence are on the wane. Human sacrifice is not something they seem to practise, although there have been reports of animals. More likely to be sexual than violent, which points to Grayling's death as a means of framing the Colsons.'

'Are you saying, due to your research, we should downplay Grayling's death as a ritual but treat it as a setup to frame the Colsons?'

'I am putting forward the possibility. The Colsons' interest in the subject is academic and not unreasonable, considering that history and culture are complex. There was the burning of witches in the past, as we all know. Belief in the devil remains, and whereas the beast has been regarded with fear and disdain, it is of some interest to the disenfranchised in society.'

'Are we looking for an idiot, or someone antisocial, or socially awkward?'

Isaac leaned back in his chair and opened the window behind him, the city's sound echoing through the room. 'What you are saying is that the Colsons are innocent.'

'Innocent of ritual sacrifice, not necessarily of murder. The man spent nights at the Colsons. Why?'

'We don't know,' Larry said.

'Then you should,' Bridget replied.

It was a theme that they had mentioned before. That the Colsons had been framed, although Grayling's apparent friendship with the couple was never fully explained.

Isaac was glad to be out of the office as he and Wendy took an early-morning flight the next day to Scotland. They met the Colsons at their croft. Wendy loved the place; Isaac wasn't so sure. His wife was becoming more adamant about moving out of the big smoke, as she referred to it, for the children's sake.

'David was a friend. We found him good company. Sometimes, he would spend the night,' Elizabeth Colson said.

'It doesn't explain why?' Isaac said. He could see that the Colsons were in for an extended stay. On a chair in the corner, a cat of indeterminate parentage, and in the kitchen window, a freshly baked cake.

'We've made an offer on the place,' Harold Colson said.

'Premium price if you're in the place.'

'Two houses in London, sell them both. Money's not the issue.'

'They won't sell for a couple of years,' Wendy said. 'Both have experienced violent death. A good solicitor for the purchasers will find that out.'

'It doesn't matter. We can offer a discount if we must for a quick sale. Once you give us access, we will rent them out while they sell. Here is home now, apart from the minor encumbrance of explaining Grant in the garden next door.'

'There'll probably be a court case you need to attend.'

'We will. What about Sorell? Any leads?' Harold asked.

'Not yet. We have two possibilities. The first is that Grayling died as a result of a satanic ritual. That's mentioned in the history books, although modern-day satanism appears benign. More dressing up in strange robes and incantations. I don't need to tell you that.'

'You don't, but most people don't understand the depth of the subject. How countries and cultures have been shaped by mainstream religion and belief in the occult. Not only satanism but primitive religions believing in spirits. Plato was adamant that the populace should believe in one God or another. He thought it gave structure to civilization, but with the lessening of traditional Christian beliefs came the possibility that satanism, devil worship, and fringe, less benevolent, more violent religious beliefs would surface. It was one avenue that we were investigating.'

'But why?' Wendy asked.

'Academic research, looking past the obvious, delving into the human psyche, the need to believe in something. Christianity has been, in the last two hundred years, largely benign. On the other hand, the devil, witchcraft, and belief in the malevolent can, given the correct circumstances, transmute from passive to aggressive.'

'Is that happening in the United Kingdom?' Isaac asked, taking a bite of a slice of the cake that had been on the window sill but was now on the table in front of them.

'It is, in small pockets of the country. Some are serious, most looking for something, although what they find will not benefit them.'

'It still doesn't explain David Grayling. Is it significant that he was the son of a vicar?'

'It lent relevance to our friendship. He had led a transient life on the street for many years, although he had a solid grounding in religion and understood our research.'

'None of which explains why he stayed the night. Unfortunately, we are forced to speculate.'

'If you must know,' Harold said, 'he reminded us of our son, who had died in his teens. David was older but had a similar personality. We found great joy in his company.'

'And then he dies, and you disappear. We see no emotion from either of you over his death.'

'You never will. Our grief is private, and since we found him in the cellar, our life has been difficult. We knew the implications of his death and how it would be interpreted. We were confused.'

'If you had been open and contacted the police, it would have been better,' Wendy said as she took another slice of cake.

'Would it? You would have investigated, found out about Grant, and the money to Fiona. What were we supposed to do? We come home from a night away and find David in the basement. We panicked and fled in a hurry, not enough time to ensure the house was secure.'

'Afterwards, what would you have done if we hadn't received an anonymous phone call?'

'Possibly what we had done with Grant. But Grant would have understood. We couldn't believe that David would. Was our reaction unexpected, considering the circumstances and what you know of us?' Harold said.

'No,' Isaac replied. 'Your reaction is understandable, but on reflection, stupid. Whether you have been truthful about your relationship with David Grayling remains unclear.'

'We have.'

Isaac and Wendy weren't so sure. Even so, they returned to London on a flight at six in the evening.

Meanwhile, Larry sat down with Aaron and Fiona Cole. A neutral location, a back room at the pub in Sevenoaks.

Larry would have preferred Fiona alone, but she had decreed that her husband would join them.

Due to the seriousness of the investigation and his predilection to make a fool of himself with alcohol, he was not going to drink but to stay with fruit juice. The juice brought a bitter taste to his mouth.

'Do you trust the Colsons?' Aaron asked.

'We remain open in our opinion of them,' Larry said.' Given the circumstances, the reason they left the house quickly is valid.'

'But they are criminals. They buried Grant in that garden. He deserved a proper burial.'

Larry had a bad feeling about Fiona. He couldn't grasp it, but instinct told him something was amiss. She was polite in conversation, attractive and well-dressed, and had an aura. Yet she had separated from Grant one year before his death, and even if he was tight with his money, she had received her share of their assets when the divorce had been finalised. This was coupled with the fact that she had not registered him as a missing person and then had him declared dead after seven years.

Not once, according to the Colsons, had they heard from the woman, but not long before Grayling had died, she had appeared at their front door, demanding money.

The Coles drank wine; Larry kept to juice. He thought it would improve his reasoning but felt it hadn't. He leant over and poured himself a glass of wine.

'How did you know the Colsons used your husband's money?'

'Chance. I made a claim on his money after seven years once he was declared legally dead. Before that, Grant had given me some money, but not enough. I checked with the bank to get Grant's contact details. We were separated and heading towards divorce. They would not tell me anything. A grovelling bank manager told me he was in contact with his client and would pass on my details.'

'But you were married for eleven years. You must have known about his businesses, assets, and the names he used.'

'I didn't. Grant was fifteen years older than me. I was a trophy wife, something I shouldn't be proud of, but there it is. He was wealthy and lived well, even if he concealed most of the money. I can't complain, but he was mean to me. It was great for the first five or six years, but he started to age faster than me. He went from wanting a Ferrari to a Mercedes Benz, from wanting a beautiful woman on his arm to spending nights at home and discussing economics.'

'Which you didn't want?'

'Which I didn't understand. If you have money, save some, but enjoy the majority. He became a Scrooge, and then he rationed the money I spent. I rebelled, argued with him, cajoled, and walked out the door. I can't blame him for being angry, and now that I am older and wiser, he might have been right.'

'Fiona has been a good wife to me,' Aaron Cole said.

Larry knew Fiona might have wanted moral support, but he wanted to go in hard and push Fiona into a corner where she would squirm, but he would not get the chance.

'A marriage breakup is always traumatic. However, after Grant had been declared dead, you could have applied for access to his bank accounts.'

'We were divorced. I applied and gained permission to enquire. I spoke to the grovelling bank manager that I mentioned before. He told me smilingly that the account had been closed, all monies transferred out of the country, and that he didn't know or wouldn't tell me where.'

'Out of the country, the money was gone. That should have indicated that Grant was still alive.'

'It didn't. The account had been closed three weeks after seeing the manager the first time, although I didn't know that for seven years.'

'You moved on with your life. How long before you met Aaron? Any other relationships in the interim? And why is there no contact with the Colsons? After all, Mrs Colson was Grant's sister.'

The answers from the woman were flawed. She either didn't care about her former husband's money, or she had access to someone else's money. It was proving difficult to probe while Fiona's husband remained.

'Tell him,' Aaron Cole said. 'He'll only find out later.'

'I'm out of the house, Grant's not returning my calls. I've got enough money for six months to rent a place in Belgravia, but I wasn't about to go out to work. I became self-employed. Remember, I was still young and desirable.'

'You found someone who would pay for your lifestyle?'

'I did. It was part of growing up, and I was not cut out for manual work or the nine-to-five grind.'

'Fiona found herself a fancy man, someone with plenty,' Aaron said.

'You don't mind?' Larry asked.

'Mind? Why should I? It was before we met. I've been married before, and I didn't expect Fiona to come to me as a vestal virgin.'

'Someone in the city,' Fiona said. 'I lived with him for two years, grew up, met Aaron. I didn't concern myself with Grant, only when Aaron and I wanted to marry. I wanted closure, even though we were divorced. There were bank accounts and insurance policies I had signed. I didn't know their full extent, but it became important to get a resolution. That was the only reason I had him declared dead. I didn't contact Harold and Elizabeth, assuming that they would have stuck their noses in, claimed that any of Grant's money belonged to them, or they would have stifled me. They never liked me, always saw me as a grubby little tart, wiggling her arse and turning Grant against his sister.'

'Were you?'

'I was everything they said about me. But compared to them, I was a saint. They were using his money and his name and profiting from it. Are you sure Grant wasn't murdered?'

It wasn't something that Homicide had found proof of, and they had discounted it as an option. But given Fiona's testimony, it was worth considering. It could be viable if Grant had found another woman, either a grubby little tart, as Fiona had described herself, or a woman of substance who would work with Grant in his business ventures and investment endeavours.

Chapter 10

Yet again, the Colsons had withheld information. There had been another woman in Grant Batholomew's life after Fiona had walked out on him. She had come forward after reading in the newspaper that Grant had died.

Siobhan Byrne had grown up outside London and lived in Kent. According to the Colsons, when pressed, it was a short-lived romance.

'Yes, I remember Grant. A long time ago, or it appears that way. We met by chance on a train. I had a recital to attend; I play the violin. Grant told me that he had a business meeting.'

'What business?'

'He didn't say. Don't read too much into the romance. It was hardly that, but it was nice for a while. I knew he had recently separated from his wife. Marriage and children had never moved me as it did others.'

'Married now?'

'No. I've had the occasional fling, and Grant was good for a while. But when it starts to get complicated or predictable, I lose interest. He was the perfect company, and we did have a few weekends away together. I know he had money, but he didn't throw it around, and sufficient is more than enough for me.'

Judging by the small cottage where the woman lived, Wendy thought sufficient was correct. It was sparsely furnished; the only luxury was an old sofa. In front of an open fire, a small dog was curled up.

'Fifteen years old, he doesn't move much,' Siobhan said as Wendy stroked it.

'Are you abreast of the news?' Wendy asked.

'I read that Grant had died and that, somehow, he's part of a murder investigation.

Devil House

'His sister might have committed a murder, and his former wife is under investigation. Do you have any observations?'

'Nothing, not really. Grant and I used to meet and spend the night together occasionally, but never in each other's house.'

'Was there a reason for that?'

'It was my decision. It was good to be with a man, but not to live with them or fall in love. I prefer solitude and my music to a long-term relationship. I didn't want commitment, nor did Grant. Apparently, his wife was not a good person.'

'She had married him for the life he could give her. She's admitted to that, and he placed restrictions on her in time. You never met her?'

'Never. I met his sister once, but I don't think she was impressed with me. She would talk to Grant but purposely ignore me.'

'Did that upset you?'

'Not particularly. Grant said they had been close as children, and he trusted her above anyone else.'

'Including you.'

'I was a casual fling. I didn't expect her to trust me, and I didn't need him in my life other than occasionally.'

'What happened?'

'To end it? I went to America, a series of concerts around the country. Three months later, we met again and had a meal and a few drinks. Maybe it could have been different, but he had been burnt, and I wasn't doing much to ease the pain. Good while it lasted.'

***

Isaac and Larry met with the man that Fiona Cole had lived with for two years after her break up with Grant.

Fiona's statement as to his wealth proved to be correct. The man was a bon vivant, a lover of life and women. In a three-storey terrace in Mayfair was the latest woman in a long string of women. She was scantily dressed.

Edward Fraser, well known in the city for the chain of upmarket restaurants he owned and for his weekly cooking show on television, made no excuses for his life.

'I love them all,' he said. 'Fiona lasted longer than most, but as you can see, I like them young.'

'Not love?' Isaac said, secretly full of admiration for the man. He had been a lothario in his youth before he met Jenny, but Fraser had taken seduction to an art form.

Fraser was dressed casually in his early fifties in an open-neck shirt and jeans.

'We needed clarification,' Larry said. 'We're investigating a murder.'

'I recognised the name on the television but didn't associate Grant Batholomew with Fiona until then. It was good while it lasted, but then, like the others, she was tired of my life and the reality that I wouldn't make an honest woman of her. Enjoy it while they can, and I wish them well when they leave. Make sure they are financially stable for a few months until they settle.'

'Never married?' Isaac asked.

'Once, in my late teens. A good person, known her since fifth grade.'

'Divorced?'

'She passed away, complications from surgery when she was twenty-five. After that, I buried myself in work, eventually resolving not to go through the trauma of losing another loved one. As with the woman you just saw, eventually, they want commitment, something I am incapable of giving. Money is not a gift; my lifestyle does not last forever, and invariably, most people become tired of it. Fiona did, found a decent man, and married him.'

'Grant Batholomew. Did you know him?'

'I did. Not that Fiona knew. I met her at a function in the city. Only later, a couple of months after she had moved in, did she mention his name.'

'Did you tell her that you knew her husband?'

'I thought it best to keep quiet. Batholomew owned the lease on one of my restaurants. I had met him once, but it was strictly professional. He might have reneged on the lease or upped the rent if he had known that Fiona was sharing my bed. I don't believe she had contact with him while she was with me. She was bitter about the man, but that's not unexpected when a marriage fails.'

There seemed no reason to believe that the man had anything to do with the recent murders, and his corroboration lent weight to the fact that Fiona Cole was a truthful witness, even if Larry still had a nagging feeling about the woman, an itch he couldn't scratch.

The young woman came in, this time dressed in a knee-length dress. 'Edward likes me to flaunt it when we're alone. I hope I hadn't offended you when you arrived,' she said.

'Not at all,' Isaac said. On the contrary, he was envious of the man and attracted to the woman, especially after the stressful conversation with Jenny since she had been jostled at the supermarket and was understandably upset by a gang of youths as they tried to grab her purse before lifting as many goods as they could before dashing out of the shop.

'Not much we can do,' an apologetic manager had said to her. 'The police, not sure they're worth the money. Too busy dealing with inflammatory comments on social media than dealing with real crime.'

'My husband's a police officer,' she had said in Isaac's defence.

'My apologies.'

'Not necessary. You're right, the city's going to hell.'

'I thought Davies was right,' the manager said. 'Get tough and hammer those who step out of line. Have you met the man?'

'Briefly.'

'Straight talker, takes a stand, not like those lily-livered…. My apologies. What division, your husband?'

'Homicide. No time for social etiquette. You do the crime, you get arrested.'

Ten minutes after she left the manager, who was still apologising, she was on the phone with Isaac, adamant that either he agreed to leave London with her and the children or she would take them and go.

Isaac had to agree with her, even the manager, and his criticism that the police were rapidly becoming as ineffective as the current government. And there was to be an election soon, and one ruling party, tired and out of ideas, would be replaced by another that wasn't tired and had plenty of ideas, most of which would do nothing to rectify the decline in social adhesion within the city.

It was a decision he would have to address at some time, but he was convinced he would not be able to make a decision that would satisfy Jenny. He wasn't ready to give up on London, not yet.

Fraser wasn't a satanist, but he warned Isaac and Larry as they prepared to leave. 'Watch out for Fiona. She's bipolar, and you don't want to see her dark side.'

'Violent?'

'Depressive, violent outbursts, and she can be destructive. She thought I was cheating on her once, put a knife through all the clothes in my wardrobe, and smashed a sculpture I was fond of.'

'Capable of murder?' Larry asked.

'It's hard to imagine, even more difficult to say, but given the right circumstances, enough motivation, and one of her dark periods, it's possible.'

Larry realised that his itch had been correct. Fiona Cole had a dark side, manifested in violence if provoked, maybe to murder. But Grayling would not have been the person at whom her anger would have been directed. He was merely a pawn in the middle, which caused Larry to query whether, if in a dark and psychotic phase of her personality, she would have been able to reason through the possibilities of how she could get the Colsons convicted of murder.

Was her vengeance that deep?

And what of the body in the garden next door? Had she known it was there, or was that extrapolating the possibilities too far?

Isaac thought it unlikely, although the reason the Colsons had buried Grant Batholomew in the garden still made no sense, money or no money. It was callous to him, and Elizabeth Colson had said she was close to her brother. A midnight burial in a garden wasn't the act of a loving sister but more that of a devious, greedy, grasping, and uncaring person.

***

Wendy took time off from searching for Cheryl Hastings, although she suspected her parents knew where she was. She wanted to refocus on the McCarthys. If Fiona Cole had periods of darkness and depressive thoughts interspersed with violent outbursts, could Janice McCarthy?

She visited the prison where the woman had been incarcerated. HMP Bronzefield, located in Middlesex, was less than an hour's drive from London, but Wendy chose to take the train, as there would be less hassle with the early-morning traffic. Opened in 2008, it took a modern approach to prison and adopted a more tolerant approach to the prisoners and their rehabilitation. However, that did not stop it from being very secure, housing serial killers and the occasional Just Stop Oil protester.

The governor, Marjorie Jenkins, remembered the event. She had taken over the governorship one year after the facility opened. Tall and slender, her hair was styled, and her nails varnished. Hardly the stereotype of a female authoritarian charged with the care of over five hundred women.

'Hard to forget. Janice Nelson was an attractive young woman who minded her business when she was here. A model prisoner, to use that cliched term,' the governor said.

The two women sat in the governor's office. Utilitarian, with few luxuries, it was the room of the no-nonsense person who had secured the position after an exhaustive hiring procedure. Twelve other candidates had applied, nine men and three women. The interviews had been burdensome; Jenkins had had three. Qualifications were checked, background checks conducted, and personality tests were given. In the end, after six weeks, Marjorie Jenkins had been appointed.

Bridget supplied the background on the governor. The appointment was not slanted towards a woman but to the most qualified and competent, a decision that had been proven correct, as Marjorie Jenkins had remained the governor since then.

'Yet she was involved in an altercation with another prisoner.'

'The other woman was in prison for the violent abuse of her child by her and her live-in boyfriend. Younger than her by a few years, he had a history of petty crime and violence. He's still behind bars, killed a man ten years later. The other woman, no need to mention her name.'

'I know it,' Wendy said.

'I'm sure you do. She was baiting Janice, not unusual in a prison where the strong prey on the weak.'

'Not exclusively a prison characteristic.'

'True, but you can't ignore it here and walk away. Janice's parents would visit weekly to ensure their daughter had extra food to eat or barter. Currency in prison. But she wasn't into that. Kept it for herself or her friends. The woman involved in the altercation was in for a long time. Either she wanted to be included as a friend, or she wanted some of the goods to eat or to barter. Janice Nelson wasn't willing to part with them. That's when the altercation happened, and the woman fell and banged her head on the ground, dead before she left the prison in the back of an ambulance. Why the interest in Janice? You alluded to a homicide; I believe I have a right to know some of the details.'

'David Grayling was murdered in what appeared to be a ritual sacrifice, devil worship. Only there are anomalies. Janice McCarthy and her husband were friends with those who owned the house. According to both parties, there was shared grief over the loss of a child.'

'Sad, but how does her time in prison relate to the murder?'

'Janice McCarthy's child, eight years old, died in a tragic accident. She fell off a swing. The pathologist, however, believed there was additional bruising on the child's body that was not consistent with the accident.'

'The girl had been beaten?'

'It wasn't presented at the inquest, possibly due to the grieving parents. The pathologist wasn't present, as he was unable to attend. Another person presented his findings; the additional bruising wasn't mentioned.'

'And the concern is that what happened in prison, coupled with Janice as a possible child beater, points to the possibility that she could be involved in the death of Grayling?'

'It's not our only theory, but it's plausible, even if it's a long bow to stretch.'

'Very long.'

'The investigation has become complex. Your insight into Janice McCarthy has been invaluable.'

Wendy left the prison, feeling it was an interesting visit but a waste of time.

Outside the McCarthy home that afternoon, she struck while the iron was hot. This time, her DCI had joined her and confided in her that his home life wasn't as good as it should be. They had sat down for lunch before visiting the McCarthys, a small Italian restaurant in Knightsbridge, a stone's throw from Harrods. The restaurant served excellent food at reasonable prices, unlike Harrods.

'It's not an easy decision to make,' Isaac said. It wasn't a conversation he would have with Larry Hill, but Wendy and he went back a long way to when he was a constable. She had seen his career as it progressed, only to stagnate in Homicide due to Commissioner Davies and his sidekick, Superintendent Caddick. Nobody in Homicide liked the man, but his presence remained, and his visits to Homicide always irritated him.

With a murder enquiry dragging, it wouldn't be long before he made his presence known with sarcastic remarks to Isaac and offers of assistance.

Commander Goddard had survived by throwing his towel in the ring with Davies, but Isaac, not adept at office politics, had steered a neutral course. So far, it had worked, but he wasn't sure how long it would last.

'Jenny's right,' Wendy said. 'You can't expect her to be happy about the situation. You were shot once, and so was Inspector Hill. No woman wants to hear that their man has been killed in the line of duty, and it's always possible. And she's right; street crime is rife, house invasion, carjacking, all signs of a decaying city. Out in the provincial towns, the problem has not taken hold.

'It will,' Isaac said as he ate his lasagne.

'Inevitable. Consider Jenny; she's your primary concern. You won't save the Metropolitan Police single-handedly, and Commander Goddard will steer a steady course to protect himself. Besides, another five to ten years, and he'll retire. It's too late for him to make too many waves. It is too early for you to do so and too foolish if you try. Davies will hang you out to dry, and the provinces won't be there for you.'

Janice McCarthy opened the front door of her house. 'Bob's not here,' she said. She cast an eye at the strikingly handsome Isaac. 'Pleased to meet you,' he said.

Inside the house, the two officers sat down.

'A few questions,' Wendy said.

'If you must.'

'Did you ever meet Fiona Cole?'

'I've never heard the name mentioned. Should I have?'
'Not necessarily. Just establishing certain facts. Fiona Cole was the former wife of Grant Batholomew.'
'Another name I hadn't heard of until you unearthed him. Don't misinterpret our association with the Colsons. We weren't bosom buddies, just persons with a similar history; tragedy had befallen us. It seemed easier with them than with others, who would invariably feel the need to tell you how their child was doing, whether they were in love or had passed their exams and were going to university. The easiest way to deal with tragedy is not to be confronted by it, by those who, in ignorance or not thinking, say something that upsets.'
'I met the governor of Bronzefield.'
'Is she still there?'
'She is. She said you were a model prisoner.'
'I was until that woman accosted me. It's tough in prison, dealing with people you would avoid outside.'
'Have the Colsons contacted you?' Isaac asked.
'They phoned, told us they were in Scotland, and weren't returning. Is that correct?'
'It is. We know where they are. What do you know about their research?'
'Nothing, really. Bob and I are certainly not academics. You must understand that shared tragedy makes for unusual friendships.'
Isaac did.
'Did they discuss it? Did you feel uneasy when it was brought up in conversation?'
'We steered clear of it, and so did they. Why would they want to research something so depressing, especially after their son died?'
'Why did you stay in this house, a view out of your front window, where…'
'Where our daughter died, that's what you were about to say.'
'It was. What's the answer?'

'A closeness to her, the last place we saw her happy and alive. Unless you've experienced tragedy, you wouldn't understand. You see dead bodies, not persons who loved and were loved. I saw our daughter in the morgue, the peacefulness in her face as if she were in a deep sleep. We prefer to focus on the good, not the bad. The Colsons might have an academic mind and the ability to rationalise. We did not.'

'What was the phone call about?'

'They asked us to keep a watch on the two houses. We said we would.'

'And you will do that, even though you were not close.'

'We will. They are selling the houses. They've asked us to supervise the removal company coming to take out their belongings to send to Scotland.'

'The furniture?'

'No. Only their research and their books. A few mementoes, some other items. They sent a detailed list. God knows how they could be so precise.'

Chapter 11

Three hours later, and armed with a copy of the list the Colsons had sent to the McCarthys, Larry and Wendy stood outside the front of the Colson house, the scene of the first murder.

Alongside them were two crime scene investigators, a woman in her forties who was an acknowledged occult expert with a Magic and Occult Science degree from the University of Exeter. Larry thought it was 'Mickey Mouse' when told about the woman's area of expertise, but Florence Bathurst was believed to be the best in her field, had been credentialled by the police, and could give evidence at a trial.

Inside, the house was stuffy. There was the Colsons' discarded clothing as they escaped, leftover food in the kitchen, and dirty dishes in the sink from when Cheryl Hastings and Barry Sorell moved in. Otherwise, nothing had changed.

Due to it being her first visit, Florence Bathurst was shown the cellar where Grayling had died. She was emotional seeing the pentagram, the Sigil of Baphomet, and the burnt-out candles.

'It's as I imagined,' she said.

Larry felt like saying it was because she had seen the photos back at Challis Street before they came, but he declined. If the woman was accredited, he had to give her some leeway.

Eager to seem relevant, Florence Bathurst continually chattered. Wendy assumed it was either nerves or derision from those who regarded her expertise as foolish and irrelevant.

'Very real, more than you would think,' she said. 'This is a prime example. Of course, they would be shocked if the horned devil appeared, but he never does. Imaginative minds, coupled with bacchanalian excess and sexual extremes, and even the most dismissive, Inspector Hill, would start to believe.'

'You don't,' Larry said.

'I maintain a healthy scepticism. We are bombarded with tales of the unknown, but proof is elusive. The subject is interesting, significantly how it shapes people and their minds. Once, when people were less educated and needed to attach significance to natural events, it was possible to frighten them with tales of Beelzebub and witchcraft. But many believe, even today, as they did in the past.

'Our history has, to some degree, been shaped by the occult. As for alchemy, turning lead into gold, it's possible if you've got a particle accelerator to knock off a few protons from the nucleus of a lead atom until only seventy-nine remain. Even then, you only end up with a few atoms.'

Upstairs, the CSIs moved around slowly. They did not need to conduct an exhaustive investigation but to wait for a lead from the police officers.

Wendy read the list and disregarded the kitchen utensils and the clothes remaining upstairs. Scrolling further down the list, she came to the books. There were several shelves and many books. Why Harold did not want to come down with the removal van, even for a day, to supervise their move would need an answer. It was as if he had an issue with the house.

'The satanic Bible,' Florence said as she flipped through the pages.

'Rare?' Wendy asked.

'You can buy it on Amazon. Anton Le Vey, the founder of the Church of Satan, authored the book. The Sigil in the cellar, he designed it.'

'Does that indicate anything?' Larry asked.

'I would have thought students of satanism would have chosen something other than a Sigil designed in the twentieth century. Is that one of the books on the list?' Florence said.

'It is,' Wendy replied.

'And you reckon that the Colsons, giving their expertise on the subject, would have searched back in history for more ancient sigils?'

'It would be logical. I would have also expected more signs around the cellar and an altar, even if it was only a cupboard with a cloth over it. And where are the robes they would have worn? Four people, you said?'

'That's what the CSIs believe.'

'Not enough. There's no precise number, but the more persons, the more likely there will be a visitation.'

'You've met people who believe strongly.'

'Some who will tell you they have seen the horned beast.'

'Rituals, what we have here?'

'Fuelled by hysteria, opioids and alcohol, Inspector. I'm not one of those deluded persons. My assessment of the Colsons, judging by the books here and their research, indicates they are not believers or sceptics but seekers of the truth.'

'You admire them?' Larry asked.

'I have an issue with persons who take a position based on prejudice or ignorance. Unfortunately, Inspector, that is how you reacted to me when we met. I hope you will allow me to investigate what we have and formulate an honest opinion. As I said, the cellar was not what I expected.

'To debase satanism, witchcraft, alchemy, and all other forms of the occult is to negate the impact that they have had over millennia. There were no witches in Salem, none in this country, only ignorance by the majority and religious zeal by those who wielded power. Two hundred years ago, the Colsons would have been dealt with brutally, with little justice.'

'But now, they will receive a fair hearing and a legal system not mired in superstition,' Larry said.

'We have progressed,' Florence Bathurst said. 'From what I've seen so far, I cannot believe the Colsons would do anything so amateurish as kill a man in the cellar, spreadeagled on the floor.'

'Elizabeth Colson's brother, buried in the garden next door?'

'Without ceremony? And were the Colsons researching the occult back then? There are other books here, Eastern religions, evolution, and psychology. Were they wealthy?'

'We believe Harold Colson came from money and worked as an accountant. Elizabeth and Harold also used Bartholomew's money and multiplied it. Also, they are clearly frugal.'

'An understatement, Inspector. Apart from the books, there is not much of value here. No wonder they don't want the furniture, but the books, there are some here that I would love to own.'

'Yet you have never heard of the Colsons?'

'I hadn't, not before I was engaged by you as your resident expert on things that go bump in the night.'

'A demeaning comment about yourself,' Wendy, who had been standing to one side, enjoying the repartee between her inspector and the expert, said.

'Not demeaning, honest. I was checked, counter-checked, subjected to extensive questioning by your legal department and Human Resources to ensure that I wasn't a fruit cake, a bloodsucking vampire, or indulged in orgiastic rituals with multiple men.'

'We need to be thorough.'

'For your information, I'm married with two children and a Christian. Historically, the occult has relevance. Whether it has a basis in reality, I wouldn't know. But a few believe in it as fervently as a devout Christian.'

'As does a bunch of ne'er-do-wells and malevolent individuals who use it for their own gratification,' Larry said.

'There are the depraved, those who would use children. Are you aware of any cases?'

'We've only found rumours.'

'You do know why?'

'The most malevolent are not the amateurs, but persons of influence.'

'Correct. The Colsons, if their research is thorough, and I have reason to believe it is, might have chanced on those persons.'

Larry realised the significance of what was being said, as did Wendy. Was the investigation to take a quantum shift into the halls of power, to those who governed the country, to the champions of industry. Wendy had another thought: Cheryl Hastings.

'There is a woman next door who found Grayling in the cellar. She was not fazed by what she found. In her youth, at eleven years of age, she was kidnapped and suffered at the hands of a debased man. Could it be that she was one of those children?'

'Ask her, but be careful. Suppressed memories may serve her well. You don't want her to remember too much. What happened to the person who kidnapped her?'

'Dead. She's disappeared. We've been trying to find her.'

'If she remembers, then she might remember persons who would not want their names revealed.'

Outside the house, Wendy phoned Bridget to intensify her efforts to scour the internet for Cheryl Hastings, fearful that she might have come to harm already. She then phoned Isaac to update him on another possible scenario: Fiona Cole was not involved, which had never made much sense, as she had money from the Colsons, and that, unless she had ongoing issues with the pair, Fiona had wanted to distance herself from them. However, the two million pounds was a lot of money, which came with questions about how Grant Batholomew, and by default, the Colsons, had so much in cash?

Had Grant Batholomew died of natural causes? Was he in agreement with the actions ultimately taken after his death?

'If Batholomew died naturally, and there was a will in place naming his sister as the sole beneficiary, then what was to be gained by hiding the body? The man was divorced, Fiona Cole had no claim on the estate, unless…' Isaac said.

'There was criminality,' Wendy ended what her DCI was saying.

'Precisely. Find Cheryl Hastings. Investigate what we can about Grant Batholomew.'

'The Colsons?'

'Let them sweat for the time being.'

'They could leave the country.'

'It's possible, but we can't hold them, not on our flimsy evidence.'

Wendy thought it was possible, or she wanted it to be. But this was an investigation that had not run its course. It could be weeks, possibly months before arrests were made.

***

In haste, Harold and Elizabeth Colson had left their research papers on a bookshelf. What was interesting, but not the initial intent in bringing Florence Bathurst in, was that a manila folder was hidden behind a voluminous book on the dark arts. In it, if not complete, was a rudimentary list of the financial status of the Colsons, stretching back fifteen years.

The initial investigation of the house had been related to murder, and that focus had been on the cellar. The remainder of the house had been checked, especially about the additional persons at the murder site. It had been four persons: initially, the Colsons, and subsequently Cheryl Hastings as the third. One more remained to be found.

'Most business is online, paperwork is unnecessary,' one of the CSIs said.

'Correct. But the Colsons were old-school.' Larry said. 'We will assume that, whereas they might be savvy with computers, they prefer to keep records handwritten on paper.

'Florence has found a manila folder. It contains information about Batholomew's finances, the property he owned, the money he had in stocks and shares, and a small amount in cash. However, it is not comprehensive, and further paperwork might reveal an anomaly in Bartholomew's death.

'Let me add, we have no evidence that Batholomew was murdered. Yet, the question remains: why in the garden?

Batholomew was free to give his wealth to whoever he wanted, and failing a will, his sister would have had the first claim.'

A large table with four chairs had been set up in the garage. On one side of the garage was another desk with a printer. There were also a couple of heaters, as the garage was not insulated. On the floor of the garage, a large carpet had been laid.

Florence Bathurst was to check the bookshelves' contents, remove them to the garage if required, and compile a comprehensive report of her findings. There was to be a twenty-four-hour presence by police officers outside the house to ensure no unwanted persons entered. The two young constables, Jim Drayton and Nadia Hussain, whom Wendy had set out to knock on doors, would be assisting.

'It might be that everything we need is on the bookshelves,' Isaac said on one of his visits. 'However, the CSIs will systematically move from room to room, checking every nook and cranny. We're not confident they will find anything, as the Colsons have not returned to the house and only asked for certain items, primarily the contents of the bookshelves. They have asked a friend to deal with this. They did not expect us to become so involved, and we must thank Florence for that.'

Larry intended to stay for the day.

Isaac left, and the assembled team got to work. Florence Bathurst went through the shelves, book by book, assisted by Nadia, who Florence had taken a shine to.

Jim Drayton worked with the CSIs, ensuring no place was missed and that protocol was not circumvented for expediency. The CSIs, understandably, found the work tedious, and moving wardrobes, beds, and other furniture, looking for the proverbial needle in a haystack, gave them no joy.

Florence sat at the table in the garage, entering the details of each book into the database, while Nadia went through each page in case a sheet of paper was hidden inside. It was laborious work and heavy. After two hours, long enough for the CSIs to prove that they would be thorough, Jim Drayton was drafted in to assist with lifting the books, as some were large and heavy, and taking them to the garage with due care and returning them once Florence and Nadia had signed off on them.

Larry was running his own race, moving ahead of the CSIs, leaving the heavy lifting to them, but casting a keen eye over each room, using his experience with the criminal class to try and think like the Colsons, who had been informed of the proceedings by the McCarthys.

Isaac had taken the phone call from an angry Harold Colson. 'What right do you have?' he demanded.

'It's a murder investigation, Mr Colson. Due care is being taken, but we need to know more about Grant Batholomew's financial status and your wife's financial records. We need to understand more than you've told us.'

'I've told you everything. We are an open book. We didn't kill David, nor did we kill Sorell or Grant. We are academics.'

'Why accountancy when you have so much money?'

'Money is relative. Life is a balance. Just because we have more than enough to live on does not mean we don't require a balance. Accountancy was sanity. The occult affects people, and our investigations into it were not without trauma, a deep-down belief that we were becoming involved in something that we shouldn't.'

'That it might be real?'

'There are malevolent people in society who do wicked things in the name of satanism. Are you aware of that?'

'We are becoming aware of it. Do you have names?'

'We suspect some.'

'How? How can your research uncover those who practise satanism and profess to be witches or wizards?'

'Satanism is mostly banal and trivial. Dressing up in fancy robes, orgiastic rituals, nothing more.'

'Hardly banal or trivial.'

'I would agree, in essence. But you are not a moderator of foolish behaviour but interested in criminal activity. Indulging in odd behaviour might be strange, but it's not a crime. As part of our research, we contacted a few satanists.'

'In particular, who? Did you attend any of their gatherings? Any blood-letting?'

'A chicken once, but nothing else.'

'Yet, there are reports and videos on YouTube about horrific actions. You must be aware of this.'

'We are, but remember, sensationalism sells, the truth doesn't. That's not to say it doesn't exist, but we've no conclusive proof.'

'Tell me about Cheryl Hastings.'

'What's to tell? She rented next door.'

'Her history?'

'None that we know of. She had a lousy boyfriend, but she clearly was well educated, but seemed to prefer living week-to-week with Sorell.'

Isaac sensed hesitation in Colson's voice, maybe because he didn't trust the man. He couldn't be sure; he needed to know.

'We need a complete rundown of Batholomew's finances, business dealings, and what you've done in the last fifteen years. And how come you could give Fiona Cole two million pounds, and why don't you expect her to return for more. Do you trust her?'

'Not for one minute. The woman's a snake. Grant knew that.'

Can you prove that he agreed with your actions after he died?'

'It was verbal. He was careful not to let her know too much about his affairs, but she lived with the man, might have seen correspondence, and had come to understand what he was up to and how he did it. She's no dummy, don't underestimate her.'

Isaac could see another message on his phone. He hadn't finished with Colson, but he could wait.

'Larry,' Isaac said. 'Development?'

'Two days, maximum, and then we're out of here. Florence has audited the books or will by the end of the day. There are loose papers, but most relate to the Colsons' studies. There are some in Arabic, but Nadia Hussain has translated them. If it's a way to hide the truth, it's a poor attempt.'

'Leonardi da Vinci used to write backwards, enough to deter most, but not enough for the determined.'

'Anyway, they refer to several properties, a share portfolio, and bank accounts with account numbers. That's all, although Bridget might make sense of them. Nadia can work with her.'

'What else?'

'There's a concealed space, back of a cupboard in the upstairs hallway.'

'And?'

'Title deeds, twenty to twenty-five thousand pounds in cash. A couple of chequebooks.'

'And Colson didn't intend coming down for them.'

'The CSIs missed it. I was looking harder, more attuned to the criminal mind.'

'Are we assuming that the Colsons assumed no one would find them?'

'They are not important in themselves, apart from the cash, not if they have copies, but lend weight to the argument that they are up to dirty tricks. It might be advisable to let Harold Colson know what we're up to, frighten him a little.'

'He knows you're in the house.'

'Their friends?'

'Not that we can blame the McCarthys.'

'No, but it gives an excuse to visit them. Fancy going over there?'

'With what we've found?'

'If you reckon, that's all. Pull the CSIs out of the house, copy what's in the place, get one of the CSIs to file them, tag them with a number, and get them over to Challis Street. Make sure the originals go back into the space.'

'A bait?'

'It depends on what they tell us. Get over to Challis Street with them ASAP, and use someone else to deliver them. Bridget can go through them. She can pull in someone from Legal and Fraud if necessary.'

'While I take a leisurely stroll through the park.'

'That's it, Larry. Get them gently warmed, and tell them we've found something that concerns us. That way, with me making Colson nervous and the McCarthys on the phone to Scotland, let's see if there's a reaction.'

Chapter 12

In the back room of the family home, Cheryl Hastings sat. She said little, ate little, and would not talk to her father but would respond to her mother in a soft voice.

Her father, who was stern but caring, and her mother, who was loving and emotional, had been through this before. The recent events had markedly affected her daughter, so they lied to the police about her presence in the house.

However, they realised that, as loving parents, they would have to take action at some stage. Another week, Cheryl would need medical intervention to deal with her parlous mental condition and the starvation diet that she was on.

In desperation, the Hastings phoned Wendy and invited her to the house. She understood why they had gone into protection mode with their daughter. She attached no blame to them; if placed in their situation, she would have done the same.

'Delayed shock?' Wendy said.

'There was no shock the first time, only sullenness, where she would sit in her room and barely talk. We listened to the experts and realised their approach was to address the situation and get her to discuss it. But she was our daughter; we knew better,' Adriana Hastings said.

'Were you right? Unresolved issues.'

'We were,' Alan Hastings said.

'No issues, all these years?'

'Yes, plenty. Bad men and, even worse, drugs. It troubled us, but we were forced to accept it, hopeful that she would come out of it in time.'

'What happened to her? Do I know the full story? Why was she not upset when she saw Grayling's body?' Wendy asked. She was determined not to get emotional, but she could feel a lump in her throat. She hoped there wouldn't be tears.

'It was hard enough dealing with what had happened. We know some of it, but there are parts of it that have never been revealed. To draw it out of her would have been too painful.'

Wendy felt the parents' loving approach might not have been the best, and the demons should have been confronted. However, she was not a psychologist but a police sergeant. Regardless, a woman sat in a room alone, unable to communicate with her parents, but she might with another.

'Mind if I speak to her?' Wendy asked.

'Gentle questioning, not a barrage,' Alan Hastings said.

'No questions at all. She's here in the house and safe. That's my primary concern. We are making progress in the murder investigation of David Grayling and Barry Sorell. Hopefully, we will not involve your daughter further.'

Wendy said it, but she did not believe it. Cheryl had been with Sorell on the night he died. There was enough evidence to bring her into Challis Street and grill her, but a conviction would require clarity about who the other person was. Even so, she did not intend to do that but to let the woman speak if she wanted to, to remain silent if she preferred.

She was pleased it was her and not Larry at the Hastings' home. His approach would have been more direct and less understanding.

Isaac had been informed of the situation and had faith in his sergeant, who had a history of dealing with troubled persons.

Wendy entered the room, carrying cups of tea for them both.

'I'm pleased to see you,' Wendy said as she sat beside the woman sitting on the edge of her bed.

'I saw Barry,' Cheryl said. 'He didn't deserve to die.'

'I know. Tell me if you want to, no pressure.'

'I didn't kill him, you know that.'

'Yes, I know,' Wendy said, but no, she didn't know, only hoped that she hadn't. 'Why return?'

'I don't know. Something in me told me to go and see him. We were alike in many ways.'

'Drink your tea.'

'I saw things next door, but it didn't upset me. Why, do you know?'

'No. Tell me what you think.'

Wendy was out of her depth. A trained counsellor or a psychologist would be the best person to help the young woman. But that would take time, time which the investigation didn't have. One wrong word, one action, no matter how minor, could see Cheryl slide into her shell. There was no option but to continue acting as she had with the runaway children in Sheffield.

Memories came flooding back to her of those she had helped, but in particular, one young girl, twelve years of age, who claimed that her father was sexually abusing her. Yet, the man was influential in the city, a prominent businessman, and a pillar of the church, and his wife was well-spoken and smartly dressed. What chance was there, a child and a junior police officer not long off the farm? Eight days later, the child was dead, beaten violently by her father, while the mother cowered in another room.

It was one of the reasons that Constable Wendy Gladstone transferred to London. The police were taking flak for their negligence, and the social worker assigned to the case, who had made the final decision to return the child to her parents, quietly resigned. It was a monumental brushing under the carpet, and the publicity it should have received, the official enquiry it justified, never happened. Just another day at the office, as far as some of her policing colleagues were concerned.

In London, she had seen similar police officers cosying up to gangsters, but she had never worked with children again. The memories were too raw.

She could vividly see that frightened child as she looked at Cheryl, holding one of her hands while the woman sipped her tea. She had read what had happened to Cheryl, the time away from the family home after she had been kidnapped, the man raping her repeatedly; not that she had ever mentioned it, but a medical examination had revealed it. And then, the man died.

Devil House

Bridget had found the police file, which Wendy had loaded onto her phone.

'It was David; he came from a religious family,' Cheryl said, putting down her tea and picking up a sandwich, which looked like it had been there for over a day.

'A vicar's son, choirboy in his father's church. Did you like him?'

'Not as much as I liked Barry, but sometimes…'

'Threesomes?'

'When Barry wasn't there. Was it wrong?'

Wendy wasn't sure what to say. She knew that it was wrong, as was taking drugs, but Cheryl's parents believed that leniency had to be shown due to the trauma of her youth. It was better to have a daughter who managed to get on with her life than a quivering wreck unable to function.

'No, I don't think so,' Wendy replied. It was the only answer she could give.

'Barry wasn't very bright, but he was good fun. David was educated and religious, even though he had reacted against his father. He told me once that he had considered sorting himself out, maybe even reuniting with his religion, but we all say that, don't we?'

Wendy had heard it many times from people when melancholy or the drugs were affecting the mind and the body. She had even heard it from the father of the daughter he had killed as he sat in the interview room, his face buried deep in his hands, sobbing. 'Why, why?' he had said. 'If I had known.'

Wendy was there when an inspector formally charged the man with the murder of his daughter.

Outside, the mother sat motionless, bolt upright on a chair. 'What now?' she said.

Wendy, in a moment of uncontrolled rage, as the woman came towards her, looking for sympathy, raised her right hand and slapped the woman hard, causing her to fall to the ground. The chief superintendent, who Wendy had thought was better than the rest in the station, informed her that her transfer was immediate and there would be no mention of the incident on her record.

The father was sentenced to life for the murder; his wife received a much shorter sentence, and Wendy was never called to give evidence at the trial.

She had not given it much thought in many years until she sat with Cheryl.

'He did terrible things.'

'Do you want to talk about this?'

'Never with my parents, but you appear to understand.'

'I have come across it before. It still troubles me.'

'Will you tell me?'

Wendy turned off her phone and advised Cheryl's parents not to come near until she left the room and to keep quiet.

'We'll leave the house, phone when you're ready,' Alan Hastings said. 'Is it okay?'

'I don't know, but Cheryl's talking.'

'Are you sure? Do you think it will help?' Wendy asked Cheryl, just to be sure.

'I am sure.'

For twenty-five minutes, Wendy recounted the young girl's story and what she had tried to do as a junior constable. How she had reacted with the mother, and that the father, after his release, had taken a train to the coast, left his clothes on the beach, walked out into the icy-cold North Sea, and never returned.

'The mother?' Cheryl asked.

'I heard that after her release, she moved away. What happened to her, I don't know.'

For the first time, and probably the last, Cheryl told Wendy all that had happened after being kidnapped, the abuse she had suffered, and how she had been rescued.

It was too vivid even for the seasoned and cynical police sergeant. She was in tears, as was the young woman. The two hugged. It was as if she hugged that little girl from so many years ago.

'Thank you,' Cheryl said. 'I believe I could eat a good meal.'

In the kitchen, Wendy cooked while Cheryl told the sergeant about her life and what she hoped for. She told her that Barry was a good person, even if he was a loser, and that David was troubled by an overbearing father who hammered religion day and night, constantly reciting passages from the Bible.

'I knew why he was with the Colsons,' Cheryl continued. 'He was intelligent, and with them, he could use his intelligence to discuss topics that he couldn't discuss when he was on the street, not with Barry, and not with me, not the way I was.'

'Can we talk? Your change is dramatic, but it might be too early.'

'You want to know about the night that Barry died?'

'Whatever you feel comfortable with,' Wendy said. She sensed a cure in the woman, but was it a reaction, a temporary respite, or would it last? She had no way of knowing, only hopeful that it was. And if it was, would it be healing for her after the guilt she had felt for so long about the young girl in Sheffield.

'I went back to the house to see Barry. I'm not sure what I was doing.'

'Where were you while you were away?'

'A friend's place. I slept rough on the floor, unsure why I had left Barry, unsure what to do. I got to the house around ten in the evening. Barry, I thought, would either have drunk himself to sleep or be high on heroin. I was fond of him in some ways. I've met bad men since I left home, even worse, after you know what. I don't want to discuss that, but it no longer controls my life.'

'I hope it remains that way.'

The two women ate pasta and minced meat with Bolognese sauce, a favourite of Wendy's sons. And judging by the gusto with which Cheryl ate, hers too.

'He was asleep, not high nor drunk. We had sex, but you must know that.'

'We know that he had sex with someone. The assumption was that it was you. Afterwards?'

'We slept for a few hours, and then I left. The house troubled me, too close to next door, and that foolishness when you found us there.'

'A new start?'

'I'm not sure. I didn't want to return home. I didn't want to stay with Barry. I wandered the streets, then returned to the house to say goodbye. That's when I found him.'

'Dead?'

'I didn't do it. I swear it. It brought back the memory of David. I was frightened.'

'You left and came here?'

'Apparently. I can vaguely remember leaving the house, then a train, and then I'm back here. I can remember my mother when I arrived, but she said nothing other than to put me in the shower, dry me down, and put me into bed.'

'Unusual that your mother did that?'

'I had the occasional episode after what had happened to me. She knew what to do. I must have looked a sight, and when you came knocking, trying to find me, they said nothing. I'm glad they didn't, but in the past, a couple of days, I would come out of it, but not with Barry. With David, I could manage, but Barry was special, and I had seen him, and it was only a few hours. The killer might have been in the house, but I couldn't be sure.'

'Do you have any idea who it might have been?'

'Apart from the faint odour of perfume, no.'

'What type?'

'I wouldn't know.'

Chapter 13

The Colson house was empty. The garage table was gone, the books were back on the shelves, and the house was dark.

In Scotland, the bait had been set, first by the McCarthys and second by Isaac's visit, accompanied by Sergeant Josie Cameron. But not before Isaac had taken her to one side in her police station and read her the riot act.

'No gossip, acting on your initiative, or telling your husband.'

He hadn't wanted to do it, but he had summed up the woman correctly, confirmed after Ivers, the local estate agent, had told him that the sergeant had engaged him in conversation a couple of days after the Colsons had been arrested. Isaac knew how it worked. Small town, tight-knit community, everybody interested in what everyone else was doing, meeting at the only pub in the area at the weekend, a few pints, or, in Scotland, a few drams of whisky, and the sergeant was a local, having been born and bred in the area.

Isaac thought the sergeant took the gentle rollicking remarkably well.

'You can trust me,' she had said.

At the croft, Isaac outlined to the Colsons what had happened at their house, that there had been an extensive search, an expert on the occult and devil worship brought in, that the crime scene investigators had gone through the place with a fine-tooth comb, and would continue to do so until the Colsons came forward and told the police in exhaustive and verifiable detail the events leading up to Grant Batholomew's death, and how they had managed to continue, using his accounts and aliases. And whether what they were doing was legal.

As a parting shot, before they left the Colsons and their croft: 'We have pulled out of the house. We will conduct an exhaustive search next week. This time, floorboards will be lifted, carpets removed, and wall cavities that look suspicious will be checked. To find the truth of your finances and the death of Grayling, a ground-penetrating radar will check your garden.'

'You can't,' Harold Colson said. 'We intend to sell the place. How can we if you destroy it?'

Isaac did not intend to tell them they did not need to remove the floorboards and carpets to get to the truth. Besides, ultraviolet light would show where there had been a disturbance on the floor, indicative of a possible hiding place. Nor did he intend to tell them that eagle-eyed Larry Hill had made a discovery.

He had cast the bait. All he needed to do was to reel in the line.

'You believe they are up to no good,' Josie Cameron asked as she drove Isaac back to the airport.

'We can't be sure. But it's damned unusual how they had so much money. If the money is illegally or fraudulently gained, it's not Homicide's concern, only if it relates to the murder. We can't be sure if they killed Grayling. Did they kill Elizabeth Colson's brother? Yet again, we don't know, and if they keep to their story, we will never be able to prove it. As for the other murder, we're drawing blanks.'

'Time to raise the heat.'

'Precisely, and that's where you come in. There may be no reaction from the Colsons, but I expect there will be. It's for you, silently and with care, to keep your eyes open. Anything untoward, you are to phone one of the team or me.'

'You can rely on me.'

'I'm certain I can.'

Isaac hoped he had instilled enough caution into the police officer, who tended to gossip. The next forty-eight hours would prove crucial.

***

Technology was to play its part. In both of the Colson houses, small cameras had been installed. Equipped with night vision and motion detectors, they would remain powered for ten hours before a technician would enter the houses and change them out.

Both houses' front and back doors had wireless alarms, and all the rooms upstairs and downstairs had cameras, emphasising the bookshelves in the primary home and Sorell and Cheryl Hastings' bedrooms. All the cameras would connect to a router in the respective houses and then relay the video to Challis Street. A team of CCTV officers would monitor for any activity.

For the operation to have any hope of success, it was necessary for there to be no obvious signs of activity.

Day One drew a blank, apart from Janice McCarthy coming over to check the house after the police and their people had left. She had rifled in a waste paper basket in the garage but only found waste left by the Colsons. She had walked through the house, down into the cellar, and acted strangely, touching the floor as if she was either scared or enjoying the thrill. She was still a marked woman, although she crossed herself on leaving, a sign that she held onto a religious belief.

The one thing of note from the woman's visit was that she was a thief. In the kitchen drawer, she took hold of an elaborately carved knife. It wasn't the murder weapon that had been confirmed by Pathology as it had a serrated blade, whereas the knife that had killed Grayling had been straight-edged. She put the knife in a bag she was carrying and left. She did not go near where the hidden documents were.

Under normal circumstances, Janice McCarthy would have been questioned soon after her visit, but this wasn't normal. Isaac busied himself with paperwork. Wendy contacted Cheryl's mother, who said she was doing fine, talking about re-engaging with her education and possibly going to university.

Wendy saw it as a delayed shock after opening up to her, and at some time, the sorrow of Sorell's death would hit her like a brick. She was ready to help again if needed, and she had to admit, albeit reluctantly, that the woman could still be a murderer.

Whether by intent or unpremeditated, after finding Sorell compromised with another woman.

Josie Cameron was on the phone to Homicide every couple of hours, talking to Larry more than the others. She was keeping away from Isaac, and even though she had taken his criticism on the chin, it still smarted.

Jenny Cook was calmer due to the more relaxed atmosphere in the office. While they waited, Isaac took a couple of hours to take their son to school and pick him up in the afternoon. It wasn't the country she wanted, but normality. Isaac knew that a position in a provincial station should mean he would have more time to connect with the family, but he would still put in long hours, the trait of a workaholic, a fact that he had recognised a long time ago.

On the second day, a phone call alerted Homicide to the fact that Harold Colson had left the croft and was booked on a midday flight to London. Bridget could find no record of his name on the boarding lists of any of the airlines. However, that wasn't conclusive, as the Colsons had become adept at using aliases and might have cancelled one ticket and purchased another.

Apart from staking out the main airports in London, which would have been impractical and would have achieved little, it was a case of wait-and-see.

Even so, if Colson intended to visit the house, he would not do it during daylight hours and would not be switching on the lights as he moved around.

At three that afternoon, Janice McCarthy visited the house, lingering long enough to pilfer two more items: a silver plate and a vase.

She also revisited the cellar, which caused concern. The governor had said the woman was a model prisoner, but Featherstone, the pathologist, believed she was capable of child abuse, and it seemed she had now acquired a fascination with murder scenes.

Bridget was documenting it, and as a former CCTV officer, she ensured that those monitoring the CCTV cameras maintained their focus.

Due to the probability that Colson would not appear until late, Isaac left the office at three in the afternoon, early enough to take the family to McDonald's and see the children to bed.

Larry stayed in the office, as did Wendy and Bridget. If something was to happen, it would be that evening.

Jim Drayton and Nadia Hussain were on standby.

At 7.30 p.m., Isaac walked back into Homicide. He carried two extra-large pizzas with him.

'Not yet?' he said.

'Nothing,' Bridget replied. 'What's the gut feeling?'

'We need a breakthrough. If this drags on much longer, we'll have Commander Goddard complaining and Caddick at my throat.'

'Heaven forbid,' Wendy exclaimed, grabbing a pizza slice.

The team didn't need to stay in the office, but Isaac was pleased to see they were there. It was a great team that he had assembled, more like family than subordinates.

At 11.05 p.m., the first hint that something was afoot. Harold Colson was sighted on foot two streets away. He stopped briefly outside the McCarthys' before walking past where their child had died, opening the gate at the rear of his house, and walking through it. He briefly walked around the side of the house, peering out at the street. He then returned to the back door, temporarily revealing a blind spot in how the cameras had been set up.

Once in the house, Colson moved through it, checking each room as he went, although he avoided the cellar. He went upstairs, slowly and methodically, until he settled in front of where Larry had found the documents. Withdrawing them, he walked down the stairs and out of the back door, all the time with an audience at Challis Street.

'Now,' Larry said.

'Give it a few minutes. Let's see what else he does,' Isaac cautioned

Colson lit a cigarette in the garden, although he wasn't known to be a smoker.

'Nerves,' Wendy said. 'Once a smoker, always a smoker.' It had been a curse of hers until she had finally kicked the habit, on doctor's orders and because the annual health checks for a serving police officer were becoming more challenging to pass. Even so, in her idle moments, she would hold a pen as she had once a cigarette.

It was good that both houses were set up for video. Colson entered the second house and lingered in the kitchen for what seemed an eternity before heading upstairs, passing the room where Sorell had died, stopping in front of an airing cupboard before entering what had been Grayling's bedroom.

Colson took hold of the bed and pushed it to one side. He then knelt on the floor, and using a screwdriver from his jacket pocket, he prised up one of the floorboards. He then took out a large metal box, which he placed in a bag he'd had folded in another jacket pocket.

Then, checking that the floorboard and bed were back in position, he went down the stairs and left by the rear door.

All eventualities had been considered, and two unmarked cars waited at strategic points in the area.

'Now,' Isaac gave the command.

Five minutes later, Colson was in the back of one of the police cars. He was handcuffed. The next stop was Challis Street, Homicide. The next person to speak to him would be Isaac Cook, and the conversation would not be casual this time.

Chapter 14

Due to the severity of the situation, Josie Cameron asked Elizabeth Colson to accompany her to London. Isaac would be told later that the sergeant had behaved impeccably since his harsh words with her and that Elizabeth Colson had come quietly and without complaint.

Six and a half hours later, six hours after her husband had arrived at Challis Street, Elizabeth Colson, accompanied by the Scottish sergeant, entered the building. She was not in handcuffs, as she had not been arrested formally nor charged.

'We have a set of documents, some in Arabic, a language you are familiar with due to your earlier research into Middle Eastern religions,' Isaac said.

The setting was interview room No. 1. Of the three interview rooms in the station, it was the most agreeable, with the sun coming through a window high on one side and a table in the middle of the room with four moderately comfortable chairs.

So far, Colson's crime was financial, not murder. Isaac thought that would change, but for now, Harold Colson was to answer questions about financial irregularities and why he and his wife had continued a business for fifteen years under the auspices of a dead man.

'There is no crime,' Colson said. 'Grant was a secretive man. He didn't flaunt his wealth, drive an expensive car, or live extravagantly. We can't blame Fiona for leaving; he treated her poorly.'

'As you did.'

'We were not responsible for his shortcomings, and they were divorced at the time of his death.'

'The metal box has been tagged but not opened. What does it contain? Will you open it for us in this room?'

'It was a ruse, the ripping up of the floorboards, wasn't it?' Colson asked.

Larry, who was alongside Isaac, could see that Colson was nervous. Legal counsel had been advised, which Colson had denied.

Larry knew that declining legal advice was either the confidence of an innocent man or the arrogance of the guilty.

'Not a ruse. We learnt about the documents at your house. Inspector Hill had found them. We even know what they say because of a constable whose first language is Arabic. We don't know why they were secreted in the house, and we didn't know about the metal chest. Did you intend to leave them there?'

'Not indefinitely. Our crimes, if there are any, are minor. Conducting a business might leave us open to censure and a hefty fine, but it's unlikely to involve prison.'

'Are you admitting to a crime?'

'No. We didn't kill anyone. And yes, at some time, I intended to return and pick up the box and the documents. The books we wanted to continue our work. That's why we asked the McCarthys to help us to arrange for them to be sent to Scotland.'

Isaac realised they had the man but little else. The documents in the first house were legal papers relating to two properties in their portfolio and exhaustive notes in Arabic detailing profit and loss on several investments, mainly shares they owned. Apart from that, there was nothing even vaguely criminal.

'Why Arabic?' Larry asked.

'Why not? I don't wish to appear flippant, but we gained gratification from our ability to write in that language and others. And if they were not hidden away, but in plain view, as sometimes they were, no one could read them.'

The metal box was brought into the room. It was in good condition, apart from being covered in dust. A padlock secured the lid.

'The key?' Isaac asked.

Colson took a key from his pocket and inserted it into the padlock. He then opened the lid. Isaac and Larry peered in.

'More documents, twenty-five thousand, three hundred and forty-six pounds in cash, the deeds to seven properties, share certificates to the value of one million, six hundred thousand and sixty-five pounds, based on their latest value, as of 5 p.m. last night,' Colson said. 'As you can see, nothing out of the ordinary.'

'Why hidden? Weren't you worried that someone would find them?'

'The money, yes. The documents were hidden in the main house, but not everyone has a special spot to store important documents.'

'You could have used a bank or a safety deposit box.'

'We do. However, we do not want to show ourselves at a bank more than necessary. We have copies of everything, and there is money in several banks. Our financial dealings are open to scrutiny, although an audit might reveal irregularities.'

Which Isaac knew would probably apply to most people when they filed their tax returns. Even he was guilty of inflating his deductions, but nothing on the scale of the Colsons, who dealt in millions.

A Fraud Squad member went through the box's contents in another room. As he did so, Colson was taken away to be reunited with his wife. Isaac realised that unless they came up with something, Colson would again walk out of the station.

One hour later, Colson was back in the interview room. Elizabeth was in another room with Wendy. The idea was that Wendy, in her friendly way, would try to engage her in conversation and form a bond with a woman who felt that she and her husband were being targeted by Fiona Cole because she believed that they and Grant had treated her unjustly.

Wendy believed the McCarthys knew more than they were telling.

'It's suspicious,' Wendy said. 'Hiding valuables under the floorboards, and then your research.'

'Why? Because we prefer our own company, we conduct research in obscure subjects, not for fame or glory, we don't use banks any more than we need to, and we don't use computers if we can avoid them?'

'It's esoteric,' Wendy said, hopeful that her understanding of the word was correct.

'We are all driven by needs. Some people collect stamps, others play golf. We expand our minds and make money. Call that a hobby if that makes you feel better, but arresting my husband and bringing him to this station in handcuffs smacks of victimization. And now, we're forced to lay bare our research and wealth. To give a detailed account to people who don't understand, who regard us as eccentric, and believe that we are murderers. When all we've done is nothing. Nothing criminal, nothing violent, nothing illegal. We're condemned due to association and prejudice. Do you believe we are guilty?'

'I'm a police officer. I maintain neutrality and deal with the crime, not the person. I can't understand why the occult fascinates people, but there are small pockets in this country where some go beyond the chanting and move to the physical.'

'We know. It's not as much as you would imagine, and most is hearsay. But, yes, some do awful things.'

'Worse than what happened to David Grayling. Tell me more about him. Were you…?'

'No. As we told you, he was knowledgeable about the Bible due to his father. If you believe in God, you must believe in the fallen angel by default. David gave us a different perspective, and even if he was estranged from his family, you can't grow up in that environment and not be affected by it. His death came as a shock to us.'

'And then Cheryl Hastings finds the body and calls the police.'

'We weren't sure how to react. Regardless of our denial, there was a surfeit of circumstantial evidence.'

Wendy knew they were correct. In Sheffield, some officers would have taken the easy route and would have seen

Devil House

them convicted. But in Challis Street, Homicide did not work that way.

However, the subsequent death of Barry Sorell would have raised doubts about their conviction if it had happened. Either the Colsons were as guilty as hell, or they were totally innocent. Wendy realised that tricks were not going to work with an educated woman.

'Tell me about your brother,' Wendy said.

'Apart from Fiona, he had no other notable relationships with women.'

'None, or were there minor infatuations?'

'None that he married. I advised him against it, not because of her. We didn't know her then. Her love for Grant was apparent in the early days of their relationship.'

'Then why advise him against marrying her?'

'Not because of Fiona, but him. Grant was excessively secretive and introverted; he would retreat into his shell at any time. He was a voracious reader, mainly the classics, and he thrived on solitude. Fiona was clearly a person who liked to go out at night. It's not that we blamed her for that, but they were chalk and cheese. He thought she would be good for him. He knew that aspects of his life were unnatural and wished to change them, but can a leopard change its spots?

'Harold and I, we're compatible because we are alike. Neither looks to others for friendship, apart from the McCarthys, but that was a shared grief, and then David, who reminded us of our son. We have never had more than a few friends and none that ever come to the house.'

'Yet you relocate to Scotland. Was that a planned move?'

'It was a considered move. As long as we had each other and our interests, we did not need the world.'

'Yet, in Scotland, you were integrating yourselves into the community.'

'We needed to be known, not regarded as the oddities who lived in that croft up the end of the lane.'

'But you were in London?'

'Not totally. Harold had his accountancy, and I occasionally went to the church. We had little in common with the people in the area, but there was no harm in that. In Scotland, in the croft, we thought that initial integration was important.'

'How did you find the people?'

'Refreshing. Sergeant Cameron talks too much. The estate agent tries to be smart and thinks he could sell coal to Newcastle, but he can't. Away from the big city, they don't have the edge. Our neighbours, a five-minute walk up the lane, are retired, as are those ten minutes down.'

'Yet Harold leaves important documents and a lot of cash in London.'

'What could we do? We panicked when we found David in the cellar, aware that someone was trying to compromise us.'

'Who? The only one it could be would be Fiona. Who else?'

'The McCarthys knew of our research. We told them once, but why would they want to do that to us?'

'Did you know that Janice McCarthy had been in prison?'

Wendy wasn't sure if she should have revealed it, but she needed a reaction.

'No. What for?'

'In her youth, dealing drugs. Served two years, an altercation with another prisoner, who fell and cracked her head on the concrete floor.'

'Dead?'

'Dead. No blame is attributed to Janice. And then, her child dies on the swings. You were living here at that time.'

'We were. I remember it well, but it was an accident.'

'It was. Did you know the child?'

'No. We didn't know the McCarthys at that time. Only later did she come over and introduce herself.'

'How did she know about your son?'

'Someone told her. Maybe at the church, as I occasionally went there. Our son's death wasn't a secret, even though we never spoke about it.'

***

In another room, a member of the Fraud Squad was going through the contents of the metal box. After an hour, he interrupted Isaac and Larry. 'Nothing untoward, except Colson's account of the cash is incorrect,' he said.

'What is your tally?' Larry asked

'Ten thousand pounds short, to the penny.'

'Which means either Colson is mistaken or someone has helped themselves to some of it.'

'I followed the correct procedures. Forensics?'

Isaac turned to Larry. 'Can you deal with it?'

Harold Colson shrugged his shoulders when informed that there would be additional questions. 'You'll not find anything against us.'

Isaac suspected that might be the case.

'A receipt for the box and the documents. I believe we are entitled to that,' Colson added.

Isaac handled Colson's request while Larry took the box to Forensics. It was urgent, and Isaac had called on Commander Goddard to use his influence to expedite it.

'I suggest you stay in London for a couple of days,' Isaac said as the Colsons left the station. 'We need to wrap this case up, and the two of you in Scotland is proving to be an encumbrance.'

'I think we can afford a good hotel,' Elizabeth Colson said.

Chapter 15

Bob McCarthy was in the garden, down on his hands and knees, pulling weeds from the ground. Wendy thought it was an attempt to maintain a distance from his wife.

'A few words with your wife,' Larry said.

'Not without me,' Bob McCarthy said as he stood up.

'It might be best,' Wendy said, 'or else we must take her to the police station.'

'Go ahead, make yourself at home.'

Inside the house, Janice McCarthy sat in front of the television, appearing engrossed in a soap opera. Wendy had noticed a moving curtain from the garden. The TV was a pretence.

'What do you want?' Janice asked. She was dressed in a blouse and jeans. The heating in the house was on, even though it wasn't cold outside.

'A few questions. We need you to elaborate on what you know about the Colsons,' Larry said as he sat close to the window, where the heat was overpowering. Wendy found it hot in the house, but it felt good on her aching legs.

Janice was tense, which Wendy put down to a guilty conscience. She had been sticking her nose in, supposedly at the Colsons' request. But why so much interest or willingness to assist when the possibility remained that the Colsons were murderers?

'For an acquaintance, you've certainly gone out of your way to help them,' Larry said.

'Neighbourly, isn't that enough?'

'You're not a neighbour, and the Colsons' house is a murder scene. Neighbourly or otherwise, people don't get involved unless there's an ulterior reason.'

Devil House

'I believe I've explained this. The Colsons are giving me some money to help them.'

'Harold Colson is in London, scurrying around in the dark. I assume he came here before he set off to retrieve documents and cash.'

'He wasn't here.'

'Janice,' Wendy said, 'we've been monitoring their houses and this one ever since you phoned them to tell them about our exhaustive search.'

'Very well. He was here. I told him to be careful, but he said it was important.'

'Why here? It's a murder investigation, not a social at the church. Your involvement is suspicious. Did you tell him about what you stole? Did you know what he was looking for?'

'He told us it was some papers. We didn't ask too much.'

'We don't believe them guilty of the murder of David Grayling,' Larry said. In the garden, he could see Bob McCarthy looking at the house. 'Does your husband know that you're a kleptomaniac?'

'A few trinkets, hardly that.'

'In prison, the woman died. You didn't kill her, but you were violent and showed great strength, or was it resilience and intense anger? Had you lost it, gone crazy, and taken your frustrations out on the woman?'

'It's prison,' Janice McCarthy said. 'The guards aren't rushing to protect you. I was sentenced for dealing drugs, not for violence. Thrown in with those people, you either sink or swim. I was forced to swim. I hit the woman, struck her, and almost broke my hand. She fell, hit her head and died. I was exonerated of any blame, and you know it, yet you continue to rehash old news.

'Let me be clear. The Colsons were not bosom buddies but shared a similar tragedy. There was an intangible bond that if people hadn't experienced what we had, they would not understand. Clearly, you have not.'

133

Wendy had to agree. A dead child was the worst thing that could happen to any parent.

Larry was conscious that if they revealed too much, Janice would be on the phone to the Colsons, and then the following interview with them would be tempered by what Janice had been told.

'These documents? Why couldn't you have sent them by registered mail to Scotland?' Larry said.

'He told me they were well hidden.'

'Any reason?'

'Why would we ask? We have paperwork in the house, at the back of a cupboard or a closed drawer, and a spare house key under a flower pot. Everyone, no doubt you, have certain documents they don't want to lose or be found by a light-fingered tradesman.'

'It's raining,' Bob McCarthy said as he entered the room. 'I'm not staying out there for you or anyone else. What you say to my wife, you can say to me.'

With that, he sat beside his wife and held her hand. 'We're a team, Janice and me. There's nothing that you can't say to her that you can't say to me.'

A display of unity, even if there was none. The look on Janice's face bore testimony to that.

'Very well,' Larry said, standing up to dominate. 'Here's what we reckon. The two of you are chummy with the Colsons due to tragedy. But that relationship has transcended into something more sinister. There were four persons in that cellar the night Grayling died. Are you the two we've been looking for?'

Wendy thought about telling him that one of the four had been Cheryl Hastings but said nothing. The man had the floor; he was calling the shots.

'It wasn't us. Sure, we knew of their research, even played along with them occasionally, reciting chants, that sort of thing.'

'But why? Evoking the devil, weren't you frightened?'

'Harold and Elizabeth thought it was bunkum. They wanted our assistance because they wanted to experience what was involved in a satanic ritual.'

'Which invariably involves sex.'

'We know.'

'Are you saying that, the four of you?'

'I'm not saying anything, nor is Janice. The Colsons were into realism. It was one night two years ago. We had all been drinking heavily. Elizabeth was spraying something in the air. Memories came flooding back, and then one thing led to another.'

'Why tell us now?' Wendy asked.

'It's not something any of us were proud of. It was the one time only. It caused conflict in our marriage, yet we continued.'

'The Colsons?'

'In the light of day, they apologised. No more was said.'

'What was Elizabeth spraying?'

'I don't know, but coupled with the alcohol and the chanting, I can only assume it was some sort of aphrodisiac or a drug. Honestly, we don't know.'

'Yet you continued to see them.'

'No more than you would a relative you didn't like. They were akin to family to us, shared experiences.'

'We should move away, do what the Colsons have done, but we can't. Our daughter is here.'

Wendy understood that sentiment. The rest she wasn't sure about. It could be the truth, or it could be what Bob McCarthy had said – bunkum.

***

Other than those of Harold Colson, there were other fingerprints on the box. One of them was known. Another was a smudged fingerprint of a constable who should have known better.

Harold Colson was told of the disparity in the cash. He was angry initially and relieved when told that the culprit was known and would be spoken to.

'Apart from that, nothing underhanded?' Colson said, almost with a look of glee on his face.

'It still doesn't explain why you come in the dead of night and prowl around like a burglar to retrieve your items. Items which are yours,' Isaac said.

'Private papers. They are not for others to see, and if I had told you about them, what would you have done? Handed them over to me? I don't think so.'

'Under the circumstances, no. But, we would have allowed you to explain. However, now the situation has changed.'

'In what way?'

'We've spoken to the McCarthys. Apart from Janice McCarthy's light-fingered pilfering, the four of you apparently acted out various rituals, including one two years ago, when the four of you went from acting to actual. Care to tell us about it?' Larry said.

'It was Elizabeth, a little too liberal with a spray she had found in one of our research books. I can't be sure what it was, but it was combined with wine, a heady dose of ritual, and make-believe. Unfortunately, we all made fools of ourselves.'

'Regrets?'

'It was not spoken about again, but yes. We all felt thoroughly ashamed. However, it is foolish but not criminal. My papers?'

'We will release those from your house after copies have been taken and signed off by you and Homicide. You will receive copies of what's in the box. But for the moment, it remains as evidence, as we must address how another person knew where the money was and why they took it.'

As Colson had always known, he and his wife could leave the police station. 'We'll be staying at a hotel for the next few days,' Harold said as he shook Isaac's and Larry's hands.

'No more midnight visits,' Larry said.

Devil House

'No need. The floorboards?'
'Not yet, not if we conclude this investigation.'

***

Wendy had the most challenging task, to confront Cheryl Hastings about why her fingerprints were on a metal box secreted under the floor and where she had obtained the key. It was going to be a difficult conversation.

In preparation, and not wanting to throw Cheryl back into her previous state of mind, Wendy met with the young woman's mother.

It was a delicate balance between policing and personal. Wendy wasn't sure she could satisfy both.

'Twenty-four hours,' Isaac had said the previous night. 'But we need an answer.'

Wendy wasn't sure it would be enough but realised that her DCI was right. It was those who remained after a murder who ultimately suffered the most, and if there was to be a relapse, then Cheryl and her parents would have to address that issue.

The two women met: Wendy outlined the situation, omitting the missing money. She didn't want the mother to prompt the daughter or even not want her to talk to her.

'She's so much better,' Adriana Hastings said. They sat in a coffee shop not far from the Hastings' home. Once they had concluded their discussion, Wendy went to the house and spoke to Cheryl.

'I need to pressure Cheryl. There is an issue that I cannot ignore. It relates to Cheryl, irrefutable proof that she discovered something.'

'Let me ask her,' Adriana said in a pleading voice.

'It can't be done. I'll be as gentle as possible. It cannot be avoided, regardless of your obvious horror at the thought of it.'

'Why tell me if you're adamant about pursuing this action?'

'Out of concern for her, I tell her mother. You need to know the possibility of what might happen. The consequences are unknown, as we still must question her about David Grayling and Barry Sorell.'

Wendy realised that talking to the mother had achieved very little. The two women left the coffee shop and drove their respective cars to the house.

'If you interfere, a police car will transfer your daughter to Challis Street. Is that clear?' Wendy said.

'Yes.'

'Good. Let me into the house, and then drive away. Don't come back, don't phone, or allow your husband anywhere near Cheryl and me.'

At the house – the mother had followed instructions and left in her car – Wendy found Cheryl sitting in the conservatory at the back of the house. The day was cold; the sun was high in the sky but weak, yet the glass-enclosed conservatory was warm and pleasant.

'I find solace here,' Cheryl said

There was a melancholy about the woman that Wendy found disturbing. When she had last left her, and subsequently from what she had heard from her mother, Cheryl re-engaged with society, planned her future, and considered attending university. The young woman wasn't unintelligent, but the life that she had led in the past, which had terminated with the death of Sorell, had had its effect.

A relapse was possible, and Wendy knew she might be responsible.

'We need to talk, a serious talk. Are you up to it?' Wendy asked, aware that the talk would not be delayed whether she was or not. The evidence of the Colsons' metal box justified being in Challis Street Police Station, not a conservatory. Wendy was conscious that Isaac was giving her leeway, and if the answers and explanations from Cheryl were not forthcoming, then it was for her to take the woman to the police station, screaming blue murder or not.

She was a thief who was not moved by death or a bloodied body.

Wendy left Cheryl and went to the kitchen. She made two cups of tea and brought them back, giving one to Cheryl.

'We know about you in the house.'

'The night Barry died?'

'Yes. We didn't know you also prised up a loose floorboard in David Grayling's room.'

'I didn't…' Cheryl blustered.

'We have proof. Your fingerprints are on the box. Forensics has confirmed it.'

'It was Barry, David.'

'It was you, Cheryl. Your wellbeing can't override the demands of a murder investigation.'

A glazed look came over the young woman as she looked around the conservatory. 'It's been hard back here. Too many memories.'

'Cheryl, please listen to me,' Wendy said as she clasped the woman's hands. 'The truth will prevail. Finding the box is one thing; taking the money is another. I'm not here to admonish or forgive. I'm here for the truth.'

'It was David who found it.'

'How?'

'David spent time with the Colsons, but you knew that. He observed and knew their secretive nature. With gentle quizzing, he realised there was more to them than they seemed. According to him, Harold Colson would ask questions about where we lived. What were the rooms like, and what was the general condition of the house?'

'Didn't they ever come in or conduct an inspection?'

'Not while I was there. There wouldn't have been a problem, and if they had asked, we would have let them, even cleaned the place.'

'Colson's asking questions. What did David tell him?'

'Not a lot, but one day I come home. It's been raining heavily outside. There are footprints in the house, as well as mud and grass. It's not us, as we all leave our shoes at the door.'

'Always?'

'Even if it was cold. Sometimes, we'd walk around wearing socks but never shoes in the house.'

'And?'

'David and I, we came in around the same time.'

'Where's Barry?'

'Flipping hamburgers. David and I followed the footprints, although the prints were hard to see upstairs. But we are determined. Nobody else was staying in the house at the time. We get down close to the carpet on the upstairs landing. We search for signs. There's a magnifying glass downstairs, which I fetch. We can see where the prints ended. There are indentations in the carpet. We follow them and end up in David's room. We see that his bed has been moved to one side.

'We move the bed and then feel around. David gets a splinter. It's a loose floorboard, but no one's seen it before. Why should they? I get a screwdriver and prise the floorboard up. There's a metal box.'

'Curiosity killed the cat, or was it more than that?'

'I'm not a thief, nor was David. Barry, I couldn't be sure, but he wasn't in the house. I take it out and open it.'

'It's padlocked.'

'It is, but I know how to pick a lock.'

'That requires an explanation.'

So far, so good, Wendy thought. Cheryl was acting rationally, with no regression yet.

'After I left home and drifted into oblivion, I squatted in North London. I can show you the place if you want. One of those who was there had a criminal record for burglary. He told me that.'

'A lover?'

'Hardly love. Don't apply your morality to me, not after what I had experienced. Thanks to you, I can deal with it, and with Barry, I could believe in the concept of love, but I'm changed. I'm not like other people. You must understand that.'

'I do. I only hope we can get through this without you relapsing.'

'We can. I stayed in that squat for eight months. I knew that he was breaking into houses to feed his drug habit.'

'And yours?'

'I was messed up. I didn't go with him when he burgled, but I enjoyed the benefits.'

'Enjoyment is not an apt word, but regardless, he shows you the tricks of the trade.'

'He did. I've still got lock-picking tools in my room if you want to see.'

'Later. You've got the box; you can open it.'

'I did open it and saw what was inside. Documents, and a lot of cash.'

'Ten thousand pounds is missing.'

'I put it into a bank account.'

'Why? It's theft.'

'Cash, hidden under floorboards. It had to be dirty money. David told me that the Colsons were not what they seemed. I didn't trust them. Polite when collecting the rent, but one day, when we left, would I get my deposit back?'

'But you must have always been conscious that Harold Colson or his wife might come and check one day.'

'I was. I left a note inside, wrapped inside one of the bundles of money.'

'What did it say?'

'The money is safe, earning interest, and that, one day, it would be returned in full. Until then, it remains our secret.'

'They would have known it was you.'

'I wrote it on a laptop, printed it, and put it in the box.'

'You must have been spaced out when you did that. Barry would never have been capable, but David was.'

'I didn't steal it. The money is still in the bank. I can show you proof.'

Wendy struggled with the concept. A house full of drug addicts, yet Cheryl doesn't take the money to feed the habit. It seemed illogical.

'David Grayling knew where it was. What was to stop him from helping himself to more?'

'How would he get into it? It was a solid padlock. A hacksaw blade wasn't going to cut through it. Besides, the son of a vicar, fire and brimstone. Stealing? Not his forte.'

'It was yours.'

'No, it wasn't. I had been on the street for a long time. Dog eat dog. I've seen what weakness gets you. I wasn't going to let another person take advantage of me.'

'The burglar boyfriend?'

'Overdose. One too many burglaries, money in his pocket, and he had a binge session with heroin, washed down with gin. Check the address, find out that I have not lied.'

Wendy messaged the address to Bridget. Less than ten minutes later, it was verified.

'The money belongs to the Colsons,' Wendy said.

'I can give you the bank statement. You can do what you want with the money. It was only for my protection.'

'And then, David dies, and you're frightened. You realise that the Colsons might not be benign. You are frightened.'

'I was mute. Now, I am frightened. Here is not safe for me. There is a murderer out there who has killed two people so far. And what about the body in the garden?'

'We can't prove how that person died.'

'But you think it might be murder.'

It would be logical to make that assumption, but it's unlikely we will be able to conclusively prove that.'

'I know what the perfume is. Remember, I told you there was a smell in the house the night Barry died.'

Wendy left the house with proof of where the ten thousand pounds was and the perfume's name. For now, Cheryl Hastings was fine, although frightened.

Wendy thought she had reason to be.

Chapter 16

Superintendent Seth Caddick made his presence known at Challis Street before midday on the last day of the month.

Detective Chief Inspector Isaac Cook's nemesis was back in Homicide. The lackey of Commissioner Alwyn Davies was trouble with a capital T. Isaac knew it wasn't social and that the man, if true to character, would attempt to enter the investigation in its closing stages, offer criticism, stick his nose in where it wasn't wanted, and disrupt the dynamics of the office.

Sergeant Wendy Gladstone despised the man; Bridget thought he was a nasty piece of work; Inspector Larry Hill believed him to be the devil incarnate, a snivelling, cowardly officer who, through incompetence and cosying up to his superiors, especially Davies, had risen through the ranks, whereas Isaac Cook, a much more competent officer, had stagnated.

And then, to throw oil onto the fire, Commander Goddard, Isaac's mentor, reluctantly threw his hand in with Davies. Although Goddard had confided to Isaac that he was sitting on the fence, awaiting developments, which gave little comfort to Isaac.

The support and the political manoeuvring that Goddard had provided were no longer there. And, coupled with Jenny, Isaac's wife, giving him strife, Isaac felt the situation was intolerable.

Another row with his wife that morning, the third in as many weeks. Homicide had become Isaac's respite, although his love remained with his wife and his children.

And now, Seth Caddick, who would report with glee to Davies. It wasn't only Isaac that he was after. Other officers were dedicated to the Metropolitan Police, committed to solving crime and making society safer, but they were dinosaurs now.

The future of the police force and political leadership in the United Kingdom were in flux. Standing firm where others were capitulating, Isaac would not change his stance and would ride out the storm, regardless of the outcome.

Wendy would have quite happily given Caddick a kick in the shins and told him to bugger off, whereas Larry would have smacked him in the face.

But Isaac had forewarned them multiple times to button their lips and let him attempt to suppress the man, to give him no opportunity to take back an actionable offence to Davies.

'Not getting far, are you, Isaac?' Caddick said. He was sitting back in his chair in Isaac's office. As tall as Isaac, he was two years younger, the child of a broken home. Davies had taken him under his wing twelve years earlier when he was a chief superintendent and Caddick, a sergeant.

It could not be denied that Davies was a skilful operator who used his wiles to deflect controversy and lay the blame on others. After all, his attempt at stern control of the streets, where crime had reduced dramatically, had been denounced by many as authoritarian, draconian, and un-British, but most in the city had applauded the result. For several months, it had become safe to venture out at night alone, and the roads had been cleared of the protesters who believed their cause was more important than the inconvenience of others.

Two days earlier, Jenny had witnessed a theft at the supermarket, a gang of hoodlums grabbing what they could and running for the door. No attempt to stop them, not by the security guard, and now, thugs on motor scooters grabbing a handbag from a woman on the street.

She was determined they needed to move out of London, and it was on Isaac's mind. Caddick was in the office, and he was gloating.

'It's under control. Why are you here, Caddick?'

'You know my job. Special appointee of the commissioner. His eyes and ears of our fine police force. How was it phrased by the commissioner? I'm sure you remember.'

'Remember? You tried to get me out the last time, set up a disciplinary to oust me.'

'You wiggled out it. Pull in favours? Goddard's not there for you; he's seen the wisdom of getting with the strength.'

Isaac could see a frontal attack by Caddick. The man was pushing for a reaction and was close to getting it. 'We're busy. Get to the point or leave,' Isaac responded.

Caddick got up from his chair and left, but not without a parting shot. 'Cook, you're floundering. Your halo's slipped, no longer the poster boy of the Metropolitan Police. I suggest you reevaluate your priorities if you intend to remain in Homicide. Otherwise, you might be back in Traffic.'

'Is that a direct threat?' Isaac could feel his fists clenching. This was no longer the man niggling him but an orchestrated attempt to cause him to act, to lean over the table and grab the man by the collar.

Larry came in. 'Don't, he said. 'The superintendent's looking for an excuse.'

'Don't worry, Hill. I've got it,' Caddick said.

Bridget gave Isaac a coffee after Caddick had left and a slice of homemade pie. 'Don't rise to the bait,' she said. 'We all know what he is.'

'How many years since the Met was regarded as the best police force in the world, the envy of others. And now?' Isaac said.

'We weather the storm, hold to our ideals. The tide will turn, and then we will be remembered. Justice goes to the just.'

And the meek shall inherit the earth, Isaac thought. He knew the reality. The rot was not settling in; it was firmly entrenched. He was one man up against many, supported by a loyal team. It wasn't going to be enough.

***

Once again, a murder investigation was thwarted by the internal machinations of the Metropolitan Police. Regardless, the investigation continued.

A calm returned after Isaac's and Caddick's confrontation as the man headed to Goddard's office.

'Our best defence?' Isaac said to the team.

'Solve these murders,' Wendy said for Homicide. This wasn't the first time they had been under pressure, and until Davies was replaced and Commander Goddard stopped sitting on the fence, it would continue.

Later that day, Fiona Cole arrived at Challis Street. It was not a request but a demand. The evidence was damning. She had questions to answer. This time, she came with a lawyer, the eminent Harriet Gordon, Kings' Counsel.

Homicide had heard of her and knew of her brilliance as a defence lawyer. She was expensive to hire, but it was known that Fiona Cole had received two million pounds from the Colsons.

Dressed in clothes that were obviously expensive and wearing stiletto heels, Fiona looked as though she was preparing for a night at the theatre, followed by a meal at the Savoy. Wealth suited her.

Harriet Gordon was in her late sixties. She wore a navy blue suit, and her hair was cut short. She wore little makeup. She showed no intention of being civil before the interview. To her, civility was not required with the police, and her defences in other cases, pointing out the Met's foibles and shortfalls were well known.

Isaac was sure that her opinion of Davies would be the same as his, although she was a strong disciplinarian who put up a rigorous defence for her clients.

'My client is here at your request,' Gordon said. 'I hope you have more than hearsay, and your evidence will be more than the incomplete brief I was given before this interview.'

Isaac hoped it was, but the woman was right. With Fiona Cole, he could have handled the interview. With Harriet Gordon, it would be touch and go, and he had still not calmed down after Commander Goddard notified him that Caddick intended to make a formal complaint about his reception in Homicide.

Wendy had spent time with Cheryl Hastings. She had the information that was to be presented. Isaac would have preferred Larry. If he had known that Harriet Gordon was to represent Fiona Cole, he would have advised that the interview be postponed until the evidence was concrete, irrefutable, and damning.

What they had was the word of a drug addict and known thief, even if the money was in a bank account. Homicide had raised a notice against the bank that the money was evidence in a murder investigation, and it could not be withdrawn. The legal department at Challis Street indicated that the notice was not cast iron and could be disputed, but given the circumstances, the bank would honour the agreement.

Isaac went through the formalities and asked each present to give their names, ranks, and titles, as in the case of Harriet Gordon. He detailed the procedure: the interview would be recorded, and a transcript would be available.

'Mrs Cole, we believe that you were in the house next door to the Colsons on the night that Barry Sorell was murdered,' Isaac said.

'The proof?' Gordon said. 'Circumstantial hearsay from a discredited witness cannot be accepted.'

'Mrs Cole, were you in the house?'

'I was not there,' Fiona Cole said.

'Your perfume is distinctive, costly, and you use it liberally. Would that be correct?'

'I always want to look my best. That's a woman's vanity. There is nothing wrong with that.'

'I would agree. However, that perfume was present in the house when Sorell died. If it wasn't you, then who was it?'

Isaac knew he was gasping for air. He was about to sink if he didn't come up with something. 'Your husband is buried in the back garden and supposedly died in the house. Do you believe that?'

'He might have. He wasn't physically strong and suffered from poor health, but as he was young, there was no reason to believe that was the cause of death, nor the pretence that he committed suicide.'

'Chief Inspector, if you have no facts, and this is a fishing exercise, I don't believe there is any requirement for my client to remain.'

'Not fishing, establishing a groundwork from which to extrapolate.'

'Then I suggest you get on with it. Wasting our time is not something I approve of.'

'Mrs Cole, you knew the house from when the Colsons lived in it?'

'Correct. I went there on several occasions with Grant. The Colsons were polite, but they disapproved of me.'

'The reason?'

'Grant was more of a loner. They felt that I was an opportunist, flaunting the goods; it was his money, not him, that I was after.'

'Were you?' Wendy asked.

'I liked the man. I came from a poor background. I did not intend to tie myself to a pauper.'

'Would you have honoured that agreement?'

'I did, up until he had tired of me. Then I left.'

'Did he support you? Did he agree to an equitable settlement at your divorce?'

'Based on what I believed to be his true worth.'

'Was it?'

'At the time, I believed that to be the case. But Grant didn't die then, did he?'

'You had no contact with him. When did you become suspicious of the Colsons?'

'I did not know in detail the extent of Grant's wealth. I suppose I didn't care, not at first. We were living well, but he did not want to involve me in his actions. I didn't ask.'

'What was he doing?' Isaac asked.

'He was buying and selling properties, trading stocks and shares. I don't believe it was illegal. He operated under certain aliases. One of those arrived at my door three months ago.'

'Do you know how? After all, it's been many years, and you've changed your name.'

'When I moved out and left Grant, I lived with another man. That you know. I left a forwarding address wherever I went. Somehow, a letter addressed to an alias of Grant's arrived at our house in Sevenoaks.'

'What did it tell you?'

'That Grant, or someone else masquerading as him, was using his name.'

'You should have assumed it was Grant.'

'I didn't know where Grant was. I knew where his sister was. They were as thick as thieves. I went to her house, laid out the facts, and that if I went to the police with proof that Grant was either alive or someone was carrying on business in his name, there would be an enquiry by His Majesty's Revenue & Customs or the police. If I had the letter, it would have been enough to raise their hackles.

'Elizabeth said that Grant was dead. I had no reason to doubt her. I didn't care whether it was the truth. I said I wanted two million pounds. They wanted to dispute it, but I had proof of them having four million and correctly assumed there was more. They paid.'

'And you believed there would be more stock certificates in the old house, and you knew where to look. Is that why you were in that house? The reason you saw Barry Sorell dead.'

'Yes.'

Harriet Gordon sat back on her chair. She said nothing.

'Why did you murder him?'

'I didn't. I panicked and left the house. Clearly, I had the mind not to leave fingerprints, and the place was a mess. And that woman, unconscious on the floor.'

'Are you saying she was there in the room with Sorell?'

'I am. I don't know if she killed him or if she found him. Whatever it was, she was on the other side of the bed on the floor. There was blood on her.'

Wendy passed over her phone. She showed Fiona Cole a photo. 'Is this her?'

'From the back, it looks like her. I didn't see her face. I can't be sure.'

'And you chose not to tell us?'

'What was there to tell. I was in the house. I saw the dead man. I didn't want to be involved.'

'That's not enough,' Larry said. 'You see a body, a woman, her face down on the floor. Instinctively, a person would check if she was dead.'

'After what happened next door? What kind of fool would stay in a house after that. Not me, that's for sure.'

'You didn't feel inclined to phone the police?'

'With what? I've got the Colsons' money. Questions would be asked.'

'For which you don't have answers.'

'We live in Sevenoaks, a married couple enjoying life. Involvement in the death, if only by witnessing the aftermath, would have impacted us.'

'No more questions,' Isaac said.

'Is that it?' Harriet Gordon acted surprised.

'For now. We have further enquiries to conduct. We will meet with Mrs Cole again.'

***

Wendy knew it could not be avoided. Cheryl Hastings would need to come to Challis Street to answer questions. There was no more she could do to defend her.

Cheryl arrived at the police station. It was after six in the evening. Her parents had brought her in a display of family unity, but the interview would be conducted with the young woman alone.

Due to the sensitivity of it and the fact that Wendy was compromised, it would be Isaac and Larry in the interview room. Wendy could stay with the parents, but this time, she would not have any part in the proceedings.

A tearful mother saw her daughter led off by Nadia Hussein to the interview room. Wendy realised there was little she could do but console the parents.

In the interview room, Cheryl sat composed. She looked straight forward, barely blinking. The time for kid gloves was over. It was time to go for the jugular.

Throughout the investigation, Cheryl Hastings had been front and centre, not lurking in the shadows. She held the lease on the house where she had lived. She had suffered terribly as a child at the hands of a sexual deviant, embracing drugs and homelessness in her teenage years. Promiscuous by her own admission, she finally ended up with Barry Sorell, attempting a more stable relationship.

Sorell, a man of little worth, treated her well, even if their life together was not the life that her parents wanted for her. It would have been doomed regardless, by apathy, disgust, and ultimately addiction. It was not intended to end in murder.

Legal aid had been called, and even though the Hastings could afford a competent lawyer, Alan Hastings was confident that it was a farce and that his daughter was innocent of all crimes.

Isaac knew that was not the case. The rental bond on the house was close to three thousand, not the ten thousand pounds she had taken. Cheryl Hastings had stolen the money, if not for herself, then for Sorell. Why might be necessary to understand, but they needed clarity on what she knew.

'You correctly identified the perfume,' Isaac said. 'The woman has admitted that she was in the house.'

'I have always told you the truth,' Cheryl replied.

Isaac was concerned that he would not be as forceful as he should have been because of Wendy's interest in the woman. He had failed twice before in prosecuting the law to its full extent, having given the benefit of the doubt to two women, both of whom were found to be murderers. One, after she shot him, he arrested; the other had disappeared.

'When we've drawn it out of you,' Isaac said.

The legal aid felt the need to be heard. A smallish man in his late twenties, he was typical of the breed: free to his client, expensive to the Ministry of Justice. Isaac did not intend to allow the man to interfere in what would need to be a vigorous interview.

He had had to deal with Harriet Gordon, who had shaken his hand on leaving the station and wished him well in the upcoming disciplinary. He wondered what she meant or how she knew Caddick was attempting to take him on again.

'Off the record,' Gordon said, 'I'm with you.'

He had seen it before. The ruthless antagonistic lawyer could separate professional from personal and would defend the most incorrigible, vicious, and least worthy person in the pursuit of a fair trial and a rigorous defence.

The legal aid wasn't a Harriet Gordon, more a caricature.

'I'll outline the situation, Miss Hastings,' Isaac said.

'Call me Cheryl.'

'Very well, Cheryl. Two women were in the house that night that Barry Sorell died. Both have admitted that. However, it's a timing issue. You have marks against your name. You showed no emotion when you found David Grayling's body. You did not tell us about the metal box and the ten thousand pounds. You must have realised that was important.'

'I couldn't tell you, could I? What would you have thought? It's true, I didn't react when I saw David, but I've explained that, and your sergeant understands. I can't be shocked.'

'This is a murder investigation. We can't let emotion be involved. If you are guilty, or if we find it is someone else, there will be an arrest. According to the other woman, she found Barry dead, and a woman, face down, was lying on the floor. She believes it was you, based on a photo shown to her,' Isaac said.

'If it wasn't you, and we were being told the truth, then there is a third woman. Is that possible? Was Barry two-timing you? Yes or no,' Larry added.

'I slept with David, so I can't blame Barry.'

Isaac hoped that Wendy's belief in the woman was well-founded, as, by her own admission, Cheryl Hastings had the morals of an alley cat.

Isaac wasn't buying the third woman. He was convinced that all persons were known to them and that bringing in another at this late juncture in the investigation would be counterproductive.

The woman sat calmly, staring into space when not questioned. Wendy, who had returned to the station, listened in an adjoining room, aware that Cheryl was retreating into her shell. She was sad as she knew there was no more she could do.

'Let us be clear on this,' Larry said. 'When did you smell the perfume? On entering the house, in the bedroom, or when you left?'

'In the room.'

'Cheryl,' Isaac said, 'there was blood everywhere, your boyfriend has been murdered, and you expect us to believe that you smelled perfume.'

'I did. I swear it.'

'It's impossible unless you can distinguish the smell of perfume from that of the blood. That smell is pungent and metallic due to the presence of iron in the haemoglobin.'

'But I did.'

'The only way possible would have been that Barry wasn't dead when you smelled the perfume and that you had sexual intercourse with Barry before killing him. Isn't that it?'

'No, no. He was dead. I swear it.'

'Then the truth. Why tell us there's perfume when clearly there wasn't?'

'It was that woman. She had been in the house, and maybe it wasn't in the bedroom.'

'But you said it was.'

'I was confused. Unable to think.'

Wendy wanted to intervene but knew she couldn't.

In another part of the police station, two persons fretted. Alan Hastings, outwardly calm, looked at his iPhone; his wife, Adriana, had tears rolling down her face, dabbing them occasionally with a handkerchief. Around them, police officers and civilians walked, talked, and helped themselves from a coffee machine in a corner of the corridor.

'How much longer?' Alan Hastings asked when Wendy came to check on them.

'Not long. It's fine,' Wendy said. She lied.

In the interview room, further attempts to get to the truth. A barrier had been erected, and it appeared impenetrable.

Isaac, in frustration, paused the meeting. The legal aid said nothing. The young woman was being badgered, and he could have used her childhood history to halt proceedings.

In a trial, the interview would be put forward as cajoling a mentally unstable witness to lie, to tell untruths when she was unable to deal with reality.

Cheryl was returned to her parents, who now sat in another room. The door was locked from the outside. Food and drink had been supplied.

In Homicide, Isaac, Larry, and Wendy sat.

'Wendy, I need you in the interrogation,' Isaac said. 'Sorry, Larry, but this will go pear-shaped if the woman regresses. Inadmissible, and thrown out of court.'

'I agree,' Larry said. 'The woman's our most valuable asset. Wendy should talk to her first.'

'Alone, no parents, no other police officers. It doesn't look good for her, does it?' Wendy said.

'She could well have killed Grayling and Sorell. The Colsons were in Scotland when Sorell died. We're certain of that.

And the Colsons are not dummies. What would they have gained by his death?'

'Not unless he knew something, although Barry Sorell was lazy and spaced out more often than not.'

'The woman Fiona Cole claimed to have seen in the room with Sorell?' Larry said.

'It's Cheryl. I'm certain of that,' Wendy said.

'Which means she murdered him.'

'It does, unless there being a third woman is correct, but that seems fanciful. I'm convinced we have met the murderer or the murderers.'

Cheryl Hastings and Wendy Gladstone met in another room. It wasn't Cheryl's bedroom this time, but it was pleasantly decorated, with comfortable chairs instead of hard, a coffee table instead of a desk bolted to the floor. A window with a view instead of a window up high.

'Cheryl, I know this is hard, but I can't help you if you don't help yourself,' Wendy said.

'I get confused. That time I was with the man, he did terrible things, beat me, and told me I was worthless. That my parents were rejoicing to be rid of me.'

'Which were all lies.'

'With your chief inspector and inspector, it was the same. I was confused, unsure what to say or if it would be true. What is the truth? I can't be sure. Did I smell the perfume in the room? Was Barry dead, or did I kill him? Was it me on the floor, or was it someone else? I see things, but I don't. That man, I thought he would kill me.'

'Would it help to talk about it? To vanquish the demons. An exorcism?'

Wendy knew that Cheryl Hastings, because of what had happened to her or despite it, had mental issues.

'Let's gain clarity,' Wendy continued. 'You find David Grayling dead. How did you know it was him?'

'I had a torch.'

'Why? You were looking for David. The back door was open, and there was electricity in the house. You could have turned on the lights. The Colsons would have been angry if you were in the house, but you couldn't have been accused of breaking, entering, or stealing, unless…'

'Once a thief, always a thief, is that it?' Cheryl said. She was having a tantrum. Her arms were flaying, and she was striking out, grabbing the door handle. 'Let me out,' she screamed.

Wendy called the station's medic. Outside the room, two officers took hold of her. Ten minutes later, an ambulance arrived, and Cheryl was transferred to St Mary's Hospital on Praed Street, Paddington.

Chapter 17

Alan and Adriana Hastings were livid and intended to complain to their local member of parliament, the press, and whoever would listen.

As the senior officer, Isaac tried to calm them, to remind them that it was a homicide investigation and that, with two deaths, questions must be asked, and people are placed in uncomfortable situations in the pursuit of justice. The Hastings were not buying it until Commander Richard Goddard sat them down in his office and explained that he had complete confidence in his people and that Sergeant Gladstone had gone above and beyond in assisting their daughter.

'We understand that,' Adriana Hastings said. 'But it's our daughter. What she went through.'

'I understand and sympathise. Your daughter is fragile; it's not that I have met her, but I have read the reports. The trauma she experienced will always remain, and whereas you, as devoted parents, have done your best, we still have two homicides to solve.

'For now, your daughter will not be troubled. However, we must talk to her in detail. Her knowledge of what happened, even if confused, is vital.'

Appeased but not happy, they left Goddard's office. Cheryl Hastings would remain in hospital for two days.

The grapevine was active in the building, or Caddick had a stooge passing information. The man waylaid the Hastings, acted as if he cared, and got the full story from them. They thought he was a good man. Little did they know.

Isaac discovered what had happened when the complaint against him for his fractious dispute with Caddick was elevated to full disciplinary action.

'Not much I can do,' Goddard said. 'I'm sitting on the fence on this one.'

Isaac phoned Jenny and told her he had had enough of the backstabbing, disloyalty, and abhorrent culture that permeated the once august police force.

Jenny knew it was his frustration speaking, not what he wanted. It was a dilemma to which she had no answer other than to pack three suitcases, put the children in her car, and drive to her parents' house. 'Two weeks, time out,' she told Isaac over the phone.

It was the first time that their friction had resulted in direct action. Isaac needed to be away from Homicide, but it wasn't possible. The situation was untenable, the solution unpalatable.

'It will get better,' Wendy said when he confided in her.

'It won't,' Isaac responded resolutely. 'Our fates are determined by political animals like Caddick. It cannot improve.'

Wendy saw a vulnerability she had not seen before. She was worried that if Isaac left or was replaced by Caddick, it would be compulsory retirement for her; for Larry Hill, either to come to heel or be out of the force due to his drinking; for Bridget, transfer to another position she would dislike.

Regardless, the investigation continued.

Fiona Cole was interviewed at her house, the McCarthys received another visit, and Cathy Hopkinson, whom Wendy had spoken to first in the street where the McCarthys lived, was again offering tea to Wendy and Larry.

Isaac was in the office, dealing with paperwork, missing his family, and reading through the directive to attend a disciplinary. To him, it was verbiage based on Caddick's hatred of him and Davies's attempt at any cost to remove from the force negative influences who did not support him one hundred per cent.

Machiavellian in concept, Machiavellian in action, Davies represented the worst of the London Met, and if Caddick sat at the man's right hand, Commander Goddard was down at his knees.

That was until Goddard walked into Isaac's office and sat down. 'We fight,' he said.

'I thought you had signed on with Davies,' Isaac said.

'Strategically, I had to. I was playing the long game. We were out on a limb, you and I. Caddick is a nobody; forget about him.'

'Why this change of heart? I thought you were lost to the enemy.'

'Isaac, give it time; wait and see. There is support from an unexpected quarter.'

'Someone we know?'

'Yes. Fight the disciplinary; do not accept that Caddick will win. Davies knows he's in trouble. His power base is weak, and he doesn't yet know the depth of it nor the ferocity of the hell that is to be visited on him.'

'Another promotion?' Isaac asked, aware that Goddard was always looking for an opportunity.

'And for you, if we pull this off.'

'What do you want from me?'

'What I've said, prepare your defence. It's unlikely that you'll attend a hearing. And for Christ's sake, get your wife to come back. Tell her it will be okay. Tell her what you must, but swear her to confidence. The powers that are forming will act swiftly.'

***

The focus was to discover who the woman was that Fiona Cole had seen Sorell with. The CSIs had revisited where he had died but came back with nothing. Considering the mess in the room and the blood, it seemed impossible that Fiona Cole could be telling the truth.

Larry didn't trust her, but consideration also had to be given to the woman who had reported Sorell's death, Oksana Akimova, a recent arrival in the country from Ukraine.

She had disappeared. She was white with blonde hair. Could she be the other woman? But that had been discounted. When Isaac spoke to her outside the house, she was clean and dressed in a light-coloured knee-length dress. Inside the home, there was no mention by the CSIs that the bathroom shower had been used or that there was blood outside of the bedroom.

Even if the woman had scrupulously cleaned herself, the CSIs would not have missed the signs, and Akimova's fingerprints were on record.

Edward Fraser had expressed his concerns about Fiona, but Homicide had not seen the unpleasant side of the woman that he had mentioned.

Larry and Wendy visited Fraser and were surprised to find another young woman in the house.

'Gone, I'm afraid,' Fraser said.

'Revolving door, Mr Fraser?' Wendy said with a smile on her face. She was in a better mood, pleased that Cheryl appeared to have no lasting effects from the grilling she had received from her chief inspector and Larry Hill.

'You're only young once,' Fraser replied. Larry could hear the easy repartee between the sophisticated man and the plain-speaking woman with her strong Yorkshire accent.

'And you're pushing the tail end of it, Mr Fraser.'

It was flippant, irreverent, and not the way to conduct an interview, but Wendy thought it appropriate. To disarm the man, to lower his defences, and to open up the conversation about Fiona Cole and what he had said about her.

'I know that, but you're not here to talk about my love life or waning libido.'

'We're here about Fiona Cole. We need to know her better.'

'You mentioned certain characteristics about her the last time we were here,' Larry said.

'I did. I wish no harm to her.'

'No harm has befallen her, but we have a situation. We believe her to have been in a house when a murder was committed. We can't be certain if she was there before, during, or after. She is adamant that it was after.'

'And it's important to know which?'

'Precisely.'

'How can I assist? She had mood swings, which could be difficult, but I can't remember her lying. Forgetting to tell the truth, especially with my credit card, but that's not a crime. She stayed as long as I gave her free rein. The same as the one who left a week ago.'

'You restricted her?'

'Controlled. At first, they buy what they need, but that need grows, and eventually, they buy clothes they never wear and shoes that stay in their boxes. When they do that, I know their appreciation of me is no longer genuine. I've become the golden goose. That's when they go.'

'Was that the case with Fiona?' Larry asked.

'Not entirely. It's not the money; it's the principle. My largesse is not unconditional.'

'Then why?'

'I believe she felt cheapened by it. Fiona has a strong moral streak. After her disappointment with her first husband, I was there on the rebound. But she wanted marriage, and eventually she found it.'

'Once again,' Larry asked, 'is she capable of violence in those dark moments? Enough to murder?'

'What drives a person to that extreme? Sure, in the heat of the moment, she might say things and lash out. We're all guilty of that, but murder, that's another level. No, I don't think she's capable of murder.'

'Able to plan?'

'Possible. She was intelligent and savvy, and I know she's been a force of good with her current husband. One thing, she left the house with a painting.'

'Valuable?'

'It was insured. I'm certain it was her. Maybe she saw it as my final payment, but she loved it.'

'You never pursued her for it?'

'I didn't know where she was. Only later, two, maybe three years, I found out she was in Sevenoaks.'

'How?'

'A chance encounter. I met her at the Royal Opera House in Convent Garden. We were attending the same opera. She introduced me to Cole. I shook hands with him, kissed her cheek, wished them well, and said goodbye.'

'Did he know who you were? Your significance?'

'Not from me. She might have told him. That was the only time I've seen her since she left me.'

'The painting?'

'A landscape. It was a Constable, one of his lesser paintings. Probably worth a King's ransom now.'

'You've not bothered to check if she has it?'

'I registered a claim with my insurance company and received a payout. There was no point in pursuing it.'

Larry and Wendy left Fraser and drove to Sevenoaks. They asked Fiona bluntly if she had the painting. There was no point in denial. It was in the hallway of the house.

'He owed it to me,' Fiona said, embarrassed that she had been caught out.

'You met him at Covent Garden. Is that correct?' Larry said.

'We did. It was polite, short, and not unpleasant.'

'Does your husband know who he was?'

'He does. I can't be held accountable for the men in my life before him. He's been married before, with a couple of children. I don't object when the children visit or when he goes to see them. Your continuing attempts to paint me as the scarlet woman are annoying. I've done nothing wrong other than want what was mine. The Colsons hold the secrets, not me.'

'Grant?' You knew he was dead, right?' Wendy asked.

'I had him legally declared dead. What else do you want me to say? He hadn't used his cards, not those I knew of. Nor had he touched his bank account. I had access to one, a few thousand pounds. I took that money, as was my right.'

***

Alan and Adriana Hastings were delighted. Their daughter had fully recovered and wanted to talk to the police. They had withdrawn their complaint against the police.

Isaac was thankful; one less issue to deal with, and the regrettable complaint had no basis in substance. People suffer during a murder investigation, get placed in awkward situations, get asked questions they do not want to answer and go mad. Cheryl Hastings had taken the last option, but the doctor had ruled her sane, with no underlying mental issues.

The Hastings knew that was incorrect. They had seen their child since she had come home from when she had been kidnapped, the hours she had spent on her own, the bottled emotions, and then puberty, where she had become promiscuous, coming home at all hours of the night, either drunk or drugged or both.

And then, that first time, she was gone. For three years, they looked for her, but she was not a missing person. Social services continued to pay her money, which she drew each month. Up and down the country until, one day, she knocked on the door, took a shower, grabbed whatever from the fridge and retreated to her room. Four days later, she came out, kissed her mother on the cheek, embraced her father, and sat down at the dining table.

'What's for lunch?' she said. 'I'm famished.'

No more questions from her parents. There was no answer about where she had been, who she had been with, or her experiences. For seven months, normality reigned. Cheryl got a part-time job in a shop, came home at six thirty from work, ate a meal with her parents, watched an inane programme on the television and went to bed.

Pleased with her return, concerned that what had been great initially had the markings of obsession, the inability to relate to people and circumstances. An avoidance of conflict, an unwillingness to go out with friends or to find a boyfriend.

The psychiatrist, who had known the child before she had become a woman and had spent time with her after her release, was circumspect. 'Be thankful. Give it time,' she said.

The Hastings had no option but to hope for the best. Their best wasn't going to be good enough.

'Last night,' Alan Hastings said on the phone. 'We came downstairs and found out she had left the house at night. And no, we don't know where she is, and to be quite frank, we'd prefer she was out there on her own than being badgered by your people.'

'But…' Wendy protested.

'Sergeant, we know you're well-meaning, and we're thankful that you helped Cheryl, but the psychiatrist who helped her when she was freed was wrong, as they are now. She will survive, not as an indulgent parent would want, but survival at any cost is better than the alternative.'

'Do you believe she would harm herself?'

'Locked up in a facility for the criminally insane, prodded and pinched, hot baths, and electric shocks. What do you reckon?'

'It's not Dickensian. She would receive the best care.'

Wendy knew it was final as far as the Hastings were concerned; it was not for Homicide. An all-points bulletin was issued: find Cheryl Hastings, then inform Homicide, Challis Street Police Station. The woman is not considered violent.

In Oxford, Alan and Adriana Hastings held hands. 'You do realise she killed Barry Sorell,' Alan said.

'Who else could it be,' Adriana replied.

There was no more to be said. They knew their lives were damned by a depraved individual. Their emotions were stunted, as were their daughter's.

Chapter 18

Commander Goddard's prediction that something was happening to rock the very foundations of the Metropolitan Police came as a shock.

The rumours were coming into Challis Street, from the holiest of holy, from New Scotland Yard. A power struggle and Alwyn Davies's position was on the line, a chance for a new broom to come in and sweep out the old.

Isaac should have been elated, but he remained sceptical. It wasn't the first time such rumours had spread, but he had received a phone call from Goddard this time. 'Say nothing, do nothing,' he'd said.

He called Larry, Wendy, and Bridget into his office. 'Let the others indulge in gossip. For you three, don't comment or offer any advice.'

'You know something?' Larry asked.

'Not officially. Let it play out. Davies, if he's under threat, is a magnificent fighter. He will not go easily. The man has powerful backers. They, if any, will determine his fate. And remember, crime dropped on his watch when he had the power.'

'And now it's escalating,' Bridget said. 'You didn't approve of what he had done.'

'It verged on the draconian, but what do we have now? And if the Met goes soft, puts in place someone soft on crime, someone who believes that a warning and a rap over the knuckles is sufficient punishment for a violent offender, then we're worse off than before.'

Wendy knew any change would be for the better, but she worried about a missing woman.

Two sightings, over a hundred miles apart, were discounted. Cheryl Hastings did not have any distinguishing features. Average height, Caucasian, brown eyes, shoulder-length brunette hair, last seen wearing jeans and a white top. A recent photo was included, but the clothes could be changed, the hair dyed and cut, and with a hat and glasses, it would not be the person they were looking for.

Wendy had advised the parents that interfering in a murder investigation and not telling them where a key witness was was illegal. But that was an idle threat. Who would convict the parents of a child who had suffered terribly and continued to have mental breakdowns? Nobody would, or maybe the hanging judge, Judge Jeffreys, but he was long dead and buried.

She had advised the Hastings that, if detained, their daughter would be held in custody, as she was clearly a reluctant witness who would abscond at the first opportunity. Wendy was also concerned that the parents had the child hidden, if not at the family home, then at a location known to them.

Taking advantage of a day away from the office, Isaac spent time with his family on Sunday. An outing to the zoo. Isaac had told Jenny what was afoot and that the long-awaited elevation to superintendent was possible. And with that, they could consider another house.

'It wasn't fun,' Jenny said. 'My parents trying to teach me how to raise children. They bought them presents they didn't need and talked childishly to them. I was glad to come back. If it's Homicide, so be it, but if you make superintendent, it's another house. Agreed?'

'Come back,' Isaac hollered as their son put out his arm to feed a banana to a monkey in a cage. 'Agreed,' he said, turning back to his wife.

Monday morning, a familiar face in the office: Superintendent Caddick. 'The disciplinary hearing is off,' he said. Then Isaac knew that the rumour about Davies being threatened had gone from rumour to actuality.

After Caddick left, Isaac phoned a friend in New Scotland Yard. to find out what was happening.

'It's true. The place is abuzz, and the media's got wind of it. A couple of reporters outside, although all they'll get today is

Devil House

cold,' Chief Inspector Farley Grainger said. 'Caddick still giving you aggravation?'

'You mean my new best friend,' Isaac replied.

'It seems the man's got a lot of new best friends. He's become a nuisance around here, trying to make out he's affable and one of us. If Davies goes, Caddick goes, and good riddance.'

'We've been here before.'

'I agree, but I saw your commander hovering around, one floor down from the high and mighty. Goddard's not a man to miss an opportunity.'

'He wants the top job, but that's a few ranks up from his current position. He'll not make it this time.'

'Not for lack of trying.'

'A favour,' Isaac said. 'You're in Fraud. Can you check out a few people for me?'

'Criminal?'

'Not sure. A couple who might be pushing the envelope. We're going nowhere fast on the investigation. A little dirt might loosen tongues.'

'Send me what you have.'

'Four persons, the couple where the first body was found. A wealthy individual, living high on the hog, pushing sixty, surrounds himself with twenty-something nymphettes.'

'Half his luck,' Grainger said. 'Any more?'

'A builder in Sevenoaks. He's probably clean.

'Send what you've got, a couple of days, and I'll see what we come up with.'

'Thanks. Keep me posted on what's happening on the top floor.'

'What, with Goddard as your boss. That man will know before us humble servants on the third floor.'

***

'Oh, yes, I knew Grant,' Cathy Hopkinson said. Teas all around, and a plate of chocolate biscuits. On the woman's lap, a cat was curled up. The yappy dog was nowhere to be seen. 'Lovely man.'

Wendy realised that Cathy, elderly, sweet, and kind, would say that about everyone on the first account. She would have said that about Dr Crippen if he had been alive and the man had been a notorious murderer a hundred years ago.

'How?' Wendy asked. 'We were told he visited rarely and tended to be secretive and antisocial, yet you refer to him as a friend.'

'Whenever he stayed with the Colsons, he would go for long walks in the morning. I was up early, and I would see him as he walked past and have a chat over the fence. Strange that you say he wasn't sociable. With me, he was perfectly fine.'

'Describe him?'

'Tall and handsome, there was a confidence about him. I thought he must be intelligent. He told me he was close to his sister but not keen on her husband.'

'He said that?'

'His sister, yes. I probably asked him about her husband.'

'Any reason why he wouldn't be keen?'

'Grant was well-spoken and had a bearing about him. Harold Colson is shorter and pudgy, a sour look on his face as if he has sucked a lemon.'

'You knew the Colsons?'

'Not particularly, nodding acquaintances. She would always speak, but never the husband.'

'Did it concern you?'

'Why should it? They lived in the neighbourhood, nothing more. Janice McCarthy knew them better, but you know that. Did you know she had been to prison?'

'The question is, how do you?'

'iPad. I researched her and her husband. Took me a few days, but after their child had died, I felt inclined.'

Technology had made significant positive advances; assisting a nosy neighbour to indulge in her favourite pastime was not one of them.

'What else did you find out?'

'Bob, her husband, works from home a lot of the time. She's got an interesting history. He seems to be a cold fish.'

Wendy had to grant that the woman was perceptive. There was a passion in Janice, and even if her youth had been traumatic, she had settled down and had come to compartmentalise her daughter's death and move forward. Why the McCarthys remained in the area still made no sense. Or was it guilt at what they had done to the child?

'Cold fish? Why do you say that?'

'Out in the garden, obsessing over it, not that it looks much better than mine.'

'You don't do your garden.'

'Perish the thought. I've got a teenager from the local school. He comes once a fortnight, does what's necessary and leaves.'

'What else did you find out about Janice?' Wendy asked. Nosy neighbours could be a force for good in a police investigation.

'There was a rumour that they beat the child.'

'From where?'

'From the child. It was five or six weeks before she died. She was over near the swings. She was sitting on one of them but not moving, her head down. I could see her from here, see everything from my bedroom upstairs.'

'Which means you could have seen the swings when their daughter died.'

'I didn't, much to my regret. I saw her on her own.'

'What happened?'

'Sometimes, I go for a walk over there. I went over to see if she was okay. She was sobbing. I asked what was wrong, the sort of thing a good neighbour should do.'

'"It's mum," she said. "She hit me." Children say things which you can't always believe. I asked her more. She said she had been upstairs doing her homework when her mother had come in and hit her for no reason.'

'You believed her?'

'Not entirely. Lucy was an attractive child, but she tended to exaggerate. Occasionally, I'd see her walking home from school. We would chat, although it was me talking and her answering. If she told me she had got an A at school, it meant a B. If she told me that her parents were happy and good to her, I knew that was a lie.'

'Did she live in a world of her own?'

'The McCarthys were good people, but they used to argue. She left him once. The child was the butter in the sandwich, slathered with attention by each parent in turn, blamed by each at another time.'

'Not uncommon,' Wendy said. She knew that strained marriages, financial difficulties, and a wistful child were often volatile and that the weak party would suffer.

'Anyway, Lucy's on the swing. I go over, and she tells me she's fine, and it's not the first time she's been hit. "Mum gets angry with Dad and then takes it out on me. It's not fair." She tells me that her father has a girlfriend, and her mother doesn't know.'

'Did you believe her?'

'I didn't. He's stormed out of the house a few times, and Janice took Lucy to spend a week with her mother. Bob had plenty of opportunities, but nothing changed. As usual, he was in the garden but seemed happier, though. Even gave me some flowers. If anyone would play up, it would have been Janice.'

'Proof?'

'She was personable and could be attractive. It wouldn't have been difficult for her, and she had been promiscuous in her youth.'

'How do you know?'

'iPad. I told you. I found out about her time in prison. I have a surname. At fifteen, shoplifting. One year later expelled from school for selling drugs in the playground. At seventeen and a half, she's in front of the magistrate for conduct unbecoming.'

'What does that mean?'

'Selling herself for a fix.'

'You didn't get all that off an iPad,' Wendy said. 'We'll come back to that. Continue with Lucy at the swings.'

'I put an arm around her, she pulled away. Initially, I thought it was due to my familiarity. "It hurts," she says.'

'Proof of more than a slap?'

'According to Lucy, it was a stick that her mother kept in the kitchen.'

Corporal punishment was often committed against a child by those who had received it when they were young. And if one knew, the other did, which meant that Bob McCarthy was complicit, whether willingly or not.

'Did you confront Lucy's mother?'

'I wanted to, but how could I? If the mother was a child beater, it was my word against hers. I knew that social services wouldn't act quickly.'

'And if you had, and social services had visited the house, then Lucy would have been hit again or locked in her room and starved. You turned a blind eye.'

'I did what was best for the child. I was right in my decision. And then, a few weeks later, the child was dead. That's when I started to investigate the McCarthys. I know you think I'm a busybody, but my intentions are good.'

Wendy wasn't sure if they were, but they would be invaluable. 'If you know so much about the McCarthys, you must know about the Colsons.'

'I've not finished with Lucy,' Cathy Hopkinson said.

'Sorry.'

'Lucy didn't usually go to the swings on her own, but that day she did.'

'You believe that due to issues at home, in her sadness, she had gone there, but this time, instead of just sitting, she had started to swing, higher and higher, until she fell.'

'I do. I saw her there once. A child needs a place to go when life gets difficult. We all do. It was an accident, which wouldn't have happened if the home had been harmonious.'

'Bob and Janice afterwards?'

'I didn't see them for months. After the inquest and the funeral, they retreated into the house. Food was delivered, and the garden was left untended. Eventually, after a long time, they emerged. Slowly. Bob went for long walks, and Janice was at the church daily. As each month passed, they changed.'

Wendy knew that Cathy Hopkinson's evidence may have resulted in charges being levelled at Janice and Bob McCarthy if she had reported what she knew. It was damning testimony. However, it wasn't relevant, on the face of it, to the current investigation into the murder of Grayling and Sorell.

***

Due to the sensitivity of the information, and that Caddick could walk into Challis Street at any time, and that New Scotland Yard was awash with rumours, and people were jockeying for position when Davies was either removed or had pulled off another miracle, Isaac and Farley Grainger met at a neutral location, fifteen miles from either place.

Grainger produced a folder from a backpack and laid it on the table in the public house. 'Four persons. There's probably more I could have found out, but you said two days was the maximum.'

It was seven in the evening. Both men had eaten a pub meal and held a pint of beer. Isaac wasn't much of a drinker, but Farley was. The man had gone out on a limb, and it would have been an affront if Isaac had not joined him for the first couple of pints.

Devil House

Farley was ready to make a night of it; Isaac wanted to get home. The similarities between Grainger and Larry Hill were striking. Although one could drink as much as the other, it was Larry who was the alcoholic. If Grainger needed to, for personal or professional reasons, he could detach from the drink for as long as required; Larry could not.

'Edward Fraser. Let's start with the easy one,' Grainger said. He slid a sheaf of papers across the table. 'That's what I have on the man.'

'A summation?'

'He started with a bistro in Croydon. Downmarket, cheap and cheerful. In his early twenties, he had the food and knew how to pull in the punters. Five years later, he's in Mayfair, which is upmarket and expensive. A TV producer comes into the place and sees that Fraser's got an easy way about him: charismatic, knowledgeable, and camera-friendly.

'Six weeks later, Fraser's on the TV. An early-morning show, a five-minute segment. The viewers love him. He's offered a contract, and it's good money. He opens another restaurant and then another. The money's coming in, and he's enjoying it.

'A bon vivant, workaholic, he can't get enough of it. He always had women, but now he's gone upmarket.'

'And young,' Isaac added. 'Criminal?'

'Nothing. The man pays his taxes and doesn't cheat on staff wages. Some of them have worked for him since the early days. I doubt if you'll find anything against him; he is too busy enjoying himself to get involved in crime, let alone murder.'

'The painting?'

'Fraser made a claim on the insurance company. It's probably valuable, but it's old history. He doesn't want to know about it. And again, no fraud.'

'Another pint?' Isaac asked.

'Don't mind if I do,' Grainger replied.

'Aaron Cole?'

'Good businessman, did it tough during the last recession. He had to lay off staff, a dispute with one of them, that he had

173

shortchanged him. The court ruled against the person laid off. Second marriage to Fiona. Two children from the first. He pays the school fees for the children. His first wife is remarried, although that marriage appears on the rocks.

'Eight years ago, one of his houses had to be substantially reworked due to shoddy construction. Although he had declared bankruptcy, Cole took the subcontractor to court and won the case, all costs to the guilty party. Cole flies close to the wind; sometimes, his wings are burnt, but he's in a dog-eat-dog business and plays it better than most. Nowadays, he builds to spec, a select clientele with the money to pay. Fiona Cole, married to Grant Batholomew, shacked up with Fraser, now married to Cole. She's the public relations of the company. Attractive?'

'And smart,' Isaac said. 'We can't be sure about her. She keeps popping up like a bad penny. She could be guilty of murder.'

'I would say it's unlikely. She's got it made it with Cole unless there are unresolved issues.'

'Aaron Cole, financially stable?'

'Close to the wind, as I said. He seems financially sound, and we've got nothing against him. I'm sure he files a return every year and pays his taxes reluctantly. The next two are more interesting.'

Isaac realised that a third pint was in order. He hoped he could handle it.

'Elizabeth Colson, née Batholomew. One brother, Grant, is deceased. Elizabeth was born two years before her brother. Upper middle class; her father was a doctor; her mother was a nurse. She still owns the family home in Dorset, which she inherited after her parents died. It is currently rented out.

'Harold Colson was born in Wales to English parents. His father was a bank manager; his mother was a housewife. Academically gifted, he went to university and graduated with a master's degree in accountancy. He worked for a firm of accountants before going out on his own. In the last fifteen years, he has taken on a small clientele, personal tax returns, not corporate. No crimes against either, until…'

'The death of Grant Batholomew.'

'We should discuss him first. No crimes against him, although technology improvements in the last ten years have allowed me to take a deeper look at him.'

'He died fifteen years ago.'

'Not according to what I've found. As you've stated, the Colsons carried on in his name, or to be correct, names.'

'How many?'

'Five that I've found. Three of those you gave me, based on the documents your inspector found.'

'The additional?'

'Correlation of names we know to financial dealings with third parties. Some are legit, some are the transference of assets, bogus loans, and transfers to bank accounts in this country and overseas. Grant Batholomew was a shrewd operator. His legacy was well managed by Harold, I assume, and Elizabeth.'

'Are these financial crimes.'

'Not yet. They could be if I delve deeper, but I've concentrated on what you want for now.'

'Good. Grant died fifteen years ago. We have a date given to us by the Colsons. Pathology, by autopsy, and Forensics, by the clothes he was buried in, and a receipt in a trouser pocket, agree that fifteen years is probably correct.'

'There is no visible change in how Bartholomew conducted business from before that time and after.'

'What sort of business? What sort of crime?'

'On the death of their father, Grant inherited two houses, a row of shops, and cash.'

'How much?'

'Current real estate valuation would be on the high side of one million, eight hundred thousand pounds. The cash was thirty-six thousand pounds in old money.'

'Substantial,' Isaac said.

'Elizabeth received the family home, a flat in London, and twenty-two thousand pounds.'

'Your conclusion?'

'Through shrewd management and frugality, Grant Batholomew had taken what was legally gained and built it up to nearly twenty-five million by the time he died. Various names have been used, and there is a probable misuse of offshore banks to avoid tax.'

'Which you would pursue if we give you the all clear.'

'Not yet, probably never. Apart from Colson's deception, there appears to be nothing criminal that we can charge him with.'

'However?' Isaac said.

'Academic research, home-based accountancy, with upward of forty-eight million pounds in known assets, and, we would have to assume, significant cash, don't gel.'

'Eccentric or criminal? What's your opinion?'

'Academic research might be feasible. But why the distraction of running a small business?'

'A front, if questions are asked. A weak defence if they are. No one would believe it.'

'And nor should we; it makes no sense.'

'It's something we've never been able to figure out. We keep trying to implicate the Colsons in the murders, and each time we try, we can't make the connection. We suspect an attempt to blacken their names, and Fiona Cole would be the most logical, but she got two million pounds from them. Why maintain a vendetta, even if you believe you were cheated out of money at the divorce? There was no reason for the Colsons to give her anything, but according to them, they gave it willingly.'

'Which means there are secrets you don't know about and I've not discovered. Give me two more days; let me dig deeper. And this time, it will be Fiona Cole,' Grainger said.

Isaac made a phone call to Challis Street. He wasn't going to risk driving home after the time in the pub, and a couple of constables could pick him up, one to drive his car. Grainger had no such issue. He was in his car and off.

Chapter 19

After the time spent with Grainger the night before, Isaac arrived late the following day in Homicide due to an unaccustomed headache and a rough tongue.

'Looks like you'll be going up in the world,' Caddick said. He was sitting in Isaac's office on his arrival.

'Not that I've heard. Social visit?' Isaac said. Bridget placed a cup of coffee in front of him.

'Wouldn't mind one myself,' Caddick said, looking at Bridget. 'Got them well-trained.'

Caddick's arrogance remained. Anyone who fell for his feigned friendship would have to be a fool.

Bridget walked out of the door, cocking her head at Caddick in a sign of disapproval, ensuring he didn't see, but her DCI did. Isaac had instructed the team, aware of what was happening at New Scotland Yard, not to assume it was a fait accompli and to be civil to Caddick.

Two weeks previously, Isaac Cook would have chucked it in and gone off to a sleepy provincial town, where the worst crime was a domestic dispute and brawls outside the pub on a Saturday night.

Now, he was excited about the future, and Caddick, who would be close to the action, was confirming that Davies's downfall was imminent.

Names were mentioned for a successor. Two sounded promising, but the third would be a diversity employee catering to modern-day ideology. Isaac didn't care if they were white, black, or whatever religion. He was black and competent, whereas the name he had heard had a poor record of achievement. If that person were to take over from Davies, the much-needed reform would happen, but it would not be a reform he would approve of.

'What are your plans, Seth?' Isaac asked.

'Don't worry about me. Something will turn up.'

Isaac wasn't worried about the man, but Caddick was right. There was always a place for a slimy arse-licker.

'Even if I grovel in the dirt,' Caddick added.

Isaac had heard reports of the man from other officers at other police stations before he had joined Davies. They were not good: planted evidence, shoddy paperwork, and even taking illegal payments had been mentioned.

If Caddick oversaw Homicide, Isaac knew that Harold and Elizabeth Colson would have been hanged, drawn, and quartered by now.

'We can pretend, but we have little in common,' Isaac said. 'To me, you represent the worst of the Met. And you believe me to be a sanctimonious, naïve fool.'

'You missed out narrow-minded, Isaac, but you're right. I'm a man who always comes out on top. You think that good policing and a supportive team are the way. I don't. We deal with the scum. They don't respect your approach. You need to show them who's boss, and if that means that sometimes we circumvent the police handbook, so much the better.'

'At least he's honest,' Larry, who had overheard the conversation, said after Caddick had left.

'His version of honest. He'll be back. No friends, only allies, and they are rapidly ducking and weaving, trying to avoid him.'

'I've got an update.'

'Something to take the taste away of that odious man.'

'It should. Fiona Cole's blown her top.'

'One of your people give you the nod?'

'Not an informer. Sergeant Eddie Machin, Sevenoaks Police Station.'

'Elaborate.'

'Apparently, Aaron Cole's sailing close to the wind.'

'Last night, my contact told me it was an occupational hazard.'

179

'It's more serious this time. A dramatic economic downturn, political turmoil, rioting on the street, and mass immigration. The people are nervous, worried that this is not a blip but a major change in the country.'

'It is. Davies, out on his ear, won't make much of a difference. Your wife? Pulling her belt in yet?'

'She senses it. One of her well-to-do friends, up to their ears in hock, is down one car, and their house is up for sale. Another couple, an attractive wife, an out-of-condition husband, and three spoiled brats, have split. She's gone back to her parents and left him with the kids. Serves them right. I've always told my wife to live within your means. Endless credit won't last forever.'

'Financially? How are you?'

'We can manage. I could do with more money. Any chance?'

'It depends on the rumour and our leader.'

'Which one? The rat, or the hawk.'

'Commander Goddard's optimistic. I assume he's the hawk. The rat is looking for allies and sees me as a possible.'

'Which you're not. Promotion in the offing?'

'It could be. Not sure I'm enthusiastic about the possible replacement for Davies.'

'There's one you wouldn't mind.'

'Long time ago. Who told you? Wendy?'

'The grapevine. You're a legend in the Met. What was it when you joined? Poster Boy, the future of the Met. They had you primed for greatness, a chance at Davies's job.'

'It stalled when Commander Goddard's mentor stepped down as commissioner and put on the ermine robe. Dead now, more is the pity.'

Fiona Cole? Details? Do we need to go to Sevenoaks?'

'I'm going. Come if you want to get away from the stench of the rat.'

***

Wendy attended Barry Sorell's funeral. Not that she had wanted to, but Cheryl Hastings was still missing. Nobody had heard from her. Alan and Adriana Hastings were adamant that they hadn't. Wendy didn't believe them, and bar monitoring their phone calls and tailing their cars, there wasn't much the police could do.

She worried for the woman but remained wary about her being innocent of the crime of murder. And if she had killed Sorell, would she be at the funeral, hiding in the bushes, or behind a gravestone, self-flagellating for her sins?

The service was short, the vicar saying a few words and a cousin of Sorell, a pretty girl in her teens, getting up to recount how he would babysit her when she was young. There was also a heavily tattooed brother dressed in a suit for the occasion but would have been more comfortable in a biker's jacket astride a Harley Davidson. Wendy thought he looked like a criminal but knew prejudice due to a person's appearance was incorrect. A day later, Bridget discovered that the brother was the manager of a small engineering company producing farm equipment.

Nadia Hussain had accompanied her, and was staying in the background, an eagle eye looking for the missing woman.

'She was here,' she said as the two women drove back to Challis Street. 'I could sense her.'

Wendy thought the woman was over-eager to prove her worth. It was she who should have sensed Cheryl but conceded that her eyes were not as sharp as when she had been young, nor were her reflexes as fast, and almost certainly, her senses were not as alert.

Wendy knew she had been able to remain in Homicide because of her DCI, and Caddick believed she was past it.

A new senior investigation officer – almost certainly Caddick, if he could inveigle his way into Homicide. And then, in a display of making his mark, Caddick would look to efficiency, cost-cutting, everyone pulling their weight, officers educated and, above all, young. She knew she would not qualify.

In Sevenoaks, on Argyle Road, Isaac, Larry, and Eddie Machin sat in the small cafeteria at the police station. It was two in the afternoon, and it was almost empty, apart from a couple of people behind the serving counter and a group of junior officers on the other side of the room, making plans for the weekend.

Isaac knew the kind of plans they were making. Which pub should we start at, and where will we find the local talent? Once, he had been one of those, although pubs didn't represent alcohol to him, and invariably, by the end of the evening, his colleagues would be too drunk to take advantage of the local talent, even if they wanted to.

'They all say they could see it coming,' Machin said. He was ginger-haired, in his twenties, and as sharp as a tack. Isaac thought he had the makings of an exemplary police officer, a possible chief inspector, even a commander. He had one advantage over Larry, a university degree. Obligatory in the police force unless exceptional experience could be shown. Larry had the experience, but there were black marks against him.

He and Larry had previously discussed it, but the inspector's reply had always been: 'I don't have the discipline; in one ear and out the next. On the street, with the flotsam of society, I'm fine. But in a classroom or sitting an exam, no way.'

Isaac would try depending on who took over from Davies, but he wasn't optimistic. He might be able to get him another pay scale, but not another rank.

'What do you reckon?' Isaac asked.

'He's been in business a long time. He must know how to weather the storm.'

Isaac wasn't sure if it was a storm or a climactic shift in the country's economy. There was a great deal of debate, uncertainty, and despair. Aaron Cole wouldn't be the first to have to deal with it. Although Isaac wasn't about to reveal it to Machin, Fiona Cole had two million pounds. If her husband was having difficulties, she could bail him out.

They found Aaron Cole in his builder's yard. The man was surveying the damage.

'What happened,' Isaac asked.

'Fiona happened,' Cole said.

'Why?' Larry asked. 'We know she can occasionally lose it, but the Colsons never mentioned it.'

'Fraser had seen it. She told me about the painting. I didn't know. I thought it wasn't worth much and that Fiona had purchased it from a flea market.'

'You've had it valued?'

'Now, for insurance purposes. Close to eighty thousand pounds at auction.'

'Financial problems?'

'Tight. We can weather the storm, or I can sell up. Fiona can't handle it when I put a clamp on her spending.'

'But she's got two million pounds. Have you considered that?'

'I have. I told her to pull her belt in for a few weeks. I'm owed money, and they're declaring bankruptcy. Unlikely to get more than a few pence in the pound. Fiona's unstable, but you know that. She has a turn, goes psycho, comes down here, gets in a forklift, and smashes up eight pallets of slate tiles, two of Italian marble, and rams my office.'

'Insurance?'

'A psycho wife? They will not cover it. I reckon we are nearly fifty thousand down, and now she's gone.'

'Schizo, or anger?'

'Not sure which, not interested at this time. I thought the two million was a godsend. Why did the Colsons give it to her?'

'We don't know, and we should.'

Fiona was gone. She had to be found, and soon. Her actions at the builder's yard showed that she was dangerous, and dangerous persons kill.

Isaac phoned the Colsons, who had remained in London, to advise them to be on the lookout. But there remained, and had for some time, the question of why the Colsons had given Fiona two million pounds and how she had received notification after fifteen years that one of Grant's aliases was being used.

Someone had brought Fiona into the picture, but why was unclear.

Isaac and Larry met with the Colsons at six that evening. This time, not at Challis Street, but in the suite they occupied at the hotel.

'Fiona's lost it,' Larry said. 'We consider her as dangerous.'

'We always found her difficult to understand,' Elizabeth Colson said.

'Why did Grant marry her? He didn't seem to be a man who needed a woman permanently.'

'She wanted him. Hasn't she told you this? A shameless hussy,' Harold Colson said.

'Maybe if she hadn't married him, he might still be alive,' Elizabeth said.

'Conjecture or fact?' Isaac asked.

'Conjecture. Grant was self-sufficient, able to spend long periods on his own, absorbed by his thoughts. He said once it was where he made the best decisions. Where he could visually see his investments, and what he should do, when and how.'

'Does that reveal something about his intelligence?'

'He was intelligent, reasoned mentally, and rarely wrote anything down.'

'That doesn't explain why he died. You said he committed suicide, and now you're implying that Fiona could have been involved. If she was, that's murder, and concealing a murder is prosecutable. Are you admitting your guilt?'

'No, we aren't. He wanted her to stay for the marriage to work, but it wasn't possible. Fiona wanted to party, but Grant did not. She wanted to spend; he knew it was foolish, and it bored him. They both came to the marriage with unreasonable expectations.'

'You make it sound as if it was a commercial transaction.'

'Marriage is a contract to love, to cherish, in sickness and health, for richer or poorer. You must know that.'

'That would be the traditional view.'

'Inspector, we've already told you. Fiona wanted someone to support her and give her a better life.'

'And love?'

'Love, on Grant's terms, was not the love she wanted. She was young and beautiful, with love to give. Grant was self-contained and solitary; Fiona was not. For the first six months, Grant enjoyed what she had to offer, but then the heady rush of lovemaking and gay abandonment dulled in him. He would cold shoulder her after the first year.'

'Shameless hussy was the term that you used. Opportunist, desperate for financial stability, a need for her husband, does not imply hussy.'

'Two years into the marriage, Grant no longer just gives her the cold shoulder; he's ignoring her. They had taken to separate bedrooms by then. Not that it worried him, but it did her.'

'She started to play up?'

'Even brought them to her bed.'

'Grant's reaction?'

'Dismay, disgust. We told him to get a grip, bring her to heel, show her attention, and give her a child. Deaf ears, I'm afraid.'

'In what way?'

'A wife was one thing, a child he couldn't countenance. His life had been structured, and he wanted it back. Eventually, he put a block on the stray men, cut her expenditure by half, and then she walked out the door after a few more years.'

'Why did she believe she was entitled to two million pounds? That's not been fully explained, not to our satisfaction.'

Elizabeth Colson looked away, Harold Colson picked up his phone and looked at the screen. Isaac and Larry noted the extraordinarily long pause. They knew it would be a revelation when the Colsons spoke next.

A tear rolled down Elizabeth's face as Harold cleared his throat.

'She knew Grant was dead,' Harold said, almost in a whisper.

'She had him declared dead at seven years,' Larry said.

'Not dead, according to the law.'

'They were divorced. Why bother with getting the law to declare him dead? She didn't need that to marry Aaron Cole.'

'Fiona wasn't that smart, didn't understand how Grant's finances were structured, didn't know that he had set her up as a director of one of his companies.'

'Not until the letter. Is that why it found her after fifteen years?'

'There was a debt to another company, which was not paid on Grant's death. We weren't liable. Grant's name was the name they had, and that of Fiona. He wasn't around, and Fiona was long gone, using her maiden name, shacking up with Fraser and others. It wasn't until she married Cole that it started to come to light.'

'How? She's a Cole now, but if she was using her maiden name, why hadn't they found her?'

'Why, we don't know. Three million pounds. An unsecured loan. Grant used them often as he preferred not to use banks, as they required tax returns and hold of any property purchased.'

'A loan shark?'

'A lender of last resort. High interest rates if a payment is missed, a visit by a couple of thugs who would show a clenched fist if the money wasn't forthcoming. Grant was going through a difficult period. He paid what he could and then disappeared. It was not difficult for him, and the lender might have given the non-payer a beating. He wouldn't kill people but preferred to keep the heat on them.

'Grant's vanished, Fiona's name on the document, but they can't find her, and they realised that even if they did – they knew Grant's nature; they knew Fiona – Fiona wouldn't have a clue what they were talking about, and she was with Edward Fraser at the time.'

'How do you know about Fraser?' Isaac asked.

'The man's on the television. In the background, we can see Fiona. We know she wouldn't be in the audience; she could barely boil an egg. We checked on him and read that he was known for his flamboyant lifestyle and young women.'

'You contacted her?'

'No reason to. Grant had used her on the document, which she wouldn't understand even if explained. Not that she was stupid, far from it, but money was Grant's responsibility, and then Fraser, and now Cole.'

'They didn't contact you, these money lenders?'

'They came to the house. They accepted that Grant was his own man, and as I said, they were not the twist-your-arm, break-bones type of lender. High interest, stiff penalties, a smack in the face. The loan sharks you refer to are criminals. These people weren't.'

'Weren't?' Larry said. 'That infers that their modus operandi has changed.'

'Fiona wasn't that hard to find, but no one had tried for many years. The lending company had transitioned from threatening to very violent. If you didn't pay, they would take what they wanted, bleed you dry, and then take you out to sea and throw you over the side.'

'An anchor around the ankles. Melodramatic, don't you think?' Isaac said.

'Is it? Fiona gets the letter courtesy of the loan sharks. It's a demand. She's unsure what to make of it, but her husband understands. He realises that it's severe and can't be ignored.

'He advises Fiona that the money must be paid and that ignoring it would be fatal. He makes a few enquiries, discovering what it means and who they are dealing with. He phones us, not that we've spoken to him before.'

'How did he know your number?'

'Fiona had the house phone number. We've not changed it. We're Mr and Mrs Average, slightly eccentric, keep to themselves.'

'You maintained the illusion while continuing with what Grant had set up: dodgy deals, shady money lenders, and false names,' Isaac said, aware that by continuing to probe, eventually even the most stalwart talks.

'Aaron Cole never came here. He explained the situation, what he knew, what he didn't. Fiona was innocent of any crime, but he would protect her at any cost.'

'You accepted what he said?'

'We had no option. The details in the letter that Fiona received were specific. Cole had found out who they were dealing with. He stayed calm, laid out the situation, and ensured we were complicit. He figured out what we were up to, not that he had an issue, and congratulated us for our ingenuity, but he wasn't going to deal with thugs at his house threatening his wife. He wanted the money owing paid and promptly, twenty-four hours, no more.'

'You agreed. You said it was over three million pounds, but you gave Fiona two,' Larry reminded the Colsons.

'We gave the money to pay the debt and gave Fiona two extra. There was no option, and then Grayling died. That's when our troubles started.'

Chapter 20

'It's MacTavish,' Commander Goddard said as he sat in Isaac's office, in the chair that had recently been vacated by Caddick.

'Has he shown his true colours?' Isaac replied. He remembered the man, the government's former whip, who played his cards close to his chest. There had been an earlier investigation, the disappearance of a beloved soap opera actress. They had found her, people had died, and eventually, she had been run over by a car as she stepped out onto the street.

Three murders during the investigation, but only one had a murderer. The other two were hushed up under the Official Secrets Act. MacTavish knew the details, but Commander Goddard and Isaac Cook did not. And now the man was back.

'Hopefully, he's a force for good.'

Isaac couldn't be sure. The man had taken a shine to him, but MacTavish, the laird of his clan and now a lord, was not a person to accept at face value.

'He won't accept anyone unless they are willing to take the hard actions,' Goddard said.

Isaac wasn't sure if he was being given a pep talk or a belief. His former mentor was agreeable in the office, but he had been distant for over a year and pretended nothing had happened.

'And you trust MacTavish after the last time? We both know what he's capable of.'

'He saved your bacon when the woman you were sleeping with was shipped overseas.'

Isaac didn't need reminding: blonde, beautiful, a murderer, or more correctly, an assassin paid to kill by her country's secret service, and by default, the government, and by further default, Angus MacTavish.

'Caddick understands better than you, Isaac. You've got to pin your support to one flag. This is not a time to wait and see the outcome. It is too late then, and those close to MacTavish will triumph. The procrastinators will be left in the dust to grovel or rot in Challis Street.'

'And you? Holding the banner high?'

'I held Davies's banner high enough. I played the game, which you are woeful at. Competency alone will not get you what you want; it never has.'

Bridget brought in a couple of coffees. 'Good to see you, Commander,' she said.

'And you, Bridget, how are you?' Goddard replied.

'Fine, thank you. We'll be seeing more of you.'

'I hope so.'

'Will we?' Isaac said as he sipped his coffee. 'Is this a renewal, or are you planning to move? The right hand of MacTavish leads to great success.'

'It does, but don't be cynical. We went along with Davies, where there was no option. Caddick would have taken your place, but we headed him off.'

'He still made superintendent.'

'So can you. This homespun morality of yours does you no credit. It might have been fine in your parents' generation, but this is a different time. The world is changing irrevocably. You either get with the strength, or you don't. What do you need from me to convince you of the truth?'

'I want to know what's going on at New Scotland Yard. Not the rumours in the corridor, but the facts.'

'Flapping ears here. The conference room, you and me. I'll tell you the state of play.'

The two men relocated. Goddard sat at the head of the table, Isaac two seats away.

'MacTavish has set up a committee. He's still got the ear of the government and the trust of the prime minister.'

'A different prime minister, a different political party,' Isaac said.

'True, but the prime minister knows MacTavish is trustworthy and committed to doing what's right. Safe hands in a crisis.'

'Is this a crisis?'

'It is. The prime minister is astute, not an ideologue. He wants the best person, regardless. He's playing politics with his party and has MacTavish onboard behind the scenes.'

'And you?'

'Not for Davies's job. It will take another six to eight years before I get a crack at it. My position will be strategic, to head up a group to reinvigorate the Met, to make it, once again, the premier police force in the world.'

'It's not possible,' Isaac said. 'It's a changed world, as you said. A diverse population means more crime and more villainy. Davies was right with his draconian approach, even if I had reservations. People won't stand for it, and you can't drive it.'

'I'll take that as an observation, not a criticism.'

'I'm saying it as I see it. It's up to you to convince me that I'm wrong. A change of government, and then it goes back to what it was.'

'MacTavish knows that, so do I. Davies is out, and a new commissioner is in. The prime minister, whoever comes next, will ensure that all powers are given to MacTavish, and it looks good to employ a former adversary. It shows the public and the police that the government is committed, that the new commissioner and his driving committee are not there because of political affiliation, but because they are the best persons for the job.'

'It's still politics.'

'Isaac, you must eliminate this idea that everything is a conspiracy. I'm not conspiratorial but determined to make a difference. Davies's supporters will remain but will toe the line and keep their heads down.'

Isaac knew they would until they saw weakness. The Met was the same as any large company in the country. A small core of highly competent persons, a bulk of good, hardworking persons, and, at the bottom, the rats and the parasites waiting for their chance.

'Caddick?'

'He's busy making friends, but they won't be the friends he wants. Davies, for all his faults, has been an exemplary police officer. His choice of lackeys has been unfortunate. After the new commissioner is installed, they will check into those closest to the previous incumbent and either demote, transfer, or move them out of the Met.'

'Or prosecute.'

'Not prosecute. That would be akin to a witch hunt, tit for tat. Bad publicity if the media knew about it.'

'And they would. What's your position, assuming this comes to fruition.'

'Someone's got to drive the reforms.'

'A new title?'

'Assistant commissioner. I'll skip deputy.'

'You won't need six years.'

'The new commissioner will have tenure. That person will need to be there for four years at the minimum.'

'You believe that great changes can be completed in that time?'

'Some changes will be made. A new generation of police officers, a new ethics code, a change in the decline in society.'

'The first two might be possible. The third cannot. It is generational. It will take more time than you have got.'

'Not if I'm the commissioner.'

'Will you be?'

'I'm certain of it, even if I must wait a few years, regardless of MacTavish, Davies, or the government.'

Isaac was conflicted. He was a police officer, not a politician or a conspiracy theorist, and not anyone's lackey. He was his own man. His satisfaction was a job well done.

'Be careful,' Jenny said that night when Isaac told her of his meeting with Commander Goddard. 'The more he rises in the Met, the more political and slippery he will become. Don't trust him as you did when he was a chief inspector and you were a wet-behind-the-ears constable.'

Isaac knew there was wisdom in what his wife said.

***

'Your wife is still missing,' Isaac said. They were in an interview room. The interrogation was being recorded.

Aaron Cole sat upright on his chair. He had worn a suit to the police station. 'She is.'

'Are you concerned?' Larry asked.

'What do you think? Of course I am. Fiona might have her faults, but running out on me isn't one of them.'

'The damage to your yard? Fiona?'

'It depends.'

'On whether we've spoken to the Colsons or not?' Isaac said. 'We know how Fiona received the letter, the threat from the money lenders.'

'Loan sharks, don't downplay who we're dealing with here.'

'Did you pay them?'

'I put it to the Colsons and told them that if we were going to deal with the wrath of the loan sharks, then we were not going it alone. I've been used to unscrupulous persons, and there have been plenty of villains in my time. These people do not disappear until they're appeased or bled you dry.'

'Metaphorically,' Isaac said.

'I knew what it was when Fiona received the letter. I made a few checks with people I know. Their advice, deal with it.'

'Did you have the money to pay?'

'I didn't, not cash. It would have forced us to sell our house, but that would have taken time. There was also a reference to other transactions and a background on Batholomew's activity. The man was dead; no way it could be him.'

'How did you know he was dead? Legally dead, a court decided that, but physically, no one knew that for certain, least of all your wife, or is that conjecture on our part?'

'Conjecture. Fifteen years, not a word of the man. I checked when Fiona and I met but could not find anything. It made no sense for a man as active as he was.'

'But secretive,' Larry said.

'Even so, there should have been some trace of him. I discovered that before she left him, he had bought a block of flats in London and used a builder mate of mine to renovate. Paid in cash, under the table.'

'A lot of that in your business?'

'In the past. Not so easy these days. Anyway, after the letter, I did a few checks and discovered that the Colsons were loaded, not that you could tell by their lifestyle. They had been seen at a few places that Batholomew owned over the years and acted as if they were the principals, and Batholomew was the silent partner. I had an avenue to get to the man.'

'You thought he was dead. You said that before,' Isaac said. 'Keep to the truth. We become suspicious when somebody lies to us.'

'I had reason to believe him dead, but I couldn't be sure. Maybe he had done a "Howard Hughes" and locked himself in the penthouse of a block of flats he owns. I said Harold and Elizabeth Colson were active. I phoned Harold, explained the situation, and received a blatant denial.'

'You weren't buying it?'

'Not a chance. I sent Fiona around to their house. She sat there and explained the situation. Showed them what the loan sharks wanted and an extra two million for her to keep quiet. Her name was on the loan document. She was taking the heat and wanted compensation.'

'They paid up?'

'Meek and mild. Fiona reckoned they were oddballs, which proved true when Harold transferred the money to my account.'

'And you paid the loan shark and squirrelled the other two million into an offshore account.'

'My fault. I can't blame anyone else. I disputed the payout figure. The yard is their handiwork.'

'You've paid them now?'

'I have, but they want more. They knew about the extra two million.'

'Which means that the Colsons told them.'

'Hell, someone did. I can't think of anyone else, although, with that sort of money, a bank manager could be bribed.'

'Fiona?'

'She blamed me for not nipping it in the bud. She's gone. Packed a suitcase, took a hundred thousand out of our joint account and fled.'

'Has she been in contact?'

'An SMS. I didn't recognise the number, so I assume she used a burner.'

'Is she safe?'

'No idea. If she goes overseas, she would be, but that would require a passport. You can check on that, so could those after me for more money. If I could, I would join her, or not. The situation is intolerable, and the long arm of the law isn't going to help.'

***

Wendy Gladstone focused on Cheryl Hastings, whose continuing disappearance was causing concern.

In Homicide, Isaac and Larry discussed the investigation. Isaac believed that the loan sharks weren't the murderers, but they had provided the ammunition for the Coles to pressure the Colsons into submission. Larry's stance was first that Cheryl Hastings was crucial to the investigation and possibly dangerous, based on her experiences as a child; second, the Colsons were guilty by association, in that the two murders had occurred in houses they owned; third, that Grant Batholomew had not died from natural causes; and fourth, Bartholomew's life insurance would be invalidated if his body had been checked by a doctor and the death certificate had stated suicide.

Larry's belief with the third was that Grant Batholomew had had a full medical two months before the date given by the Colsons, that there was life insurance, and that Elizabeth Colson had been the beneficiary.

'The money was paid, four hundred thousand pounds,' Larry said.

'Where did this policy come from? What happens if there is no death certificate?' Isaac asked.

'I asked Bridget to see what she could find. Someone as pedantic and meticulous as Batholomew would have considered every contingency. There was no death certificate when Batholomew died, but then, after seven years, he was declared dead. The life insurance was paid at that time.'

'It was Fiona Cole who had him declared dead. Maybe she thought the money would go to her if she knew about the policy.'

'She gained access to Batholomew's primary account, but the cupboard was bare.'

'No funds?'

'A couple of hundred pounds.'

'A windfall to Elizabeth, which she might not have expected.'

'Except Fiona had the court declaration, not the Colsons. A claim on the insurance company would have had to come from Fiona.'

'Which meant she knew there was a policy. What happens if she's not the recipient?'

'Assuming the paperwork is in order, it's sent to the beneficiary, who receives a cheque.'

'I don't see how it advances the investigation,' Isaac said. 'I don't have an issue with Fiona Cole's logic. Do you?'

'She received a letter from the insurance company stating the policy number, that the money had been paid, and there would be no further correspondence. Don't you see it?'

'Explain,' Isaac said.

'Batholomew had numerous bank accounts. She knows of one. It is understandable if he was drawing from it regularly for daily use. But how does she know about the life insurance if she's not the beneficiary?'

'Point taken, although it seems minor. Do you see something I don't?'

'Fiona must know where the life insurance money went. She's not the person to let sleeping dogs lie. She must have confronted the Colsons, but neither she nor the Colsons mentioned it.'

'Are you suggesting they paid her off back then? Did Fiona threaten to go to the police to find out where Batholomew was? Did Fiona suspect or know? And if she did, why did she keep quiet? Are we attributing actions to the woman that would show her malevolence, deceitfulness, and probable criminality?'

'I think we are,' Larry said.

Chapter 21

Homicide did not need Commander Goddard to keep them posted on the machinations in New Scotland Yard. Changing the commissioner of the Metropolitan Police was big news, exacerbated by Alwyn Davies's public relations campaign and his willingness to stand in front of a microphone and a camera and give his views on the current state of crime and criminal investigation in London and throughout the country.

To Isaac, he was idiosyncratic and not easily defined. Davies stood for law and order, the right of the individual to better himself, and he had done a lot to ensure new officers were welcomed into the force and those graduating from the police academy got to shake his hand as they passed out. Yet, he surrounded himself with stooges who worshipped at his feet.

Machiavellian, Isaac knew, although the rank and file never felt the force of the man's invective or sleight of hand, he reserved that for those who threatened him or did not prostrate themselves at the mention of his name.

Richard Goddard had been one of those. Goddard's mentor had been the previous commander, but he was dead. A moving ceremony at the cathedral, where a police guard stood outside as his coffin passed. Davies attended and gave a moving eulogy on how the late commissioner had shaped the force into what it was and his pride when he became his successor. In the congregation, Isaac imagined Davies choking on the saccharine words.

If he had been in Davies's office when the man met with his team, he would have realised that saccharine came nowhere near the truth.

Around Davies, a core group of police officers would assist him in defending his position. Caddick at his right hand. Also present was Assistant Deputy Commissioner Alfie Wigg, a plain-speaking man in his fifties, balding, carrying ten kilos more than he should, who hailed from Newcastle, in the north-east. Alongside him, on the other side of Davies's desk, Chief Superintendent Mary Ayton, her dulcet voice belying her vicious trait, the ability to bring a female officer to tears or to make a burly constable quiver at the knees. Driven to succeed in a man's world, she had risen through the ranks rapidly, even faster than Isaac when he had been in favour.

One more person made up the group. Deputy Commissioner Ian Jephson is the most formidable of those who sided with Davies. A bear of a man, well over six foot, with a bellowing voice. He was neither charismatic nor likeable, and his promotions had come through tough policing and more than one commendation for dealing with violent criminals.

Larry and Isaac were not the only police officers shot in the line of duty; Jephson had taken a bullet to the stomach, another that had grazed his skull, and another in the leg, the reason he walked with a limp. It had been Jephson who arrested five men who had broken into a jeweller's and stolen eight million pounds in uncut diamonds; who, when confronted by a terrorist after the zealot had killed four with a knife, had grabbed the man, twisted the knife away, and broken his neck. The subsequent inquest had cleared him of all blame, and he had received a medal for bravery from a grateful monarch.

'Bloody well-deserved,' he had said outside the palace. 'Those bastards deserve to die.' Jephson did not care for people, only power. Once he had rid the Met of Davies, a man he despised, the commissioner's position was his. But then, he despised everyone other than his wife of forty years.

Jephson was one of the names that Goddard had mentioned as a possible successor.

'Your defence, Commissioner?' Chief Superintendent Mary Ayton asked. She wanted to be the top dog, but she knew that for a woman to succeed, she would need a flawless record, not a record in Human Resources that had registered complaints against her from her staff or ex-staff. Nobody lasted long if they criticised or complained. She hated Davies passionately, although she wasn't about to say it.

Davies regarded her as competent and determined and knew she could not be trusted. He knew his support base was weak, but he had had worse odds before.

'We take down MacTavish,' Davies said.

'Lord, former government whip, laird of his clan. A tough call,' Wigg said.

'That's why we're here, Alfie. You people are the best.'

'But someone as powerful as MacTavish?' Mary Ayton said. 'Do we have some dirt on him?'

'MacTavish wants to make the Met into a home for the inept. Over my dead body,' Davies said. 'I've known the man for a long time. He's getting old and doesn't have the influence or bark he once had. We can deal with him.'

'The government?'

'They're not even the same party, diametrically opposed to him, but the prime minister is weak as water. A lap dog to MacTavish.'

'You need to split them, throw in an aspersion, and sow dissent,' Jephson said but thought that Davies had lost it. Once, the man would have stood his ground and taken on all comers, but now he needed a team to do the dirty work for him.

Jephson's concern was strengthening his position. He knew he was sitting on the fence, and he knew the metal of the commissioner. The man was a fighter and wouldn't hesitate to alienate, sideline, and destroy anyone who got in his way. He was determined not to be one of those.

Out of his depth with the heavy hitters in the office, Caddick was not a man who kept quiet. He had something to say, and not even Jephson would interrupt, knowing that Davies and Caddick had a history stretching back years.

Caddick was the person Davies trusted, and for good reason. Alfie Wigg was younger than Ian Jephson by six years. Wigg was one rank below Jephson but in good health, whereas, as was known in New Scotland Yard, Jephson was a heavy smoker and an even heavier drinker. Not that either impaired his policing, but the ruddy face and the extended belly, coupled with a hoarse cough in the morning until he had had his early-morning hit of coffee, were clear indications of poor health and early death.

Commissioners of the Met invariably lasted more than five years, whereas Jephson looks like he was at death's door.

Wigg, by contrast, was a young fifty who ran five miles daily, didn't drink or smoke, had been married to the same woman for over thirty years, and was always smartly turned out in his uniform. He would be the more palatable choice for the top job, But how? He wasn't sure, and he, like Jephson, was playing a wait-and-see game.

Chief Superintendent Mary Ayton, in her late forties, had been married twice. She had two children in their twenties, who were both a credit to her. She had earned her rank through good management, although she had also gained enemies along the way as she had weeded out more than a few pieces of deadwood in the Met. For now, she realised that loyalty to the leader was paramount and necessary.

'Destroy MacTavish's power base,' Caddick said.

'How do you intend to do that?' Mary Ayton asked.

'Divide and conquer.'

'Divide who? MacTavish has the support of the prime minister.'

'But not his party, and if there's an election, win or lose, we discredit MacTavish and his people,' Davies said. 'Even so, if we agree with Caddick, how can we change the situation?'

'Change the prime minister. MacTavish does not belong to his party or sit in parliament but in the House of Lords,' Caddick said.

'Caddick's right, although with a change of government, we need to ensure support there,' Wigg said.

'A commissioner is appointed by the King on the recommendation of the home secretary.'

'Who doesn't make that recommendation without the prime minister's approval.'

'We all know the fool's going to lose the next election. Either another election and soon, or we change out the prime minister and the home secretary,' Davies said.

It was a dangerous strategy, and none of those in the office who reported to the commissioner was enthusiastic about the proposal, realising that if it backfired, there would be a cleansing of the Met's old guard and replacement with a new, apart from Caddick.

He knew where his future lay, not dealing with Ayton, who despised him, or Wigg, who knew him for what he was, and not with Jephson. The man had collared him in the corridor before the meeting and laid out the facts. 'Caddick, be very careful. There'll be no place for you in what I envisage for New Scotland Yard.'

'Caddick,' Davies said, 'it's your idea. It has merit, but how? MacTavish's influence is regarded across the political divide as incorruptible and decent. Taking down a prime minister is easier said than done.'

'A three-pronged attack. Inveigle your way into MacTavish's inner sanctum, sow dissent in the rank and file of the PM's party.'

'The third?' Jephson asked. 'Caddick, let's hear it, give us facts.'

'They wouldn't dare remove the commissioner if crime escalated in the city, and the Met showed their reinforced resolve to deal with it.'

'We've been there before,' Mary Ayton said.

'I didn't say draconian.'

'Unacceptable,' Davies said. 'What you're suggesting is against everything I stand for.'

The others in the office said no more. The meeting concluded with no clear strategy, except for each to prepare a strategy document and to reconvene in one week.

'Caddick, remain,' Davies said as the others filed out.

With the door closed and Caddick sitting down, Davies spoke. 'What did you have in mind?'

'I thought you were against it.'

'Last resort, the final breath of a dying man. The other three support me now, but they will jump ship when the end is inevitable. You, however, I trust.'

'Always,' Caddick said.

'Seth, don't say something you don't mean. You've been promoted above your rank. Without me, you would be flayed, demoted, thrown out of the force, or sent somewhere so far away that you'd be lucky to see daylight for six months. How about training the police in Iraq? Now, what's the idea?'

'If the threat against you is so great, and there is a crime of such magnitude that only you can deal with, they will be forced to reconsider.'

'And I emerge as the hero, on a white horse and in shining armour. You couldn't organise that, even if you wanted to, and I certainly couldn't agree.'

'But you will. You'll not relinquish your post that easily, and we both know it.'

'Caddick, I've underestimated you. You're more devious than I thought possible. Deaths?'

'Almost certainly.'

'Persons that don't concern us?'

'Concern or don't concern. Does it matter?'

'Goddard's working with MacTavish.'

'Goddard is friendly with DCI Cook again.'

'Forget them, focus on MacTavish. Any dirt on him that could stick?'

'There is a folder. Can you get to it?'

'It depends how deep it is.'

'What I suggest will be the last resort,' Caddick said. 'I'll send you a case file. Read it carefully. My information is sketchy. We need to fill in the blanks.'

***

For five days, Caddick did not appear in Homicide. Isaac thought it suspicious but was thankful. There had been developments. Fiona Cole had been found.

With a respite from searching for Cheryl Hastings, Wendy had used Bridget to search Grant Batholomew's known aliases. A couple had been used by the Colsons, and a third had not. A small hotel on the south coast, an easy drive from London. The weather was mild for the time of year; Fiona was sitting in the sun on the hotel balcony.

'Why?' Wendy asked.

'Have you spoken to Aaron?'

'We have. Hiding out here won't do you much good. If these people want to find you, they will, and you've left your husband to deal with them.'

'It was Aaron; he thought he could be smart. These people are not in the building trade. They are not interested in the price of concrete. Hard cash, stick to the agreement, and be thankful if you get out with your shirt still on. Then Aaron wants to dispute the payment, which will go up by the day. We had the money, we could have paid them off, even given them the two million, but, oh no, not Aaron.'

'You could not guarantee they would have left alone even if you gave them what they wanted. When Grant borrowed the money, they could have been little men in back offices. But now, the country is infested with rogues from the four corners of the planet. English gentility and a sense of fair play have gone out the window.'

'You might be right, and Aaron's been a good man.'

'You've never had children?'

'When I was with Grant, I thought about it, but since then, no. I never saw my life as anything other than a succession of men after Grant, with the highs and then the lows. I thought it was never stable enough for children. I did love Grant, not initially, as I was desperate, but he grew on me, and then, once he had sated his lust, he turned away. I never thought him highly sexed, more of a roll on, roll off lover.'

'Marriage is more than sex. Companionship is important, and so is trust.'

'I gave him both, but he changed. It was subtle. He started checking how much I was spending. He would return clothes I'd bought and ensure the wine in the house didn't cost more than a certain price.'

'Wise money management,' Wendy said.

'He did not tell me that, not that I would have been interested. I was young. It seemed important to look good.'

'And he was forced to deal with unscrupulous people to fund his ventures and to satisfy your whims. Have you thought he might have wanted you to stay but didn't know how or what to say? Introvert, unable to express his emotions or to talk to you.'

'The Colsons, they killed him, I'm sure of it.'

'How? We believe it's possible, apart from Elizabeth's affection for her brother.'

'Affection, sure, they were unbelievably close. It doesn't mean they didn't kill him.'

'Without proof, what can we do?'

'I have proof,' Fiona said. 'In Sevenoaks.'

Wendy phoned Isaac, updated him about what she had been told, and that she was driving back to Sevenoaks to the bank where the Coles had an account.

Fiona read the letter she retrieved from a safety deposit box.

Dear Fiona,

It has been some months since we corresponded. I realise you are with Edward Fraser, so I have your address. I need to let you know that my health is not good, and I might not survive for more than a few months.

I do not need sympathy, nor do I want you to come and see me. I will make a provision for you after I die. Legally, I do not have to, but I was as much to blame for our marriage breakdown as you were.

On my death, my assets will be apportioned between you and my sister. She will receive the majority, but you will receive a substantial amount. Do not worry about how much; it will allow you to live without financial worries.

This money will not be in cash but in trust. Money will be drawn monthly, and any extraneous expenses must be approved by a solicitor I have appointed. You will receive his name in a subsequent letter.

If you need to purchase a car or a house, those requests will be approved subject to certain checks on the value and the legality.

'How can he trust a solicitor if he's dead?' Wendy asked.

'I never received the name of the solicitor. What could I do? I'm a dunce with money, relying on the men in my life to deal with it. Aaron's always been generous, but I'm not as extravagant as I was with Grant.'

'You've left him in the lurch.'

'I was angry and frightened.'

'The letter, is there more?'

Fiona continued.

I've two in mind for the solicitor, but I've not decided which will best serve my purposes and yours.

Needless to say, I do not have explicit trust in Harold, Elizabeth's husband, but decisions have to be made. In the next week, I should have finalised all to our satisfaction.

Do not look for me at where we used to live or at Elizabeth's. I will be at neither.'

'It sounds fine', Wendy said.

'Grant didn't write it.'

'Are you sure?'

'Grant would never start a letter with "Dear", not even with me. Nor would he have trusted a solicitor. He abhorred them. It would only be Elizabeth and Harold that he trusted. The letter says that he has reservations about him. He did not. He thought he was a dullard but a good match for Elizabeth. Also, the letter's typed. Grant preferred handwritten, and he rarely used a computer.'

'And you've not mentioned this since before Grant died? When did he die? Does this letter tell you?'

'I kept the letter. It had to be the Colsons who wrote it. I can't be sure whether it was before Grant died or after, but if you reckon he's been dead for fifteen years, then the letter dates from that period.'

'Did you contact the Colsons?'

'Never. The past was behind me, I didn't want to know, and I didn't believe the letter.'

Chapter 22

The pathologist who had conducted the autopsy reiterated what he had said before. 'Fifteen years, give or take a year. Grant Batholomew, adult male. No physical injuries, no bone breakage, no body trauma due to a bullet or a knife. If you want me to prove it's murder, I can't.'

Isaac had to accept the man's expertise. The murder of Batholomew, if it had occurred, would not be solved by anything other than a confession from the Colsons, and that was unlikely.

Fiona Cole could not be discounted for the murder of Sorell, but why would she kill him? It made no sense. By her own admission, she was not proactive, and her life, if pleasant and she had enough money and a social life, was fine.

Wendy wasn't convinced by the woman's account of the letter from Grant and her insistence that it was a fake. It was dated fifteen years previously, and it tallied with the timing of the burial of the body.

Even if Fiona thought it was fake, she had proven that contacting the Colsons wasn't an issue.

Isaac visited the scene of the first murder. The cellar had been cleaned and painted, and the house was for sale.

The estate agent who was present when he visited was circumspect. 'I'll try, but who wants to buy a house after what happened here?'

Isaac knew it would sell at the right price, and the Colsons were flexible. He didn't offer a comment, and if he hadn't shown his warrant card, the murder would not have been mentioned, and the typical spiel would have been uttered from the woman's mouth: great potential, ideal family home, a school within walking distance, make a bundle if you fix the décor, imagine what this room would look like with new curtains.

Isaac hoped that potential purchasers had a good solicitor who would conduct checks on the property and that they would talk to the neighbours.

The Colsons, who had relocated to Scotland, were annoyed when Isaac and Wendy spoke to them on a video hookup.

'Fiona, always trouble,' Elizabeth said.

'Maybe she is,' Wendy replied. 'However, she had a letter that purported to come from Grant. Forensics have checked it and confirmed. The paper is from an A4 printer and can be dated to around the time Grant died.'

'We didn't send it. Besides, they were divorced. Why would he have cared about her? After all, she moved out on him.'

'Did she?' Isaac asked, 'Or was she driven out? Did you have leverage over her, knew something that Grant didn't?'

'Such as? Do you think Edward Fraser was not around before she left? Ask him about the letter? He could have sent it.'

Isaac ended the video call and turned to Wendy. 'Cheryl Hastings, find her. Drag her parents into Challis Street if you must. This round-robin of everyone accusing each other is going nowhere.'

'Need help?' Caddick said as he stuck his head around the corner.

'Caddick, bugger off. We don't need you now, never will.'

'You've not been keeping your ear to the ground. That's obvious.'

'What's happened?'

'The commissioner's fighting back. MacTavish's out on a limb.'

Isaac didn't know or care. Frustrated with the situation, he had lost his temper. He had shouted at Caddick the second time; he could have hit him.

The man beat a retreat. Isaac phoned Commander Goddard.

***

Wendy threatened a search warrant. The Hastings complained, phoned their local member of parliament, and pleaded with Wendy to show compassion and how much they respected her. All to no avail.

Wendy drove to Oxford. The door to the Hastings' home opened, and Wendy entered. The search warrant was not used.

'How long?' Wendy asked.

'We didn't see her for eleven days,' Alan Hastings said. 'Then she knocked on the door. We've cleaned her up the best we could.'

Wendy could see why they had protected their daughter. In the corner of a bedroom, curled up like a baby, the body of an adult female with a child's mind. Cheryl Hastings had suffered a complete relapse, and her speech was garbled.

'She needs care, not the care you can give her,' Wendy said.

'We know best,' Adriana Hastings said.

'You don't. Compassion might have been right when she was a child, but now she's an adult. This could be regressive, and nothing you can do will help.'

Wendy made the call. An ambulance appeared within the hour. As the vehicle pulled away, Cheryl lifted her head from the stretcher. 'I did it,' she said.

'Did what?'

'I killed Barry.'

'Why?'

'I caught him with another woman.'

'Do you know who it was?'

'From Ukraine. She phoned me, and I told her to go to the house and ask for Barry.'

'She was in the room?'

'I was angry, hit her hard with my fist. Then I killed Barry. I didn't want to, but I couldn't help myself.'

'Fiona Cole, did you see her?'

'Only the Ukrainian woman.'

'We knew,' Adriana Hastings said.
'It was your duty to tell us,' Wendy replied.
'It wasn't. It's why we never had pets.'
'Because if Cheryl had a relapse, she would kill them.'
'Not only kill but mutilate,' Alan Hastings said.
Wendy took hold of Cheryl's hand. 'David Grayling?'
'It wasn't me.'

It was a confession. Whether the woman would be able to write and sign it was uncertain. Regardless, and even if her parents attempted to avoid the inevitable, she would be confined to a high-security psychiatric hospital if sentenced for the murder.

Wendy had hoped for a different outcome, but as with the young girl in Sheffield, Cheryl's fate was predetermined by a man many years before.

***

Attempts to find Oksana Akimova proved unsuccessful. Wendy thought it was because the woman was new in the country, seeking work, or trafficked, and that she had paid the cost of staying at the house in kind rather than in cash. Payment of rent by sexual favours was not unknown in the country.

'We have to assume that Cheryl Hastings is telling the truth,' Isaac said. 'But why did the other woman stay?'

'You don't understand, DCI,' Wendy said. 'She did not sleep with Sorell or come to this country out of want but due to desperation. She was neither a criminal nor a bad person, just trying to survive. Also, delayed shock from what she saw, able to stay rational when we interviewed her.'

'And after?'

'I can't bear to think about it. Cheryl was enough for me.'

'We assume that Fiona Cole saw the Ukrainian woman?'

'It doesn't explain the perfume. Cheryl discovers Barry in bed with Oksana Akimova. She kills one and hits the other. Akimova revives, grabs her clothes on the other side of the room, and leaves. She has no blood on her, which seems unlikely. Cheryl leaves the house and disappears, not seeing Fiona but smelling her. This means Fiona is in the house before Cheryl and leaves soon after, but how do they avoid each other? Cheryl would have been confused after killing Barry, or maybe she didn't register. She leaves, no blood on her either.'

'It depends if she used a small knife or a long blade.'

'It was from the kitchen. It wasn't that long. She could have used some of Akimova's clothes to clean herself. The woman was out on the street, dressed in a flimsy dress.'

'You didn't check her belongings?' Isaac asked.

'We had a dead body in the house, and she had phoned it in. She gave a statement. We took her phone number and address in London. There was no reason to detain her; besides, we were occupied in the house. It was clear she wasn't the murderer, and I was organising a search of the area.'

'You are convinced it was Cheryl Hastings who killed Sorell?'

'I've always regarded her as a suspect. Her background damned her.'

'Yet you gave her leeway.'

'There was no evidence and no proof that she had ever been violent. It was her that phoned to tell us to check the cellar.'

'Anonymously, the next day,' Isaac said. He wasn't sure whether his sergeant had acted correctly or emotion had played a part. 'You could have held the Ukrainian woman, but you are right. She's probably had enough of being hassled, and we had nothing on her. Even so, I believe we erred. She could have been the killer. We wouldn't have known.'

'We would have. Her fingerprints were not on the knife, and according to Fiona Cole, the woman was a short distance from Sorell. If she was trafficked, prostituted, or illegal in the country, that might be grounds for deportation. She could have hoodwinked us.'

'We know that Cheryl smelled the perfume, and Fiona saw Sorell dead and Akimova lying nearby.'

'Which means that Fiona Cole was in the house when Sorell was murdered. She must have heard, even if she didn't see it.'

'And left before Akimova came to, grabbed her clothes, dressed, and then phoned us.'

'Tight on timing. How did Fiona get away unless she went next door?'

Isaac could see flaws in his sergeant's logic. If a frenzied attack, the murderer would have wildly stabbed the man, and there was a probability that the killer would leave fingerprints. If the murder had been calculated and calmly implemented, then the killer would have had their hand on the knife handle and not on the body. Blood splattering might have occurred, but the murderer would have effectively been unmarked.

There seemed little doubt that Cheryl Hastings's confession would be accepted along with the evidence, although Isaac knew that if Harriet Gordon was acting as the defence barrister in her murder trial, and given the evidence they had, Cheryl Hastings could be found not guilty.

He was keenly aware that if Caddick read through the reports of the murder investigation and if he was smart enough, he might see clear evidence of poorly executed police procedures.

Isaac hoped the man was as incompetent as he thought he was.

***

Wendy, suitably chastised, even though Isaac hadn't directly accused her of negligence, took it upon herself to remedy the situation. She enlisted Bridget, who spent five hours that evening combing the city on her computer for Oksana Akimova. If the woman was legally in the country and not selling herself to men, it should be possible to find her.

Bridget had proven the first, but not the second. She focused on beauty salons, as the woman had said that she was a beautician looking for work in London and that, due to the situation in her homeland, Oksana Akimova had been given refugee status.

Wendy phoned salons close to Notting Hill, where the woman had said she wanted to work, but with no success. Bridget thought there was an easier way. If the woman was working and paying taxes, she would find her name on a database.

'Beauty Essence, 24 Heath Street, Hampstead,' Bridget said.

Wendy left the office and drove to the beauty salon. A young woman at reception asked, 'Do you have an appointment?'

'Could I have one for tomorrow afternoon?'

She did not want a manicure or a massage, but she could see Oksana at the back of the salon. The woman was busy, and Wendy did not want to flash her warrant card, which would have caused embarrassment to the woman and possibly dismissal. People's reaction to a murder investigation, even if the person was a witness, would be to raise questions, and scandal by association was not something the establishment might want to deal with.

Wendy took a seat in a coffee shop across the road and waited. After ninety minutes, she saw Oksana Akimova leave the salon and walk down the road.

'Oksana,' Wendy shouted.

The woman turned her head.

'Sergeant Gladstone, Homicide, Challis Street. If you've got a moment?'

'Fifteen minutes, but why?'

'We need to understand the events when Sorell died. You were there. We have the person responsible, but another person was in the house that day.'

'I was there. I saw him dead.'

'You were calm.'

'From where I had come from? People have died, even my brother. Our house in Kharkiv was hit by a rocket. Death is only too common.'

'We have a confession. Would you come back to the house for a reenactment?'
'If I must.'
'It's important.'
'When?'
'Sunday. Are you working?'
'No.'
'Your phone doesn't work, any reason?'
'I got an account with Vodafone, a number change.'
Wendy took the number and the address where the woman lived. She would pick her up at eight in the morning on Sunday. She phoned Nadia Hussain to ask if she would put in extra time.

For two and a half hours, Wendy lingered in the area. And then Nadia took over. Oksana left the salon at seven in the evening, hopping on a bus. Nadia jumped on the same bus and flashed her warrant card at the bus driver. He nodded.

Five stops later, Oksana got off the bus and walked for ten minutes before entering a terraced house. It was the same address that she had given Wendy. It didn't mean that she would stay.

Nadia called for backup. Jim Drayton arrived, and the two settled in for the night in his car. Wendy phoned every hour but received the same answer: 'Nothing. We know she's there. Every so often, she looks out of the window.'

At three twenty in the morning, Oksana Akimova left the building. She was carrying a small suitcase. Nadia and Drayton had been forewarned of the possibility. Nadia followed on foot, and Drayton drove the car, remaining far behind. He didn't need to see Nadia, as she had a GPS tracker in her pocket. She was also wired for sound, and the two constantly communicated.

At Hampstead Railway Station, Oksana took a train. Nadia maintained the pursuit. After changing trains twice, Oksana took a taxi. Nadia quickly put a magnetic tracker on the rear of the vehicle. Jim Drayton drew up alongside Nadia, and the two took off in pursuit. They had the taxi's registration number.

Wendy, who had had a restless night, kept in contact with the two constables. Once, she would have followed a suspect, but Oksana knew her, and a long night travelling across the city in pursuit wasn't something she could manage now.

It was six fifteen before Wendy arrived at Oksana Akimova's current location. In front of her, an imposing block of flats, circa 1950s, austere and foreboding. Nadia was asleep as she and Jim Drayton took turns to watch where the woman had entered.

Wendy got in the car's back seat, causing Nadia to wake up. 'Sorry about that,' she said.

'No need to be,' Wendy replied. 'Did you?'

'Just before she got in the taxi, I slipped it into a bag over her shoulder.'

Wendy phoned for backup and then phoned her DCI. 'Oksana Akimova's done a runner,' she said.

Half asleep, Isaac struggled to understand what he was being told. Alongside him, Jenny continued to sleep. He got out of bed, rubbed his eyes and entered another room.

'Run that past me again,' he said.

'Oksana Akimova, the Ukrainian woman that you spoke to. I've found her. She was working in Hampstead, living in the area, and paying her taxes.'

'At six in the morning?'

'Yesterday, late in the afternoon. Constables Hussain and Drayton have spent the night keeping a watch on her. She did a runner just after three this morning. They followed.'

'Are you certain she's running?'

'It's mighty suspicious. I'm bringing her into the station. I told her yesterday afternoon about the reenactment on Sunday. She agreed, and then she disappeared.'

'You've tried to phone her?'

'Not yet. I will in the next fifteen minutes.'

***

A long way north of London, early in the morning, another phone rang. Not that of a police officer, but a lord.

'What is it?' MacTavish said. He was in his late seventies, in poor health, and under doctor's orders to exercise more, to drink less, and not to gorge on fatty food. He chose to ignore the directives.

Sitting in his bed, he realised that the doctor might be right. He felt dreadful, and the smell of whisky was on his breath. There had been a meeting of the clan the previous night, and he, as the laird, could not claim lousy health as a reason not to down his whisky with every toast, nor could he decline to eat the venison and grouse and have a double helping of dessert. After all, he had always been a larger-than-life character who commanded respect due to his bearing and position.

'Davies is up to something,' the voice said.

'At this time of the morning?'

'He's in his office. He's been there since four this morning.'

'On his own?'

'Just him. Davies doesn't come in early unless it's vital.'

'Unless you've got an ear in the room, it doesn't help us, does it?'

'Whatever Davies does, it will be dramatic.'

'Thank you, Chief Superintendent. Keep me posted,' MacTavish said. He knew who his money was on to take over from Davies.

Mary Ayton knew she was playing a dangerous game. She knew which side she preferred but didn't know who would emerge victorious. And that MacTavish, the master manipulator who was the driving force behind removing Davies, was not the government, the prime minister, or the home secretary, and it would take some time to remove the commissioner.

She made another phone call. 'Be prepared,' she said. 'Davies is up to something. I don't know what.'

'Thank you,' Richard Goddard said. 'Whatever it is, it will be unexpected and dramatic.' There was no more anyone could do except wait and see.

***

Nadia stayed in the car. Wendy and Jim Drayton took the elevator in the block of flats. The muted signal inside the metal construction of the elevator meant they had to stop every couple of floors for the doors to open to allow the GPS tracker to get a clear signal.

Eventually, they locked onto a flat on the thirteenth floor. Wendy made a phone call.

'Yes,' a woman replied in accented English.

'Oksana, it's Wendy Gladstone. Where are you?'

'In bed, at home.'

'I suggest you open the door. We're outside the flat.'

There was no concern about the woman absconding again. There was no exit for her, and Wendy and Drayton stood outside.

The door opened. Wendy and Drayton entered. 'A lot of explaining to do,' Wendy said.

'You'd not understand,' Oksana said.

'Who else is here?'

Another woman appeared from one of the bedrooms. She did not speak English, and Oksana translated for her. 'Oksana is my friend. She asked me for help with a room for the night.'

Wendy took a seat. 'Oksana, tell your friend to make tea for us.' She turned to Drayton. 'Ask Nadia to come up. I don't want the women feeling intimidated by your presence.'

Drayton understood that the friend might be in the country illegally. He drank a cup of tea before Nadia arrived and then left. One of the additional officers Wendy had called for stood outside the apartment.

'Is your friend an illegal?' Wendy asked. 'Oksana, don't lie. We will check.'

'She has applied for refugee status. She came to England as a tourist, and the war started back home.'

'Proof?' Nadia said. 'I know the process,' she said to Wendy.

'Constable Hussain's right. Does she have proof?'

The friend went to the kitchen, opened a door, took out an envelope and gave it to Wendy.

'Nadia, you check,' Wendy said as she gave her the envelope.

'This flat?' Wendy asked.

'Mariana is allowed to stay here. While her status is being processed, the local council has found housing for her.'

'On her own?'

'There are two more women, but they are not here now.'

'The paperwork's in order,' Nadia said. 'You do realise?'

'I do,' Wendy said. 'Oksana, did you do what Mariana and, no doubt, her two flatmates are doing?'

'I was granted refugee status before I arrived in England. I spoke English, I had a skill.'

'Then why were you at the house with Sorell and Cheryl Hastings?'

'We are all vulnerable. You have not only let in refugees; you've let in the criminal gangs and the traffickers.'

'You've not answered my question,' Wendy reminded her.

'I have. Mariana must do what is necessary. I did not.'

'You moved into the house; you had sexual intercourse with Barry Sorell instead of paying the rent.'

'I paid the rent.'

'How?'

Oksana handed over her phone after she had brought up her bank account. 'You can see the deduction from my account. You can see who it was paid to,' she said.

'It doesn't show the name, but I recognise the account. It's Cheryl Hastings,' Wendy said. 'Okay, we have to give you the

219

benefit of the doubt, and you did answer your phone. It doesn't explain why you are here.'

'I move often, speak English, and understand how my country's women are treated in London. If I told the police, you would arrest some of the people involved in trafficking women.'

'But you won't,' Wendy said.

'I don't want to be involved. I will not testify in court or make myself more visible than I am.'

'If you told us what you know, we could investigate.'

'And in the meantime, I have a family in my country. They are more important to me than finding a murderer. I received a phone call last night, telling me to be careful and that I had been seen talking to a police officer.'

Wendy knew the criminals could always identify authority figures and persons who threatened them. Oksana's story was plausible, although Wendy could not be sure if it was true. And if it was, what action should they take? Had Homicide uncovered persons involved in sex trafficking? What should they do? It was out of her understanding. She needed advice. She phoned the only person she could trust.

Isaac listened carefully and spoke to Oksana. She handed the phone back to Wendy.

'She received a message, correct?'

'That's what she said.'

'Scan the messages and the phone calls on the phone, and send them to Bridget.'

Catch 22. Either they left Oksana with Mariana, allowing them to vanish, or Homicide took them to the police station. Both options were flawed, and if Oksana had been observed in Hampstead, there was no reason she hadn't been followed, and the people watching her knew where she was and that the police were with her.

Wendy outlined her concerns. Isaac offered to give them twenty-four-hour protection. However, they both knew that if what Oksana was saying was true, then those they were protecting them from would not have any compunction about killing a police officer, nor would they have qualms about killing the two Ukrainians, either with a bullet or slow torture while they extracted what Oksana and, to a lesser degree, Mariana knew.

Isaac made the decision. 'Bring them to Challis Street.'

When told by Oksana, Mariana reacted severely and refused to leave the flat. Oksana accepted her fate. 'I've got the day off,' she said.

Wendy felt uneasy about Oksana, just as Larry did with Fiona Cole. She hoped she was wrong.

Mariana Belousova sat in the interview room at Challis Street with a translator. Oksana had been translating at the flat, but she could have been giving her interpretation of what her friend was saying or something totally different.

Mariana was confirmed as having the correct documentation to remain in London. Also, the flat belonged to the council, and three women lived there. Mariana had supplied the names, but they could be false, as Mariana's could be.

If involved in crime, Oksana Akimova appeared to be the more credible or the smartest, and proficient English would have to be a bonus. Was Oksana more than a friend but an employer? The beauty salon lent her credibility and provided a good cover.

After all, Harold Colson prepared tax returns at home, even though he and his wife had substantial assets and money.

However, Oksana Akimova's activities were not the primary concern of Homicide: murder was.

Chapter 23

After five days under observation at the hospital, Cheryl Hastings started to talk coherently. She wanted to see Wendy.

Wendy arrived at the hospital at ten in the morning. She had intended to be there thirty minutes earlier, but there had been a protest blocking the road, which the police dealt with promptly, and then an accident when a car back-ended a truck. She could sense a change in the city in that the police were uncharacteristically prompt in clearing the road, using a taser on one protester and a headlock on another. Softly, softly, it wasn't.

She thought it might be part of Davies's fightback, not the draconian measures he had employed before, but tougher than when he had been forced to back off. The car accident she put down to impatience and anger.

In Cheryl Hastings' room, there was a big bunch of flowers. The room was bright and pleasant, although outside, there was a police officer, and a bolted door was past him at the end of the corridor. It wasn't prison, nor was it a high-security psychiatric hospital, but it was not a place that the woman could escape from.

'How are you?' Wendy asked.

'Fine.'

Wendy knew that fine was not a description she would have used. The changes in the woman, her impassiveness when confronted with violent death, her confession in the back of an ambulance, and her parents' corroboration were clear signs of internal trauma.

'Cheryl, you confessed to a murder. I need to know the full story.'

Regardless of the woman's confession and the evidence pointed towards that conclusion, certain anomalies needed to be resolved. Her doctor had warned against prolonged questioning, and her parents, who were outside the room, were now defending their daughter's actions but not claiming that she was innocent.

'I don't know what I said.'

'You disappeared, and then you returned in a dishevelled state. Your parents cover for you, which is understandable. But it's your boyfriend who's dead. What do you feel?'

'Sad.'

'You rented a room to Oksana Akimova. Is that correct?'

'She phoned and gave me her credit card details. She was in bed with Barry.'

'Are you certain? After all, you hadn't met her. How could you be sure it was her?'

'It had to be her. Who else could it be?'

'The perfume. You remember that?'

'I do.'

'What if I tell you it belonged to Grant Batholomew's former wife and that she was in the house with you?'

'I never met her. I wouldn't know her any more than I would Oksana.'

'Oksana is in her twenties. She is blonde and slim. Batholomew's widow is in her forties. She's brunette but could have been blonde. Older than the Ukrainian woman and not as slim.'

'How could I tell? And what would the older woman want with Barry?'

'It's an interesting question for which I don't have an answer. It would explain the smell of the perfume. Oksana Akimova has never admitted to being in the room with Sorell, only to discovering the body. Fiona Cole saw a woman in the room with him. You've admitted to hitting the woman, but you weren't capable of looking at her. You don't know who it was.'

'What would you have done? Would you have sat down with them and discussed the matter. I was wrong, I reacted. I don't know who the woman was, but I know Barry.'

'You slept with Grayling and admitted that you would not have been surprised if Barry slept with another woman. According to Sorell and you, you had moved out.'

'Not for long, just a few days. Barry's not a man that women lust after, but he was decent and good to me. I wanted to be with him, but I couldn't, not long term.'

'Because of your childhood?'

'Because I'm mad. Do you think I can ever forget?'

'No, but Barry Sorell's dead. Why did you admit to killing him?'

'I did kill him, and I did hit that woman. I know when I'm rational and sane. And when I'm not, I know I can be capable of terrible deeds.'

'Including burglary with a former boyfriend?'

'That and more.'

'Why are you telling me this?'

'I can sense that I'm getting worse. I need professional help. My parents mean well, and you have been great to me, but I know that others will suffer because of me.'

'Including the woman who was with Barry?'

'When I'm crazy, I can turn in an instant. Crazy, I have no fear. I know the guilt of what happened to Barry, and it hurts.'

***

Further checks of Mariana Belousova revealed that her documents were expertly forged.

Homicide believed she had been trafficked. The two other women sharing the flat with her did not return that night and were not seen again. Oksana Akimova was legally in the country, there was no record of prostitution, and she had a degree in English from the Taras Shevchenko National University of Kyiv in Ukraine.

It still didn't explain why she would have moved from Hampstead, out of fear, to a place that would be known by criminal elements.

Mariana Belousova would be held in custody pending a decision on her status in the United Kingdom. Isaac believed she would receive permission to stay. Her country was at war. She had come to London as a victim.

Oksana Akimova was more complex.

'We still have a timing issue,' Isaac said in the interview room. Wendy had joined him as she knew more about the woman and Cheryl Hastings.

'I gave my evidence. I phoned the police.'

'Outside the house, you were dressed in a flimsy dress, even though it was cold.'

'I told you, I don't have many possessions.'

'If you're frightened of criminals, why go to the house where three women lived who were selling themselves?' Wendy asked.

'I didn't intend to stay long.'

'That's not an answer.'

'It is the only answer. I am watched, and they know where I work.'

'Which means you're either involved with them or attempting to bring them down.'

'I am neither. I am involved with an organisation that is committed to helping victims of trafficking.'

'You've not told us this before,' Isaac said.

'I haven't, and I did not intend to. I was at Sorell's house, not for a long-term stay.'

'You believe it has been used to house trafficked women?'

'There was a Bulgarian woman, Iva Arsenova, at the house. You detained her.'

'That is correct.'

'She was sent back to Bulgaria. Two men were arrested in London. One died before incarceration; the other is in prison.'

'Iva Arsenova?' Wendy asked.

'She was killed in Sofia, the capital of Bulgaria. It was two weeks ago. She talked. I will not, but I will do what I can to help the women.'

'Do you have proof of this?'

'I will give you a name. You can phone the woman; she will confirm who I am.'

'Assuming it's the truth,' Wendy said. 'You can't keep moving from one place to the next every few days.'

'I don't intend to. I have done what I can. I will work in the beauty salon and become a model English citizen.'

Isaac thought the sentiment was fine, although what was a model English citizen? Did such a person exist? He wasn't sure.

'Will you be left alone?' Wendy asked.

'I have become too visible. But they might think that my involvement with the police makes it dangerous for them to kill me.'

Isaac knew that criminal gangs didn't worry about the police. They believed they were above the law and that Oksana Akimova was unsafe. He knew Wendy would keep tabs on the woman, but it would not be enough.

***

Oksana Akimova's credentials were confirmed, that she had passed on information through the organisation she had mentioned, which had resulted in the arrest of two men. One had died before coming to trial, and the other was in prison and would be deported once his sentence was served.

None of this would assist the woman who had returned to the beauty salon in Hampstead but not back to her previous accommodation. Wendy feared for the woman, although she had consented to meet at Sorell and Cheryl Hastings' house on a gloomy Sunday morning.

Due to the possibility that Cheryl had been telling the truth and Fiona had been in the house, Oksana would retrace her movements. Fiona would come later, and if necessary, another reenactment would be held when both women were present.

On Sunday, Oksana approached the front door, reached into the letterbox, and pulled on a string; a key was attached. She then unlocked the door and announced who she was in a loud voice.

'There was no answer. Cheryl had told me there might not be anyone at home, and if there wasn't, to go upstairs and take the room at the far end of the landing,' Oksana said.

Isaac and Wendy did not intend to ask questions as the woman reenacted the day she had arrived at the house. The three climbed the stairs, Oksana having a look in the bathroom.

'I checked to see if it was clean. It wasn't, but it was acceptable.'

Proceeding further, looking left and right, checking the other rooms as she went until she reached Sorell's room.

'That's when I saw him. I froze, unable to think straight. The sight of death didn't concern me, but the violence did.'

'And then?' Wendy felt it was time to ask questions.

'I backed away and fled. I didn't want to be involved, but I couldn't ignore it. After five or ten minutes, I phoned the police.'

'Civic duty? Or was there more to it?'

'Nothing more. It was England. I didn't expect to see a body in that condition. I realised that the man hadn't died naturally or by his own hand. It was murder. I was in the country legally. I had no option but to do the right thing.'

'Why this house? Why rent here?'

'I told you at the police station. Iva Arsenova.'

'You continue to tell us that your involvement in the trafficking of women is passive. Staying in this house indicates something else.'

'My sister was trafficked.'

'To the United Kingdom?'

'I know where and when and what happened to her.'

'This house?'

'Not this house. Iva Arsenova.'

'She was Bulgarian,' Isaac said.

'I know the date Iva arrived in this country was the same as my sister's. Why do you think the police arrested two men?'

'One who was tried and convicted. His conviction was based on police evidence. There were no witnesses at his trial.'

'No one would stand in a court and give evidence against him.'

'The one who died before trial?'

'He was a weak man. He would have given evidence against the other man. They killed him; they would kill me if they knew the truth.'

'You detailed what you knew about your sister and Iva Arsenova.'

'I gave evidence, enough for the police to arrest the men and for one to be convicted. They don't know about my sister.'

'And then you play your hand and come to the house looking for Iva and find a murder,' Wendy said.

'I did. If I had given it more thought, I would not have contacted the police. I was below the radar before; I'm not now. If they come for me, so be it, but I'll not shirk my duty.'

'Did you notice the smell of perfume in the house?'

'No.'

'Another person in the room? Not dead or bloodied?'

'I only saw the man.'

The National Crime Agency confirmed what Oksana Akimova had said. Superintendent Aisha Khan of the Modern Slavery Human Trafficking Unit gave Oksana one piece of advice: 'Don't go it alone.'

Isaac passed on the advice to her. Wendy knew she wouldn't heed it.

***

Fiona Cole walked around the house, although not with the same diligence as the other woman. Wendy had to remind her that it was not a casual stroll but a murder reenactment.

'I know,' Fiona said. 'I'm aware of my responsibilities. I've already told you what happened the day I arrived. In the bedroom, there was a dead body and a woman on the floor.'

In the kitchen, Fiona tarried before heading up the stairs and walking along the landing. She stopped at Sorell's bedroom. 'That's where I saw him and the woman on the floor.'

Isaac could see an anomaly. Oksana Akimova had seen a dead body but not another person lying nearby. Cheryl Hastings mentioned the person, and Fiona Cole was also adamant she had seen someone. Someone was lying, but that had been obvious from the start.

The situation had changed. Oksana Akimova had credibility. She had gone from a suspect to a trusted person. The organisation she worked with gave her a glowing reference. The superintendent at the National Crime Authority had said that the information they had received was qualified, precise, and valued. The superintendent also added that they expected to receive further details. If they did, Isaac realised that Oksana Akimova's remaining time in London might be short.

'Fiona,' Wendy said,' we know three women were in the house. One is the murderer, by her confession, although she could be mistaken.'

'She doesn't know if she killed the man or not? That makes no sense.'

Wendy had to agree, but it was a possibility. Could Cheryl be delusional? In her addled mind, did the truth get altered? Did she have memories of events, unable to disseminate the truth? Could she be innocent?

'Level with us,' Isaac said. 'You're in this house. Why? The Colsons next door have given you two million pounds, and now we know also the money to pay off the loan sharks. What's so important about this house?'

'I knew Grant had to be dead.'

'How?'

'Grant wouldn't have allowed himself to be compromised. My trust in him.'

'And you believed the Colsons had taken their eyes off the ball and placed you in an embarrassing position?'

'I did. I needed to know why.'

229

'So, you come into this house and see Barry Sorell in bed.'
'I knew about the box in the end room.'
'How?'
'It was Grant who used it. Elizabeth knew about it, but he trusted her and Harold. They thought I was dumb, but I saw Grant move the bed once, and I saw the metal box. What was in it had to be important.'
'After fifteen years?'
'Why not?'
'We know about the box, also other documents in the other house. Did you know that?'
'No. Back then, they didn't own the other house…'
'Let me put it to you, Fiona. You came into this house determined to find more, confident that if the Colsons could pay you and the loan sharks, there was a lot more money, and you wanted it,' Isaac said.
'Why not? He used my name without my knowledge and caused Aaron and me to become the target of people who would kill. You know about his yard?'
'We do. Initially, he said it was you.'
'What else could he say? The truth? We're not dealing with a bank here, but vermin of the worst kind. We wanted them off our backs, and Aaron tries to get smart.'
'It doesn't explain why this house.'
'I knew Grant was dead.'
'How?'
'It was three years after we divorced. I saw Harold in the city, in a bank.'
'Did he see you?'
'No, but I watched him. After he left, I went into the bank and checked Grant's account. It wasn't his regular account, but it was in the name of an alias. It was a joint account. I asked the cashier to check the balance. It was down eight thousand pounds. Only one person could have taken the money, and that person would have needed to know the alias, the account number, and have the necessary identification.'

'How long had the money been there?'

'Ever since we divorced. Grant hadn't bothered to close the account, which wouldn't have been possible without my consent, nor had he withdrawn funds. I assume he had forgotten about it, but I'm short of money. I visited the bank, saw Harry, and then the cashier. "You've just missed your husband," she said. No way would Grant allow anyone to withdraw money from his accounts. That's when I knew he was dead.'

'What did you do about it?'

'What could I do? I withdrew close to five thousand and walked out of the bank. I knew contacting the Colsons would be a waste of time. Grant couldn't do any wrong in their eyes, but I could.'

'But then, there's a murder at the Colsons, and you're skulking around. Fiona, you killed Barry Sorell, didn't you?'

'No.'

Wendy stood in the way of the woman, who was frantic about exiting the house. 'Why did you kill him? Did they see you? And even if they did, what does it matter? What did you think they could do.'

'I recognised both of them.'

'Where, when, how?'

'I thought the Colsons were out. It was a week after they had given me the money.'

'What were you looking for?'

'It was owed to me.'

'What was?'

'My share of Grant's money. There had to be more. If there was a box in one house, there was bound to be another next door. It was late at night. I was quiet as I entered the house. I could hear noise from below me. I was scared but followed it and saw them down there.'

'Who?'

'A man on the floor, another man standing to one side, and that woman astride the man on the floor. They were chanting; the air was heavy with the smell of marijuana and something else. There were three, but they didn't see me, or I didn't think they had, as if they were in a hypnotic trance. And then I'm in this house, and the man who plunged the knife into the other man, he sees me, and he's got a knife.

'I wrestled with him and realised that he remembered me. I grabbed the knife from him and killed him. It was self-defence.'

'Was it?'

'I recognised the woman. She's asleep, but she wakes up as I kill Sorell. I struck her as she got up, and she fell down.'

'The blood?'

'Not while I was there, nor while the woman is in the bed with him.'

'Why didn't you tell us about next door before?'

'I was in shock for a while, and then I thought I must be dreaming or delusional, or maybe it had been the marijuana in the room.'

'It's obvious,' Wendy said. 'Mrs Cole intended to pressure the Colsons for more money, but they'd disappeared.'

'It's still murder, Fiona,' Isaac said.

'It's self-defence, I swear it.'

Isaac conceded that it probably was.

Fiona Cole was transported to Challis Street, where she would sign a confession and be charged. There would be a prison term, but considering the complexity of the murder investigation, it was unlikely it would be for long, not if she hired Harriet Gordon for her defence.

***

Six days later, when Wendy and Homicide were confident that Fiona had killed Sorell and he had killed Grayling, she drove to Oxford.

'Thank you, Sergeant,' Alan Hastings said. 'We've placed her in care at the best psychiatric hospital in the country. We tried to protect her and help her deal with what ailed her. Now, we will trust the medical centre, although we do not believe they will have more success than us.'

On the way out, Adriana Hastings kissed her on the cheek. 'Thank you,' she said.

Wendy did not intend to tell them that their daughter had been straddled over David Grayling in a satanic ritual. She knew it would be revealed at Fiona Cole's trial, but she hoped the Hastings' interest in that cul-de-sac in London would no longer exist by then.

***

Five weeks later, Alwyn Davies stood before a hastily organised press conference at New Scotland Yard.

'Ladies, gentlemen, and assembled media, we are all aware of the tragic events of yesterday when a suicide bomber blew himself up in front of the entrance to the Horse Guards Parade in Whitehall. Ten people have died. Three were UK nationals, and the others were tourists visiting the city.

'Let me offer my condolences and the sorrow of all serving officers at New Scotland Yard and all police stations in London and throughout the country.'

Hands went up from the assembled throng. Davies ignored them and continued.

'Due to the severe escalation of violence in the city and possible further threats, I am setting up a group of my most talented officers to deal with the current situation. Regardless, measures have been taken. Namely, first, a heightened police presence throughout the city; second, anyone lurking, creating dissent, or committing a criminal activity will be questioned and detained; third, the judiciary has been charged with increased powers and will act promptly; fourth, anyone who is here on a student, tourist, or refugee visa and is found to be involved in any activities contrary to the laws of this country will be deported, in most cases within days of arriving from wherever they have come from. Fifth, anyone who resists arrest and attempts to avoid capture will be treated as a terrorist. The armed police officers will not hesitate to shoot. Not to wound but to kill. We cannot know if someone is a suicide bomber. We do not intend to find out the hard way. We have identified two of the man's accomplices. They are dead. They died resisting arrest.

'Let me say this to everyone here, in London, in the United Kingdom, and worldwide: we will not tolerate a recurrence of what happened. If you come to this country to create trouble, expect summary action. Our response will be to fight fire with fire.

'Anyone who doubts this will bear the full brunt of the power of the Metropolitan Police. An organisation I have the privilege of leading and intend to lead for many years.

'I have met with the prime minister in Downing Street. He has given me his unqualified support and authorised me to take whatever actions my leadership team and I believe are necessary. Thank you.'

Davies turned around and walked back inside the building. He knew what he had just said would make it impossible for others to take him down.

On the other side of town, a man known to Angus MacTavish but not to Commander Goddard and his team, smiled. It had been a great success. He did not concern himself that two of his followers and ten innocent people had died.

He made a phone call. 'Our agreement remains.'

'It does,' Seth Caddick said. 'Your plans?'

'I will take my place alongside Angus MacTavish. He will know who I am. Whether others do, it does not matter.'

'Which name will you use?'

'Lord Ibrahim Ali Alsworthy, or possibly my adopted birth name, Benjamin Marshall, the son of the previous lord and an actress by the name of Marjorie Frobisher. I will not be denied.'

Caddick knew what he had done, what Davies had not wanted to know about. How to control the Islamic jihadist convert, he wasn't sure. Caddick phoned Detective Chief

Inspector Isaac Cook. 'I believe you will need to treat me with more respect from now on,' he said.

'I'm aware that you were responsible for the two jihadists' deaths. Does that mean you will be promoted?'

'It does. Tell Goddard I've got him in my sights.'

Isaac phoned Jenny and updated her on what Caddick had said. 'The new house is no longer possible,' she said.

'Wait and see,' Isaac replied. He realised that Davies, once again, had snatched victory from the jaws of defeat.

The End

Phillip Strang

ALSO BY THE AUTHOR

DI Tremayne Thriller Series

Death Unholy – A DI Tremayne Thriller – Book 1

All that remained were the man's two legs and a chair full of greasy and fetid ash. Little did DI Keith Tremayne know that it was the beginning of a journey into the murky world of paganism and its ancient rituals. And it was going to get very dangerous.

'Do you believe in spontaneous human combustion?' Detective Inspector Keith Tremayne asked.

'Not me. I've read about it. Who hasn't?' Sergeant Clare Yarwood answered.

'I haven't,' Tremayne replied, which did not surprise his young sergeant. In the months they had been working together, she had come to realise that he was a man who had little interest in the world. When he had a cigarette in his mouth, a beer in his hand, and a murder to solve he was about the happiest she ever saw him, but even then, he was not one of life's most sociable people. And as for reading? The occasional police report, an early-morning newspaper, turned first to the racing results.

Death and the Assassin's Blade – A DI Tremayne Thriller – Book 2

It was meant to be high drama, not murder, but someone's switched the daggers. The man's death took place in plain view of two serving police officers.

He was not meant to die; the daggers were only theatrical props, plastic and harmless. A summer's night, a production of Julius Caesar amongst the ruins of an Anglo-Saxon fort. Detective Inspector Tremayne is there with his sergeant, Clare Yarwood. In the assassination scene, Caesar collapses to the ground. Brutus defends his actions; Mark Antony rebukes him.

They're a disparate group, the amateur actors. One's an estate agent, another an accountant. And then there is the teenage school student, the gay man, the funeral director. And what about the women? They could be involved.

They've each got a secret, but which of those on the stage wanted Gordon Mason, the actor who had portrayed Caesar, dead?

Death and the Lucky Man – A DI Tremayne Thriller – Book 3

Sixty-eight million pounds and dead. Hardly the outcome expected for the luckiest man in England the day his lottery ticket was drawn out of the barrel. But then, Alan Winters' rags-to-riches story had never been conventional, and some had benefited, but others hadn't.

Death at Coombe Farm – A DI Tremayne Thriller – Book 4

A warring family. A disputed inheritance. A recipe for death.

If it hadn't been for the circumstances, Detective Inspector Keith Tremayne would have said the view was outstanding. Up high, overlooking the farmhouse in the valley below, the panoramic vista of Salisbury Plain stretching out beyond. The only problem was a body near where he stood with his sergeant, Clare Yarwood, and it wasn't a pleasant sight.

Phillip Strang

Death by a Dead Man's Hand – A DI Tremayne Thriller – Book 5

A flawed heist of forty gold bars from a security van late at night. One of the perpetrators is killed by his brother as they argue over what they have stolen.

Eighteen years later, the murderer, released after serving his sentence for his brother's murder, waits in a church for a man purporting to be the brother he killed. And then he is killed.

The threads stretch back a long way, and now more people are dying in the search for the missing gold bars.

Detective Inspector Tremayne, his health causing him concern, and Sergeant Clare Yarwood, still seeking romance, are pushed to the limit solving the murder, attempting to prevent more.

Death in the Village – A DI Tremayne Thriller – Book 6

Nobody liked Gloria Wiggins, a woman who regarded anyone who did not acquiesce to her jaundiced view of the world with disdain. James Baxter, the previous vicar, had been one of those, and her scurrilous outburst in the church one Sunday had hastened his death.

And now, years later, the woman was dead, hanging from a beam in her garage. Detective Inspector Tremayne and Sergeant Clare Yarwood had seen the body, interviewed the woman's acquaintances, and those who had hated her.

Burial Mound – A DI Tremayne Thriller – Book 7

A Bronze-Age burial mound close to Stonehenge. An archaeological excavation. What they were looking for was an ancient body and historical artefacts. They found the ancient body, but then they found another that's only been there for years, not centuries. And then the police became interested.

It's another case for Detective Inspector Tremayne and Sergeant Yarwood. The more recent body was the brother of the mayor of Salisbury.

Everything seems to point to the victim's brother, the mayor, the upright and serious-minded Clive Grantley. Tremayne's sure that it's him, but Clare Yarwood's not so sure.

But is her belief based on evidence or personal hope?

The Body in the Ditch – A DI Tremayne Thriller – Book 8

A group of children play. Not far away, in the ditch on the other side of the farmyard, lies the body of a troubled young woman.

The nearby village hides as many secrets as the community at the farm, a disparate group of people looking for an alternative to their previous torturous lives. Their leader, idealistic and benevolent, espouses love and kindness, and clearly, somebody's not following his dictate.

An old woman's death seems unrelated to the first, but is it? Is it part of the tangled web that connects the farm to the village?

Detective Inspector Tremayne and Sergeant Clare Yarwood soon discover that the village is anything but charming and picturesque. It's an incestuous hotbed of intrigue and wrongdoing. And what of the farm and those who live there. None of them can be ruled out, not yet.

The Horse's Mouth – A DI Tremayne Thriller – Book 9

A day at the races for Detective Inspector Tremayne, idyllic at the outset, soon changes. A horse is dead, the owner's daughter is found murdered, and Tremayne's there when the body is discovered.

The question is, was Tremayne set up, in the wrong place at the right time? He's the cast-iron alibi for one of the suspects, and he knows that one murder can lead to two, and more often than not to three.

The dead woman had a chequered history, though not as much as her father, and then a man commits suicide. Is he the murderer, or was his death the unfortunate consequence of a tragic love affair? And who was in the stable with the woman just before she died? More than one person could have killed her, and all of them have secrets they would rather not be known.

Tremayne's health is troubling him. Is what they are saying correct, that it is time for him to retire, to take it easy and put his feet up? But that's not his style, and he'll not give up on solving the murder.

Montfield's Madness – A DI Tremayne Thriller – Book 10

A day at the races for Detective Inspector Tremayne, idyllic at the Jacob Montfield, regarded by the majority as a homeless eccentric, a nuisance by a few, had pushed a supermarket trolley around the city for years.

However, one person regards him as a liability.

Eccentric was correct, a nuisance, for sure, mad, plenty thought that, but few knew the truth, that Montfield is a brilliant man, once a research scientist. And even less knew that detailed within a notebook hidden deep in the trolley, there is a new approach to the guidance of weapons and satellites—a radical improvement on the previous and it's worth a lot to some, power to others, accolades to another.

And for that, one cold night, he died at the hand of another. Inspector Tremayne and Sergeant Clare Yarwood are on the case, but so are others, and soon they're warned off. Only Tremayne doesn't listen, not when he's got his teeth into the investigation, and his sergeant, equally resolute, won't either. It's not only their careers on the line, but their lives.

DCI Isaac Cook Thriller Series

Murder is a Tricky Business – A DCI Cook Thriller – Book 1

A television actress is missing, and DCI Isaac Cook, the Senior Investigation Officer of the Murder Investigation Team at Challis Street Police Station in London, is searching for her.

Why has he been taken away from more important crimes to search for the woman? It's not the first time she's gone missing, so why does everyone assume she's been murdered?

There's a secret; that much is certain, but who knows it? The missing woman? The executive producer? His eavesdropping assistant? Or the actor who portrayed her fictional brother in the TV soap opera?

Murder House – A DCI Cook Thriller – Book 2

A corpse in the fireplace of an old house. It's been there for thirty years, but who is it?

It's murder, but who is the victim and what connection does the body have to the house's previous owners. What is the motive? And why is the body in a fireplace? It was bound to be discovered eventually but was that what the murderer wanted? The main suspects are all old and dying or already dead.

Isaac Cook and his team have their work cut out, trying to put the pieces together. Those who know are not talking because of an old-fashioned belief that a family's dirty laundry should not be aired in public and never to a policeman – even if that means the murderer is never brought to justice!

Murder is Only a Number – A DCI Cook Thriller – Book 3

Before she left, she carved a number in blood on his chest. But why the number 2 if this was her first murder?

The woman prowls the streets of London. Her targets are men who have wronged her. Or have they? And why is she keeping count?

DCI Cook and his team finally know who she is, but not before she's murdered four men. The whole team are looking for her, but the woman keeps disappearing in plain sight. The pressure's on to stop her, but she's always one step ahead.

And this time, DCS Goddard can't protect his protégé, Isaac Cook, from the wrath of the new commissioner at the Met.

Murder in Little Venice – A DCI Cook Thriller – Book 4

A dismembered corpse floats in the canal in Little Venice, an upmarket tourist haven in London. Its identity is unknown, but what is its significance?

DCI Isaac Cook is baffled about why it's there. Is it gang-related, or is it something more?

Whatever the reason, it's clearly a warning, and Isaac and his team are sure it's not the last body that they'll have to deal with.

Murder is the Only Option – A DCI Cook Thriller – Book 5

A man thought to be long dead returns to exact revenge against those who had blighted his life. His only concern is to protect his wife and daughter. He will stop at nothing to achieve his aim.

'Big Greg, I never expected to see you around here at this time of night.'

'I've told you enough times.'

'I've no idea what you're talking about,' Robertson replied. He looked up at the man, only to see a metal pole coming down at him. Robertson fell down, cracking his head against a concrete kerb.

Two vagrants, no more than twenty feet away, did not stir and did not even look in the direction of the noise. If they had, they would have seen a dead body, another man walking away.

Murder in Notting Hill – A DCI Cook Thriller – Book 6

One murderer, two bodies, two locations, and the murders have been committed within an hour of each other.

They're separated by a couple of miles, and neither woman has anything in common with the other. One is young and wealthy, the daughter of a famous man; the other is poor, hardworking and unknown.

Isaac Cook and his team at Challis Street Police Station are baffled about why they've been killed. There must be a connection, but what is it?

Murder in Room 346 – A DCI Cook Thriller – Book 7

'Coitus interruptus, that's what it is,' Detective Chief Inspector Isaac Cook said. In a downmarket hotel in Bayswater, on the bed lay the naked bodies of a man and a woman.

'Bullet in the head's not the way to go,' Larry Hill, Isaac Cook's detective inspector, said. He had not expected such a flippant comment from his senior, not when they were standing near to two people who had, apparently in the final throes of passion, succumbed to what appeared to be a professional assassination.

'You know this will be all over the media within the hour,' Isaac said.

'James Holden, moral crusader, a proponent of the sanctity of the marital bed, man and wife. It's bound to be.'

Murder of a Silent Man – A DCI Cook Thriller – Book 8

A murdered recluse. A property empire. A disinherited family. All the ingredients for murder.

No one gave much credence to the man when he was alive. In fact, most people never knew who he was, although those who had lived in the area for many years recognised the tired-looking and shabbily-dressed man as he shuffled along, regular as clockwork on a Thursday afternoon at seven in the evening to the local off-licence.

It was always the same: a bottle of whisky, premium brand, and a packet of cigarettes. He paid his money over the counter, took hold of his plastic bag containing his purchases, and then walked back down the road with the same rhythmic shuffle.

Murder has no Guilt – A DCI Cook Thriller – Book 9

No one knows who the target was or why, but there are eight dead. The men seem the most likely perpetrators, or could have it been one of the two women, the attractive Gillian Dickenson, or even the celebrity-obsessed Sal Maynard?

There's a gang war brewing, and if there are deaths, it doesn't matter to them as long as it's not their death. But to Detective Chief Inspector Isaac Cook, it's his area of London, and it does matter.

It's dirty and unpredictable. Initially, the West Indian gangs held sway, but a more vicious Romanian gangster had usurped them. And now he's being marginalised by the Russians. And the leader of the most vicious Russian mafia organisation is in London, and he's got money and influence, the ear of those in power.

Murder in Hyde Park – A DCI Cook Thriller – Book 10

An early-morning jogger is murdered in Hyde Park. It's in the centre of London, but no one saw him enter the park, no one saw him die.

He carries no identification, only a water-logged phone. As the pieces unravel, it's clear that the dead man had a history of deception.

Is the murderer one of those that loved him? Or was it someone with a vengeance?

It's proving difficult for DCI Isaac Cook and his team at Challis Street Homicide to find the guilty person – not that they'll cease to search for the truth, not even after one suspect confesses.

Six Years Too Late – A DCI Cook Thriller – Book 11

Always the same questions for Detective Chief Inspector Isaac Cook — Why was Marcus Matthews in that room? And why did he share a bottle of wine with his killer?

It wasn't as if Matthews had amounted to much, apart from the fact that he was the son-in-law of a notorious gangster, the father of the man's grandchildren.

Yet the one thing Hamish McIntyre, feared in London for his violence, rated above anything else, was his family, especially Samantha, his daughter. However, he had never cared for Marcus, her husband.

And then Marcus disappeared, only for his body to be found six years later by a couple of young boys who decide that exploring an abandoned house is preferable to school.

Grave Passion – A DCI Cook Thriller – Book 12

Two young lovers out for a night of romance. A shortcut through the cemetery. They witnessed a murder, but there was no struggle, only a knife through the heart.

It has all the hallmarks of an assassination, but who is the woman? And why was she beside a grave at night? Did she know the person who killed her?

Soon after, other deaths, seemingly unconnected, but tied to the family of one of the young lovers.

It's a case for Detective Chief Inspector Cook and his team, and they're baffled on this one.

The Slaying of Joe Foster – A DCI Cook Thriller – Book 13

No one challenged Joe Foster in life, not if they valued theirs. And then, the gangster is slain and his criminal empire up for grabs.

A power vacuum; the Foster family is fighting for control, the other gangs in the area aiming to poach the trade in illegal drugs, to carve up the empire that the father had created.

It has all the makings of a war on the streets, something nobody wants, not even the other gangs.

Terry Foster, the eldest son of Joe, the man who should take control, doesn't have his father's temperament or wisdom. His solution is slash and burn, and it's not going to work. People are going to get hurt, and some of them will die.

The Hero's Fall – A DCI Cook Thriller – Book 14

Angus Simmons had it made. A successful television program, a beautiful girlfriend, admired by many for his mountaineering exploits.

And then he fell while climbing a skyscraper in London. Initially, it was thought he had lost his grip, but that wasn't the man: a meticulous planner, his risks measured, and it wasn't a difficult climb, not for him.

It was only afterwards on examination that they found the mark of a bullet on his body. It then became a murder, and that was when Detective Chief Inspector Isaac Cook and his Homicide team at Challis Street Police Station became interested.

Phillip Strang

The Vicar's Confession – A DCI Cook Thriller – Book 15

The Reverend Charles Hepworth, good Samaritan, a friend of the downtrodden, almost a saint to those who know him, up until the day he walks into the police station, straight up to Detective Chief Inspector Isaac Cook's desk in Homicide. 'I killed the man,' he says as he places a blood-soaked knife on the desk.

The dead man, Andreas Maybury, was not a man to mourn, but why would a self-professed pacifist commit such a heinous crime. The reasons aren't clear, and then Hepworth's killed in a prison cell, and everyone's ducking for cover.

Guilty Until Proven Innocent – A DCI Cook Thriller – Book 16

Gary Harders' conviction two years previously should have been the end of the investigation. A clear-cut case of murder, and he had confessed to the crime and accepted his sentence without complaint. But now, the man's conviction was about to be overthrown, but why? And why is Harders not saying that his confession was police coercion? His prints are on the murder weapon, but Forensics has found another set.

Not only is there proof of either the Forensics department's error, incompetency or conspiracy, but Commissioner Alwyn Davies is getting tough on crime, draconian tough.

Detective Chief Inspector Isaac Cook and Chief Superintendent Richard Goddard are under pressure to take sides, aware that a positive return ensures promotion, but at the cost of their respective souls.

Davies has powerful backers, persons willing to make a deal with the devil. To allow violent putdown of those who disrupt the

Devil House

streets and removal of those who cause unsolicited and anti-social crime.

The plan has merits, a return to the safe society of decades past, but where will it stop. Who will say it's time to ease off, and then, what's the Russian mafia got to do with it? Too much from what DCI Cook can see, but he's powerless.

Murder Without Reason – A DCI Cook Thriller – Book 17

DCI Cook faces his greatest challenge. The Islamic State is waging war in England, and they are winning.

Not only does Isaac Cook have to contend with finding the perpetrators, but he is also being forced to commit actions contrary to his mandate as a police officer.

And then there is Anne Argento, the prime minister's deputy. The prime minister has shown himself to be a pacifist and is not up to the task. She needs to take his job if the country is to fight back against the Islamists.

Vane and Martin have provided the solution. Will DCI Cook and Anne Argento be willing to follow it through? Are they able to act for the good of England, knowing that a criminal and murderous action is about to take place? Do they have an option?

Sergeant Natalie Campbell Thriller Series

Dark Streets – Book 1

A homeless man, Old Joe's death was not unexpected. Not until it was found to be murder.

This was Darlinghurst Road, Kings Cross, once a hub of inequity, of strip joints and gentleman's clubs, of licensed premises and restaurants. But now, the area is changing, going upmarket, another enclave for those that can afford it, not a place for the homeless, nor is it a place of murder, but then there is another murder in Point Piper, upmarket and exclusive; a woman, her throat cut.

Detective Gary Haddock's a seasoned hand in Homicide, but he's baffled by the murders that continue. Statistically, Sydney's Eastern Suburbs doesn't have murder, but after four, are they serial or random, and if they are serial, why?

Sergeant Natalie Campbell from Kings Cross Police Station is wet behind the ears when she pairs with Haddock but soon learns she is more astute than he is, although she's a risk taker. He has to protect her, but she will take the investigations forward.

Pinchgut – Book 2

An old fort in Sydney Harbour – the body of a woman missing for seventeen years. It's murder, but after so long, can it be solved?

Sergeant Natalie Campbell and Inspector Haddock are resolute that it can. But then, there's the complication of the murdered woman's father, the bombastic, bullying Bernie Cornell. One of Australia's richest men, but he's closing in on death due to old age and ill health.

There's no shortage of intrigue, no shortage of potential murderers.

Devil House

Island Shadows – Book 3

The island was a prison in colonial days, then a shipbuilding facility, and now it's a venue for concerts and tourists, with some camping overnight and others wandering around the engineering workshops or the prison ruins.

Death wasn't uncommon in the island's earlier, more violent days, but not in the present, and not at a heavy metal concert.

Lead singer Alan Greenworthy is reclusive and mysterious except when he's on stage, but now he's dead.

Was the murderer the woman he had just made love to or a jealous paramour, or was the motive more obscure? And would others die?

It's another challenging case for Sergeant Natalie Campbell and Inspector Haddock.

Steve Case Thriller Series

The Haberman Virus – Book 1

A remote and isolated village in the Hindu Kush Mountain range in North Eastern Afghanistan is wiped out by a virus unlike any seen before.

A mysterious visitor clad in a spacesuit checks his handiwork, a female American doctor succumbs to the disease, and the woman sent to trap the person responsible falls in love with him – the man who would cause the deaths of millions.

Hostage of Islam – Book 2

Three are to die at the Mission in Nigeria: the pastor and his wife in a blazing chapel; another gunned down while trying to defend them from the Islamist fighters.

Kate McDonald, an American, grieving over her boyfriend's death and Helen Campbell, whose life had been troubled by drugs and prostitution, are taken by the attackers.

Kate is sold to a slave trader who intends to sell her virginity to an Arab Prince. Helen, to ensure their survival, gives herself to the murderer of her friends.

Prelude to War – Book 3

Russia and America face each other across the northern border of Afghanistan. World War 3 is about to break out and no one is backing off.

And all because a team of academics in New York postulated how to extract the vast untapped mineral wealth of Afghanistan.

Steve Case is in the middle of it, and his position is looking very precarious. Will the Taliban find him before the Americans get him out? Or is he doomed, as is the rest of the world?

Standalone Novels

Malika's Revenge

Malika, a drug-addicted prostitute, waits in a smugglers' village for the next Afghan tribesman or Tajik gangster to pay her price, a few scraps of heroin.

Yusup Baroyev, a drug lord, enjoys a lifestyle many would envy. An Afghan warlord sees the resurgence of the Taliban. A Russian white-collar criminal portrays himself as a good and honest citizen in Moscow.

All of them are linked to an audacious plan to increase the quantity of heroin shipped out of Afghanistan and into Russia and ultimately the West.

Some will succeed, some will die, some will be rescued from their plight and others will rue the day they became involved.

Verrall's Nightmare

Historians may reflect on what happened, psychoanalysts may debate endlessly, and although scientists would attempt to explain, none would conclusively get the measure of all that had occurred.

Others, less knowledgeable, aficionados of social media, would say that Benedict Verrall was mad, or else the events in a small hamlet in the south of England never occurred and that it was a government conspiracy. That Samuel Whittingham was a figment of Verrall's imagination and the storms and their devastation, unprecedented in their scope and deaths, were freaks of nature, not of evil.

The truth, however, was more obscure, and that Verrall was neither mad nor was he malicious. Although he was responsible for instigating what was to happen, that hadn't been his intention.

He did not believe in the paranormal or the metaphysical, but then, he had not considered the brain tumour pressing down on his brain.

Or was it Verrall's madness, either the dream or the nightmare? That will be for the reader to decide.

ABOUT THE AUTHOR

Phillip Strang was born in the late forties, the post-war baby boom in England; his childhood years, a comfortable middle-class upbringing in a small town, a two hours' drive to the west of London.

His childhood and the formative years were a time of innocence. Relatively few rules, and as a teenager, complete mobility due to a bicycle – a three-speed Raleigh – and a more trusting community. It was the days before mobile phones, the internet, terrorism and wanton violence. An avid reader of Science Fiction in his teenage years: Isaac Asimov, and Frank Herbert, the masters of the genre. Still an avid reader, the author now mainly reads thrillers.

In his early twenties, the author, with a degree in electronics engineering and an unabated wanderlust to see the world left England's cold and damp climes for Sydney, Australia – the first semi-circulation of the globe, complete. Now, forty years later, he still resides in Australia, although many intervening years spent in a myriad of countries, some calm and safe – others, no more than war zones.

Printed in Great Britain
by Amazon